P. G. Wodehouse

'The ultimate in comfort reading because nothing bad ever happens in P.G. Wodehouse land. Or even if it does, it's always sorted out by the end of the book. For as long as I'm immersed in a P.G. Wodehouse book, it's possible to keep the real world at bay and live in a far, far nicer, funnier one where happy endings are the order of the day' *Marian Keyes*

'You should read Wodehouse when you're well and when you're poorly; when you're travelling, and when you're not; when you're feeling clever, and when you're feeling utterly dim. Wodehouse always lifts your spirits, no matter how high they happen to be already' *Lynne Truss*

'P.G. Wodehouse remains the greatest chronicler of a certain kind of Englishness, that no one else has ever captured quite so sharply, or with quite as much wit and affection' *Julian Fellowes*

'Not only the funniest English novelist who ever wrote but one of our finest stylists. His world is perfect, his stories are perfect, his writing is perfect. What more is there to be said?' *Susan Hill*

'One of my (few) proud boasts is that I once spent a day interviewing P.G. Wodehouse at his home in America. He w̶a̶s̶ ̶e̶x̶a̶c̶t̶l̶y̶ I'd expected: a lovely, modest ma̶ ̶ ̶ ̶ ̶ ̶ ̶ ̶ ̶ ̶ ̶ ̶ ̶ ̶ e of his own novels. It's dangerou̶ ̶ ̶ ̶ ̶ ̶ ̶ ̶ ̶ ̶ ̶ e a writer, but I'll risk it with him'

'The inc̶o̶ ̶ ̶ ̶ ̶ ̶ ̶ ̶ ̶ ̶ ̶ ̶ ̶ ̶ ̶ ̶ ̶ all ages, sha̶ ̶

'A genius . [...] a credible world that, s[...] what a delight it always is to enter it and the temptation to linger there is sometimes almost overwhelming' *Alan Ayckbourn*

'Wodehouse was quite simply the Bee's Knees. And then some' *Joseph Connolly*

'Compulsory reading for anyone who has a pig, an aunt – or a sense of humour!' *Lindsey Davis*

'I constantly find myself drooling with admiration at the sublime way Wodehouse plays with the English language' *Simon Brett*

'I've recorded all the Jeeves books, and I can tell you this: it's like singing Mozart. The perfection of the phrasing is a physical pleasure. I doubt if any writer in the English language has more perfect music' *Simon Callow*

'Quite simply, the master of comic writing at work' *Jane Moore*

'To pick up a Wodehouse novel is to find oneself in the presence of genius – no writer has ever given me so much pure enjoyment' *John Julius Norwich*

'P.G. Wodehouse is the gold standard of English wit' *Christopher Hitchens*

'Wodehouse is so utterly, properly, simply funny' *Adele Parks*

'To dive into a Wodehouse novel is to swim in some of the most elegantly turned phrases in the English language' *Ben Schott*

'P.G. Wodehouse should be prescribed to treat depression. Cheaper, more effective than valium and far, far more addictive' *Olivia Williams*

'My only problem with Wodehouse is deciding which of his enchanting books to take to my desert island' *Ruth Dudley Edwards*

The author of almost a hundred books and the creator of Jeeves, Blandings Castle, Psmith, Ukridge, Uncle Fred and Mr Mulliner, P.G. Wodehouse was born in 1881 and educated at Dulwich College. After two years with the Hong Kong and Shanghai Bank he became a full-time writer, contributing to a variety of periodicals including *Punch* and the *Globe*. He married in 1914. As well as his novels and short stories, he wrote lyrics for musical comedies with Guy Bolton and Jerome Kern, and at one time had five musicals running simultaneously on Broadway. His time in Hollywood also provided much source material for fiction.

At the age of 93, in the New Year's Honours List of 1975, he received a long-overdue knighthood, only to die on St Valentine's Day some 45 days later.

P. G. WODEHOUSE
Mr Mulliner Speaking

arrow books

Published by Arrow Books 2008

5 7 9 10 8 6 4

First published in the United Kingdom in 1929 by Herbert Jenkins Ltd

Arrow Books
The Random House Group Limited
20 Vauxhall Bridge Road, London, SW1V 2SA

www.randomhouse.co.uk

www.wodehouse.co.uk

Addresses for companies within The Random House Group Limited can be found at: www.randomhouse.co.uk/offices.htm

The Random House Group Limited Reg. No. 954009

A CIP catalogue record for this book
is available from the British Library

ISBN 9780099514060

The Random House Group Limited supports The Forest Stewardship Council® (FSC®), the leading international forest certification organisation. All our titles that are printed on Greenpeace approved FSC® certified paper carry the FSC® logo. Our paper procurement policy can be found at www.randomhouse.co.uk/environment

Typeset by SX Composing DTP, Rayleigh, Essex
Printed in the UK by CPI Bookmarque, Croydon, CR0 4TD

Mr Mulliner Speaking

CONTENTS

The conversation in the bar-parlour of the Angler's Rest, which always tends to get deepish towards closing-time, had turned to the subject of the Modern Girl; and a Gin-and-Ginger-Ale sitting in the corner by the window remarked that it was strange how types die out.

'I can remember the days,' said the Gin-and-Ginger-Ale, 'when every other girl you met stood about six feet two in her dancing-shoes, and had as many curves as a Scenic Railway. Now they are all five foot nothing and you can't see them sideways. Why is this?'

The Draught Stout shook his head.

'Nobody can say. It's the same with dogs. One moment the world is full of pugs as far as the eye can reach; the next, not a pug in sight, only Pekes and Alsatians. Odd!'

The Small Bass and the Double-Whisky-and-Splash admitted that these things were very mysterious, and supposed we should never know the reason for them. Probably we were not meant to know.

'I cannot agree with you, gentlemen,' said Mr Mulliner. He had been sipping his hot Scotch and lemon with a rather abstracted air: but now he sat up alertly, prepared to deliver judgement. 'The reason for the disappearance of the dignified, queenly type of girl is surely obvious. It is Nature's method of ensuring the continuance of the species. A world full of the sort of young woman that Meredith used to put into his novels and du Maurier into his pictures in *Punch* would be a world full of permanent spinsters. The modern young man would never be able to summon up the nerve to propose to them.'

'Something in that,' assented the Draught Stout.

'I speak with authority on the point,' said Mr Mulliner, 'because my nephew, Archibald, made me his confidant when he fell in love with Aurelia Cammarleigh. He worshipped that girl with a fervour which threatened to unseat his reason, such as it was: but the mere idea of asking her to be his wife gave him, he informed me, such a feeling of sick faintness that only by means of a very stiff brandy and soda, or some similar restorative, was he able to pull himself together on the occasions when he contemplated it. Had it not been for . . . But perhaps you would care to hear the story from the beginning?'

People who enjoyed a merely superficial acquaintance with my nephew Archibald (said Mr Mulliner) were accustomed to set him down as just an ordinary pin-headed young man. It was only when they came to know him better that they discovered their mistake. Then they realised that his pinheadedness, so far from being ordinary, was exceptional. Even at the Drones Club, where the average of intellect is not high, it was often said of Archibald that, had his brain been constructed of silk, he would have been hard put to it to find sufficient material to make a canary a pair of cami-knickers. He sauntered through life with a cheerful insouciance, and up to the age of twenty-five had only once been moved by anything in the nature of a really strong emotion – on the occasion when, in the heart of

Bond Street and at the height of the London season, he discovered that his man, Meadowes, had carelessly sent him out with odd spats on.

And then he met Aurelia Cammarleigh.

The first encounter between these two has always seemed to me to bear an extraordinary resemblance to the famous meeting between the poet Dante and Beatrice Fortinari. Dante, if you remember, exchanged no remarks with Beatrice on that occasion. Nor did Archibald with Aurelia. Dante just goggled at the girl. So did Archibald. Like Archibald, Dante loved at first sight: and the poet's age at the time was, we are told, nine – which was almost exactly the mental age of Archibald Mulliner when he first set eyeglass on Aurelia Cammarleigh.

Only in the actual locale of the encounter do the two cases cease to be parallel. Dante, the story relates, was walking on the Ponte Vecchia, while Archibald Mulliner was having a thoughtful cocktail in the window of the Drones Club, looking out on Dover Street.

And he had just relaxed his lower jaw in order to examine Dover Street more comfortably when there swam into his line of vision something that looked like a Greek goddess. She came out of a shop opposite the club and stood on the pavement waiting for a taxi. And, as he saw her standing there, love at first sight seemed to go all over Archibald Mulliner like nettlerash.

It was strange that this should have been so, for she was not at all the sort of girl with whom Archibald had fallen in love at first sight in the past. I chanced, while in here the other day, to pick up a copy of one of the old yellowback novels of fifty years ago – the property, I believe, of Miss Postlethwaite, our courteous and erudite barmaid. It was entitled *Sir Ralph's Secret*, and its heroine, the Lady Elaine, was described as a superbly handsome girl, divinely tall, with a noble figure, the arched Montresor nose, haughty eyes beneath delicately pencilled brows, and that indefinable air of aristocratic aloofness which marks the daughter of a hundred Earls. And Aurelia Cammarleigh might have been this formidable creature's double.

Yet Archibald, sighting her, reeled as if the cocktail he had just consumed had been his tenth instead of his first.

'Golly!' said Archibald.

To save himself from falling, he had clutched at a passing fellow-member: and now, examining his catch, he saw that it was young Algy Wymondham-Wymondham. Just the fellow-member he would have preferred to clutch at, for Algy was a man who went everywhere and knew everybody and could doubtless give him the information he desired.

'Algy, old prune,' said Archibald in a low, throaty voice, 'a moment of your valuable time, if you don't mind.'

He paused, for he had perceived the need for caution. Algy was a notorious babbler, and it would be the height of rashness to give him an inkling of the passion which blazed within his breast. With a strong effort, he donned the mask. When he spoke again, it was with a deceiving nonchalance.

'I was just wondering if you happened to know who that girl is, across the street there. I suppose you don't know what her name is in rough numbers? Seems to me I've met her somewhere or something, or seen her, or something. Or something, if you know what I mean.'

Algy followed his pointing finger and was in time to observe Aurelia as she disappeared into the cab.

'That girl?'

'Yes,' said Archibald, yawning. 'Who is she, if any?'

'Girl named Cammarleigh.'

'Ah?' said Archibald, yawning again. 'Then I haven't met her.'

'Introduce you if you like. She's sure to be at Ascot. Look out for us there.'

Archibald yawned for the third time.

'All right,' he said, 'I'll try to remember. Tell me about her. I mean, has she any fathers or mothers or any rot of that description?'

'Only an aunt. She lives with her in Park Street. She's potty.'

Archibald started, stung to the quick.

'Potty? That divine... I mean that rather attractive-looking girl?'

'Not Aurelia. The aunt. She thinks Bacon wrote Shakespeare.'

'Thinks who wrote what?' asked Archibald, puzzled, for the names were strange to him.

'You must have heard of Shakespeare. He's well known. Fellow who used to write plays. Only Aurelia's aunt says he didn't. She maintains that a bloke called Bacon wrote them for him.'

'Dashed decent of him,' said Archibald, approvingly. 'Of course, he may have owed Shakespeare money.'

'There's that, of course.'

'What was the name again?'

'Bacon.'

'Bacon,' said Archibald, jotting it down on his cuff. 'Right.'

Algy moved on, and Archibald, his soul bubbling within him like a welsh rabbit at the height of its fever, sank into a chair and stared sightlessly at the ceiling. Then, rising, he went off to the Burlington Arcade to buy socks.

The process of buying socks eased for awhile the turmoil that ran riot in Archibald's veins. But even socks with lavender clocks can only alleviate: they do not cure. Returning to his rooms, he found the anguish rather more overwhelming than ever. For at last he had leisure to think: and thinking always hurt his head.

Algy's careless words had confirmed his worst suspicions. A girl with an aunt who knew all about Shakespeare and Bacon must of necessity live in a mental atmosphere into which a lame-brained bird like himself could scarcely hope to soar. Even if he did meet her – even if she asked him to call – even if in due time their relations became positively cordial, what then? How could he aspire to such a goddess? What had he to offer her?

Money?

Plenty of that, yes, but what was money?

Socks?

Of these he had the finest collection in London, but socks are not everything.

A loving heart?

A fat lot of use that was.

No, a girl like Aurelia Cammarleigh would, he felt, demand from the man who aspired to her hand something in the nature of gifts, of accomplishments. He would have to be a man who Did Things.

And what, Archibald asked himself, could he do? Absolutely nothing except give an imitation of a hen laying an egg.

That he could do. At imitating a hen laying an egg he was admittedly a master. His fame in that one respect had spread all over the West End of London. 'Others abide our question. Thou art free,' was the verdict of London's gilded youth on Archibald Mulliner when considered purely in the light of a man who could imitate a hen laying an egg. 'Mulliner,' they said to one another, 'may be a pretty minus quantity in many ways, but he can imitate a hen laying an egg.'

And, so far from helping him, this one accomplishment of his would, reason told him, be a positive handicap. A girl like Aurelia Cammarleigh would simply be sickened by such coarse buffoonery. He blushed at the very thought of her ever learning that he was capable of sinking to such depths.

And so, when some weeks later he was introduced to her in the paddock at Ascot and she, gazing at him with what seemed to his sensitive mind contemptuous loathing, said:

'They tell me you give an imitation of a hen laying an egg, Mr Mulliner.'

He replied with extraordinary vehemence:

'It is a lie – a foul and contemptible lie which I shall track to its source and nail to the counter.'

Brave words! But had they clicked? Had she believed him? He trusted so. But her haughty eyes were very penetrating. They seemed to pierce through to the depths of his soul and lay it bare for what it was – the soul of a hen-imitator.

However, she did ask him to call. With a sort of queenly, bored disdain and only after he had asked twice if he might – but she did it. And Archibald resolved that, no matter what the mental strain, he would show her that her first impression of him had been erroneous; that, trivial and vapid though he might seem, there were in his nature deeps whose existence she had not suspected.

For a young man who had been superannuated from Eton and believed everything he read in the Racing Expert's column in the morning paper, Archibald, I am bound to admit, exhibited in this crisis a sagacity for which few of his intimates would have given him credit. It may be that love stimulates the mind, or it may be that when the moment comes Blood will tell. Archibald, you must remember, was, after all, a Mulliner: and now the old canny strain of the Mulliners came out in him.

'Meadowes, my man,' he said to Meadowes, his man.

'Sir,' said Meadowes.

'It appears,' said Archibald, 'that there is – or was – a cove of the name of Shakespeare. Also a second cove of the name of Bacon. Bacon wrote plays, it seems, and Shakespeare went and put his own name on the programme and copped the credit.'

'Indeed, sir?'

'If true, not right, Meadowes.'

'Far from it, sir.'

'Very well, then. I wish to go into this matter carefully. Kindly pop out and get me a book or two bearing on the business.'

He had planned his campaign with infinite cunning. He knew that, before anything could be done in the direction of winning the heart of Aurelia Cammarleigh, he must first establish himself solidly with the aunt. He must court the aunt, ingratiate himself with her – always, of course, making it clear from the start that she was not the one. And, if reading about Shakespeare and Bacon could do it, he would, he told himself, have her eating out of his hand in a week.

Meadowes returned with a parcel of forbidding-looking volumes, and Archibald put in a fortnight's intensive study. Then, discarding the monocle which had up till then been his constant companion, and substituting for it a pair of horn-rimmed spectacles which gave him something of the look of an earnest sheep, he set out for Park Street to pay his first call. And within five minutes of his arrival he had declined a cigarette on the plea that he was a non-smoker, and had managed to say some rather caustic things about the practice, so prevalent among his contemporaries, of drinking cocktails.

Life, said Archibald, toying with his teacup, was surely given to us for some better purpose than the destruction of our brains and digestions with alcohol. Bacon, for instance, never took a cocktail in his life, and look at him.

At this, the aunt, who up till now had plainly been regarding him as just another of those unfortunate incidents, sprang to life.

'You admire Bacon, Mr Mulliner?' she asked eagerly.

And, reaching out an arm like the tentacle of an octopus, she drew him into a corner and talked about Cryptograms for forty-seven minutes by the drawing-room clock. In short, to sum the thing up, my nephew Archibald, at his initial meeting with the only relative of the girl he loved, went like a sirocco. A Mulliner is always a Mulliner. Apply the acid test, and he will meet it.

It was not long after this that he informed me that he had sown the good seed to such an extent that Aurelia's aunt had invited him to pay a long visit to her country house, Brawstead Towers, in Sussex.

He was seated at the Savoy bar when he told me this, rather feverishly putting himself outside a Scotch and soda: and I was perplexed to note that his face was drawn and his eyes haggard.

'But you do not seem happy, my boy,' I said.

'I'm not happy.'

'But surely this should be an occasion for rejoicing. Thrown together as you will be in the pleasant surroundings of a country house, you ought easily to find an opportunity of asking this girl to marry you.'

'And a lot of good that will be,' said Archibald moodily.

'Even if I do get a chance I shan't be able to make any use of it. I wouldn't have the nerve. You don't seem to realize what it means being in love with a girl like Aurelia. When I look into those clear, soulful eyes, or see that perfect profile bobbing about on the horizon, a sense of my unworthiness seems to slosh me amidships like some blunt instrument. My tongue gets entangled with my front teeth, and all I can do is stand there feeling like a piece of Gorgonzola that has been condemned by the local sanitary inspector. I'm going to Brawstead Towers, yes, but I don't expect anything to come of it. I know exactly what's going to happen to me. I shall just buzz along through life, pining dumbly, and in the end slide into the tomb a blasted, blighted bachelor. Another whisky, please, and jolly well make it a double.'

Brawstead Towers, situated as it is in the pleasant Weald of Sussex, stands some fifty miles from London: and Archibald, taking the trip easily in his car, arrived there in time to dress comfortably for dinner. It was only when he reached the drawing-room at eight o'clock that he discovered that the younger members of the house-party had gone off in a body to dine and dance at a hospitable neighbour's, leaving him to waste the evening tie of a lifetime, to the composition of which he had devoted no less than twenty-two minutes, on Aurelia's aunt.

Dinner in these circumstances could hardly hope to be an unmixedly exhilarating function. Among the things which helped to differentiate it from a Babylonian orgy was the fact that, in deference to his known prejudices, no wine was served to Archibald. And, lacking artificial stimulus, he found the aunt even harder to endure philosophically than ever.

Archibald had long since come to a definite decision that

what this woman needed was a fluid ounce of weed-killer, scientifically administered. With a good deal of adroitness he contrived to head her off from her favourite topic during the meal: but after the coffee had been disposed of she threw off all restraint. Scooping him up and bearing him off into the recesses of the west wing, she wedged him into a corner of a settee and began to tell him all about the remarkable discovery which had been made by applying the Plain Cipher to Milton's well-known Epitaph on Shakespeare.

'The one beginning "What needs my Shakespeare for his honoured bones?"' said the aunt.

'Oh, that one?' said Archibald.

'"What needs my Shakespeare for his honoured bones? The labour of an Age in pilèd stones? Or that his hallowed Reliques should be hid under a starry-pointing Pyramid?"' said the aunt.

Archibald, who was not good at riddles, said he didn't know.

'As in the Plays and Sonnets,' said the aunt, 'we substitute the name equivalents of the figure totals.'

'We do what?'

'Substitute the name equivalents of the figure totals.'

'The which?'

'The figure totals.'

'All right,' said Archibald. 'Let it go. I daresay you know best.'

The aunt inflated her lungs.

'These figure totals,' she said, 'are always taken out in the Plain Cipher, A equalling one to Z equals twenty-four. The names are counted in the same way. A capital letter with the figures indicates an occasional variation in the Name Count. For instance, A equals twenty-seven, B twenty-eight, until K equals ten is reached, when K, instead of ten, becomes one, and T instead of nineteen, is one, and R or Reverse, and so on, until

A equals twenty-four is reached. The short or single Digit is not used here. Reading the Epitaph in the light of this Cipher, it becomes: "What need Verulam for Shakespeare? Francis Bacon England's King be hid under a W. Shakespeare? William Shakespeare. Fame, what needst Francis Tudor, King of England? Francis. Francis W. Shakespeare. For Francis thy William Shakespeare hath England's King took W. Shakespeare. Then thou our W. Shakespeare Francis Tudor bereaving Francis Bacon Francis Tudor such a tomb William Shakespeare."'

The speech to which he had been listening was unusually lucid and simple for a Baconian, yet Archibald, his eye catching a battle-axe that hung on the wall, could not but stifle a wistful sigh. How simple it would have been, had he not been a Mulliner and a gentleman, to remove the weapon from its hook, spit on his hands, and haul off and dot this doddering old ruin one just above the imitation pearl necklace. Placing his twitching hands underneath him and sitting on them, he stayed where he was until, just as the clock on the mantelpiece chimed the hour of midnight, a merciful fit of hiccoughs on the part of his hostess enabled him to retire. As she reached the twenty-seventh 'hic', his fingers found the door-handle and a moment later he was outside, streaking up the stairs.

The room they had given Archibald was at the end of a corridor, a pleasant, airy apartment with French windows opening upon a broad balcony. At any other time he would have found it agreeable to hop out onto this balcony and revel in the scents and sounds of the summer night, thinking the while long, lingering thoughts of Aurelia. But what with all that Francis Tudor Francis Bacon such a tomb William Shakespeare count seventeen drop one knit purl and set them up in the other alley stuff, not even thoughts of Aurelia could keep him from his bed.

Moodily tearing off his clothes and donning his pyjamas, Archibald Mulliner climbed in and instantaneously discovered that the bed was an apple-pie bed. When and how it had happened he did not know, but at a point during the day some loving hand had sewn up the sheets and put two hair-brushes and a branch of some prickly shrub between them.

Himself from earliest boyhood an adept at the construction of booby-traps, Archibald, had his frame of mind been sunnier, would doubtless have greeted this really extremely sound effort with a cheery laugh. As it was, weighed down with Verulams and Francis Tudors, he swore for a while with considerable fervour: then, ripping off the sheets and tossing the prickly shrub wearily into a corner, crawled between the blankets and was soon asleep.

His last waking thought was that if the aunt hoped to catch him on the morrow, she would have to be considerably quicker on her pins than her physique indicated.

How long Archibald slept he could not have said. He woke some hours later with a vague feeling that a thunderstorm of unusual violence had broken out in his immediate neighbourhood. But this, he realized as the mists of slumber cleared away, was an error. The noise which had disturbed him was not thunder but the sound of someone snoring. Snoring like the dickens. The walls seemed to be vibrating like the deck of an ocean liner.

Archibald Mulliner might have had a tough evening with the aunt, but his spirit was not so completely broken as to make him lie supinely down beneath that snoring. The sound filled him, as snoring fills every right-thinking man, with a seething resentment and a passionate yearning for justice, and he climbed out of bed with the intention of taking the proper steps through the recognized channels. It is the custom nowadays to disparage the educational methods of the English public-school and to maintain that they are not practical and of a kind to fit the growing boy for the problems of after-life. But you do learn one thing at a public-school, and that is how to act when somebody starts snoring.

You jolly well grab a cake of soap and pop in and stuff it down the blighter's throat. And this Archibald proposed – God willing – to do. It was the work of a moment with him to dash to the washstand and arm himself. Then he moved softly out through the French windows onto the balcony.

The snoring, he had ascertained, proceeded from the next room. Presumably this room also would have French windows: and presumably as the night was warm, these would be open. It would be a simple task to oil in, insert the soap, and buzz back undetected.

It was a lovely night, but Archibald paid no attention to it. Clasping his cake of soap, he crept on and was pleased to discover, on arriving outside the snorer's room, that his surmise had been correct. The windows were open. Beyond them, screening the interior of the room, were heavy curtains. And he had just placed his hand upon these when from inside a voice spoke. At the same moment the light was turned on.

'Who's that?' said the voice.

And it was as if Brawstead Towers with all its stabling, outhouses and messuages had fallen on Archibald's head. A mist rose before his eyes. He gasped and tottered.

The voice was that of Aurelia Cammarleigh.

* * *

For an instant, for a single long, sickening instant, I am compelled to admit that Archibald's love, deep as the sea though it was, definitely wobbled. It had received a grievous blow. It was not simply the discovery that the girl he adored was a snorer that unmanned him: it was the thought that she could snore like that. There was something about those snores that had seemed to sin against his whole conception of womanly purity.

Then he recovered. Even though this girl's slumber was not, as the poet Milton so beautifully puts it, 'airy light', but rather reminiscent of a lumber-camp when the wood-sawing is proceeding at its briskest, he loved her still.

He had just reached this conclusion when a second voice spoke inside the room.

'I say, Aurelia.'

It was the voice of another girl. He perceived now that the question 'Who's that?' had been addressed not to him but to this newcomer fumbling at the door-handle.

'I say, Aurelia,' said the girl complainingly, 'you've simply got to do something about that bally bulldog of yours. I can't possibly get to sleep with him snoring like that. He's making the plaster come down from the ceiling in my room.'

'I'm sorry,' said Aurelia. 'I've got so used to it that I don't notice.'

'Well, I do. Put a green-baize cloth over him or something.'

Out on the moonlit balcony Archibald Mulliner stood shaking like a blancmange. Although he had contrived to maintain his great love practically intact when he had supposed the snores to proceed from the girl he worshipped, it had been tough going, and for an instant, as I have said, a very near thing. The relief that swept over him at the discovery that Aurelia could still justifiably remain on her pinnacle was so profound that it made him feel filleted. He seemed for a moment in a daze. Then he was brought out of the ether by hearing his name spoken.

'Did Archie Mulliner arrive to-night?' asked Aurelia's friend.

'I suppose so,' said Aurelia. 'He wired that he was motoring down.'

'Just between us girls,' said Aurelia's friend, 'what do you think of that bird?'

To listen to a private conversation – especially a private conversation between two modern girls when you never know what may come next – is rightly considered an action incompatible with the claim to be a gentleman. I regret to say, therefore, that Archibald, ignoring the fact that he belonged to a family whose code is as high as that of any in the land, instead of creeping away to his room, edged at this point a step closer to the curtains and stood there with his ears flapping. It might be an ignoble thing to eavesdrop, but it was apparent that Aurelia Cammarleigh was about to reveal her candid opinion of him: and the prospect of getting the true facts – straight, as it were, from the horse's mouth – held him so fascinated that he could not move.

'Archie Mulliner?' said Aurelia meditatively.

'Yes. The betting at the Junior Lipstick is seven to two that you'll marry him.'

'Why on earth?'

'Well, people have noticed he's always round at your place, and they seem to think it significant. Anyway, that's how the odds stood when I left London – seven to two.'

'Get in on the short end,' said Aurelia earnestly, 'and you'll make a packet.'

'Is that official?'

'Absolutely,' said Aurelia.

Out in the moonlight, Archibald Mulliner uttered a low, bleak moan rather like the last bit of wind going out of a dying duck. True, he had always told himself that he hadn't a chance, but, however much a man may say that, he never in his heart really believes it. And now from an authoritative source he had learned that his romance was definitely blue round the edges. It was a shattering blow. He wondered dully how the trains ran to the Rocky Mountains. A spot of grizzly-bear shooting seemed indicated.

Inside the room, the other girl appeared perplexed.

'But you told me at Ascot,' she said, 'just after he had been introduced to you, that you rather thought you had at last met your ideal. When did the good thing begin to come unstuck?'

A silvery sigh came through the curtains.

'I did think so then,' said Aurelia wistfully. 'There was something about him. I liked the way his ears wiggled. And I had always heard he was such a perfectly genial, cheery, merry old soul. Algy Wymondham-Wymondham told me that his imitation of a hen laying an egg was alone enough to keep any reasonable girl happy through a long married life.'

'Can he imitate a hen?'

'No. It was nothing but an idle rumour. I asked him, and he stoutly denied that he had ever done such a thing in his life. He was quite stuffy about it. I felt a little uneasy then, and the moment he started calling and hanging about the house I knew that my fears had been well-founded. The man is beyond question a flat tyre and a wet smack.'

'As bad as that?'

'I'm not exaggerating a bit. Where people ever got the idea

that Archie Mulliner is a bonhomous old bean beats me. He is the world's worst monkey-wrench. He doesn't drink cocktails, he doesn't smoke cigarettes, and the thing he seems to enjoy most in the world is to sit for hours listening to the conversation of my aunt, who, as you know, is pure goof from the soles of the feet to the tortoiseshell comb and should long ago have been renting a padded cell in Earlswood. Believe me, Muriel, if you can really get seven to two, you are onto the best thing since Buttercup won the Lincolnshire.'

'You don't say!'

'I do say. Apart from anything else, he's got a beastly habit of looking at me reverently. And if you knew how sick I am of being looked at reverently! They will do it, these lads. I suppose it's because I'm rather an out-size and modelled on the lines of Cleopatra.'

'Tough!'

'You bet it's tough. A girl can't help her appearance. I may look as if my ideal man was the hero of a Viennese operetta, but I don't feel that way. What I want is some good sprightly sportsman who sets a neat booby-trap, and who'll rush up and grab me in his arms and say to me, "Aurelia, old girl, you're the bee's roller-skates!"'

And Aurelia Cammarleigh emitted another sigh.

'Talking of booby-traps,' said the other girl, 'if Archie Mulliner has arrived he's in the next room, isn't he?'

'I suppose so. That's where he was to be. Why?'

'Because I made him an apple-pie bed.'

'It was the right spirit,' said Aurelia warmly. 'I wish I'd thought of it myself.'

'Too late now.'

'Yes,' said Aurelia. 'But I'll tell you what I can and will do.

You say you object to Lysander's snoring. Well, I'll go and pop him in at Archie Mulliner's window. That'll give him pause for thought.'

'Splendid,' agreed the girl Muriel. 'Well, good night.'

'Good night,' said Aurelia.

There followed the sound of a door closing.

There was, as I have indicated, not much of my nephew Archibald's mind, but what there was of it was now in a whirl. He was stunned. Like every man who is abruptly called upon to revise his entire scheme of values, he felt as if he had been standing on top of the Eiffel Tower and some practical joker had suddenly drawn it away from under him. Tottering back to his room, he replaced the cake of soap in its dish and sat down on the bed to grapple with this amazing development.

Aurelia Cammarleigh had compared herself to Cleopatra. It is not too much to say that my nephew Archibald's emotions at this juncture were very similar to what Mark Antony's would have been had Egypt's queen risen from her throne at his entry and without a word of warning started to dance the Black Bottom.

He was roused from his thoughts by the sound of a light footstep on the balcony outside. At the same moment he heard a low woofly gruffle, the unmistakable note of a bulldog of regular habits who has been jerked out of his basket in the small hours and forced to take the night air.

> 'She is coming, my own, my sweet!
> Were it never so airy a tread,
> My heart would hear her and beat,
> Were it earth in an earthy bed'

whispered Archibald's soul, or words to that effect. He rose from his seat and paused for an instant, irresolute. Then inspiration descended on him. He knew what to do, and he did it.

Yes, gentlemen, in that supreme crisis of his life, with his whole fate hanging, as you might say, in the balance, Archibald Mulliner, showing for almost the first time in his career a well-nigh human intelligence, began to give his celebrated imitation of a hen laying an egg.

Archibald's imitation of a hen laying an egg was conceived on broad and sympathetic lines. Less violent than Salvini's *Othello*, it had in it something of the poignant wistfulness of Mrs Siddons in the sleep-walking scene of *Macbeth*. The rendition started quietly, almost inaudibly, with a sort of soft, liquid crooning – the joyful yet half-incredulous murmur of a mother who can scarcely believe as yet that her union has really been blessed, and that it is indeed she who is responsible for that oval mixture of chalk and albumen which she sees lying beside her in the straw.

Then, gradually, conviction comes.

'It looks like an egg,' one seems to hear her say. 'It feels like an egg. It's shaped like an egg. Damme, it *is* an egg!'

And at that, all doubting resolved, the crooning changes; takes on a firmer note; soars into the upper register; and finally swells into a maternal pæan of joy – a 'Charawk-chawk-chawk-chawk' of such a calibre that few had ever been able to listen to it dry-eyed. Following which, it was Archibald's custom to run round the room, flapping the sides of his coat, and then, leaping onto a sofa or some convenient chair, to stand there with his arms at right angles, crowing himself purple in the face.

All these things he had done many a time for the idle

entertainment of fellow-members in the smoking-room of the Drones, but never with the gusto, the *brio*, with which he performed them now. Essentially a modest man, like all the Mulliners, he was compelled, nevertheless, to recognize that to-night he was surpassing himself. Every artist knows when the authentic divine fire is within him, and an inner voice told Archibald Mulliner that he was at the top of his form and giving the performance of a lifetime. Love thrilled through every 'Brt-t't-t't' that he uttered, animated each flap of his arms. Indeed, so deeply did Love drive in its spur that he tells me that, instead of the customary once, he actually made the circle of the room three times before coming to rest on top of the chest of drawers.

When at length he did so he glanced towards the window and saw that through the curtains the loveliest face in the world was peering. And in Aurelia Cammarleigh's glorious eyes there was a look he had never seen before, the sort of look Kreisler or somebody like that beholds in the eyes of the front row as he lowers his violin and brushes his forehead with the back of his hand. A look of worship.

There was a long silence. Then she spoke.

'Do it again!' she said.

And Archibald did it again. He did it four times and could, he tells me, if he had pleased, have taken a fifth encore or at any rate a couple of bows. And then, leaping lightly to the floor, he advanced towards her. He felt conquering, dominant. It was his hour. He reached out and clasped her in his arms.

'Aurelia, old girl,' said Archibald Mulliner in a clear, firm voice, 'you are the bee's roller-skates.'

And at that she seemed to melt into his embrace. Her lovely face was raised to his.

'Archibald!' she whispered.

There was another throbbing silence, broken only by the beating of two hearts and the wheezing of the bulldog, who seemed to suffer a good deal in his bronchial tubes. Then Archibald released her.

'Well, that's that,' he said. 'Glad everything's all settled and hotsy-totsy. Gosh, I wish I had a cigarette. This is the sort of moment a bloke needs one.'

She looked at him, surprised.

'But I thought you didn't smoke.'

'Oh yes, I do.'

'And do you drink as well?'

'Quite as well,' said Archibald. 'In fact, rather better. Oh, by the way.'

'Yes?'

'There's just one other thing. Suppose that aunt of yours wants to come and visit us when we are settled down in our little nest, what, dearest, would be your reaction to the scheme of socking her on the base of the skull with a stuffed eelskin?'

'I should like it,' said Aurelia warmly, 'above all things.'

'Twin souls,' cried Archibald. 'That's what we are, when you come right down to it. I suspected it all along, and now I know. Two jolly old twin souls.' He embraced her ardently. 'And now,' he said, 'let us pop downstairs and put this bulldog in the butler's pantry, where he will come upon him unexpectedly in the morning and doubtless get a shock which will do him as much good as a week at the seaside. Are you on?'

'I am,' whispered Aurelia. 'Oh, I am!'

And hand in hand they wandered out together onto the broad staircase.

In a mixed assemblage like the little group of serious thinkers which gathers nightly in the bar-parlour of the Angler's Rest it is hardly to be expected that there will invariably prevail an unbroken harmony. We are all men of spirit: and when men of spirit, with opinions of their own, get together, disputes are bound to arise. Frequently, therefore, even in this peaceful haven, you will hear voices raised, tables banged, and tenor Permit-me-to-inform-you-sir's competing with baritone And-jolly-well-permit-me-to-inform-*you*'s. I have known fists to be shaken and on one occasion the word 'fathead' to be used.

Fortunately, Mr Mulliner is always there, ready with the soothing magic of his personality to calm the storm before things have gone too far. To-night, as I entered the room, I found him in the act of intervening between a flushed Lemon Squash and a scowling Tankard of Ale who had fallen foul of one another in the corner by the window.

'Gentlemen, gentlemen,' he was saying in his suave, ambassadorial way, 'what is all the trouble about?'

The Tankard of Ale pointed the stem of his pipe accusingly at his adversary. One could see that he was deeply stirred.

'He's talking Rot about smoking.'

'I am talking sense.'

'I didn't hear any.'

'I said that smoking was dangerous to the health. And it is.'

'It isn't.'

'It is. I can prove it from my own personal experience. I was once,' said the Lemon Squash, 'a smoker myself, and the vile habit reduced me to a physical wreck. My cheeks sagged, my eyes became bleary, my whole face gaunt, yellow and hideously lined. It was giving up smoking that brought about the change.'

'What change?' asked the Tankard.

The Lemon Squash, who seemed to have taken offence at something, rose and, walking stiffly to the door, disappeared into the night. Mr Mulliner gave a little sigh of relief.

'I am glad he has left us,' he said. 'Smoking is a subject on which I hold strong views. I look upon tobacco as life's outstanding boon, and it annoys me to hear these faddists abusing it. And how foolish their arguments are, how easily refuted. They come to me and tell me that if they place two drops of nicotine on the tongue of a dog the animal instantly dies: and when I ask them if they have ever tried the childishly simple device of not placing nicotine on the dog's tongue, they have nothing to reply. They are non-plussed. They go away mumbling something about never having thought of that.'

He puffed at his cigar in silence for a few moments. His genial face had grown grave.

'If you ask my opinion, gentlemen,' he resumed, 'I say it is not only foolish for a man to give up smoking – it is not safe. Such an action wakes the fiend that sleeps in all of us. To give up smoking is to become a menace to the community. I shall not readily forget what happened in the case of my nephew Ignatius. Mercifully, the thing had a happy ending, but...'

* * *

Those of you (said Mr Mulliner) who move in artistic circles are possibly familiar with the name and work of my nephew Ignatius. He is a portrait-painter of steadily growing reputation. At the time of which I speak, however, he was not so well-known as he is to-day, and consequently had intervals of leisure between commissions. These he occupied in playing the ukulele and proposing marriage to Hermione, the beautiful daughter of Herbert J. Rossiter and Mrs Rossiter, of 3 Scantlebury Square, Kensington. Scantlebury Square was only just round the corner from his studio, and it was his practice, when he had a moment to spare, to pop across, propose to Hermione, get rejected, pop back again, play a bar or two on the ukulele, and then light a pipe, put his feet on the mantelpiece, and wonder what it was about him that appeared to make him distasteful to this lovely girl.

It could not be that she scorned his honest poverty. His income was most satisfactory.

It could not be that she had heard something damaging about his past. His past was blameless.

It could not be that she objected to his looks for, like all the Mulliners, his personal appearance was engaging and even – from certain angles – fascinating. Besides, a girl who had been brought up in a home containing a father who was one of Kensington's leading gargoyles and a couple of sub-humans like her brother Cyprian and her brother George would scarcely be an exacting judge of male beauty. Cyprian was pale and thin and wrote art-criticism for the weekly papers, and George was stout and pink and did no work of any kind, having developed at an early age considerable skill in the way of touching friends and acquaintances for small loans.

The thought occurred to Ignatius that one of these two

might be able to give him some inside information on the problem. They were often in Hermione's society, and it was quite likely that she might have happened to mention at one time or another what it was about him that caused her so repeatedly to hand the mitten to a good man's love. He called upon Cyprian at his flat and put the thing to him squarely. Cyprian listened attentively, stroking his left side-whisker with a lean hand.

'Ah?' said Cyprian. 'One senses, does one, a reluctance on the girl's part to entertain one's suggestions of marriage?'

'One does,' replied Ignatius.

'One wonders why one is unable to make progress?'

'One does.'

'One asks oneself what is the reason?'

'One does – repeatedly.'

'Well, if one really desires to hear the truth,' said Cyprian, stroking his right whisker, 'I happen to know that Hermione objects to you because you remind her of my brother George.'

Ignatius staggered back, appalled, and an animal cry escaped his lips.

'Remind her of George?'

'That's what she says.'

'But I can't be like George. It isn't humanly possible for anybody to be like George.'

'One merely repeats what one has heard.'

Ignatius staggered from the room and, tottering into the Fulham Road, made for the Goat and Bottle to purchase a restorative. And the first person he saw in the saloon-bar was George, taking his elevenses.

'What ho!' said George. 'What ho, what ho, what ho!'

He looked pinker and stouter than ever, and the theory

that he could possibly resemble this distressing object was so distasteful to Ignatius that he decided to get a second opinion.

'George,' he said, 'have you any idea why it is that your sister Hermione spurns my suit?'

'Certainly,' said George.

'You have? Then why is it?'

George drained his glass.

'You ask me why?'

'Yes.'

'You want to know the reason?'

'I do.'

'Well, then, first and foremost,' said George, 'can you lend me a quid till Wednesday week without fail?'

'No, I can't.'

'Nor ten bob?'

'Nor ten bob. Kindly stick to the subject and tell me why your sister will not look at me.'

'I will,' said George. 'Not only have you a mean and parsimonious disposition, but she says you remind her of my brother Cyprian.'

Ignatius staggered and would have fallen had he not placed a foot on the brass rail.

'I remind her of Cyprian?'

'That's what she says.'

With bowed head Ignatius left the saloon-bar and returned to his studio to meditate. He was stricken to the core. He had asked for inside information and he had got it, but nobody was going to make him like it.

He was not only stricken to the core, but utterly bewildered. That a man – stretching the possibilities a little – might resemble George Rossiter was intelligible. He could also understand that a man – assuming that Nature had played a scurvy trick upon him – might conceivably be like Cyprian. But how could anyone be like both of them and live?

He took pencil and paper and devoted himself to making a list in parallel columns of the qualities and characteristics of the brothers. When he had finished, he scanned it carefully. This is what he found he had written:

GEORGE	CYPRIAN
Face like pig	Face like camel
Pimples	Whiskers
Confirmed sponger	Writes art-criticism
Says 'What ho!'	Says 'One senses'
Slaps backs	Has nasty, dry snigger
Eats too much	Fruitarian
Tells funny stories	Recites poetry
Clammy hands	Bony hands

He frowned. The mystery was still unsolved. And then he came to the last item.

GEORGE	CYPRIAN
Heavy smoker	Heavy smoker

A spasm ran through Ignatius Mulliner. Here, at last, was a common factor. Was it posible...? Could it be...?

It seemed the only solution, and yet Ignatius fought against it. His love for Hermione was the lodestar of his life, but next to it, beaten only by a short head, came his love for his pipe. Had he really to choose between the two?

Could he make such a sacrifice?

He wavered.

And then he saw the eleven photographs of Hermione

Rossiter gazing at him from the mantelpiece, and it seemed to him that they smiled encouragingly. He hesitated no longer. With a soft sigh such as might have proceeded from some loving father on the Steppes of Russia when compelled, in order to ensure his own safety, to throw his children out of the back of the sleigh to the pursuing wolf-pack, he took the pipe from his mouth, collected his other pipes, his tobacco and his cigars, wrapped them in a neat parcel and, summoning the charwoman who cleaned his studio, gave her the consignment to take home to her husband, an estimable man of the name of Perkins who, being of straitened means, smoked, as a rule, only what he could pick up in the street.

Ignatius Mulliner had made the great decision.

As those of you who have tried it are aware, the deadly effects of giving up smoking rarely make themselves felt immediately in their full virulence. The process is gradual. In the first stage, indeed, the patient not only suffers no discomfort but goes about inflated by a sort of gaseous spiritual pride. All through the morning of the following day, Ignatius, as he walked abroad, found himself regarding such fellow-members of the community as had pipes and cigarettes in their mouths with a pitying disdain. He felt like some saint purified and purged of the grosser emotions by a life of asceticism. He longed to tell these people all about pyridine and the intense irritation it causes to the throats and other mucous surfaces of those who inhale the tobacco smoke in which it lurks. He wanted to buttonhole men sucking at their cigars and inform them that tobacco contains an appreciable quantity of the gas known as carbon monoxide, which, entering into direct combination with the colouring matter of the blood, forms so staple a compound as to render the corpuscles incapable of carrying oxygen to the tissues. He yearned to make it clear to them that smoking was simply a habit which with a little exercise of the will-power a man could give up at a moment's notice, whenever he pleased.

It was only after he had returned to his studio to put the finishing touches to his Academy picture that the second stage set in.

Having consumed an artist's lunch consisting of two sardines, the remnants of a knuckle of ham, and a bottle of beer, he found stealing over him, as his stomach got onto the fact that the meal was not to be topped off by a soothing pipe, a kind of vague sense of emptiness and bereavement akin to that experienced by the historian Gibbon on completing his *Decline and Fall of the Roman Empire*. Its symptoms were an inability to work and a dim feeling of oppression, as if he had just lost some dear friend. Life seemed somehow to have been robbed of all motive. He wandered about the studio, haunted by a sensation that he was leaving undone something that he ought to be doing. From time to time he blew little bubbles, and once or twice his teeth clicked, as if he were trying to close them on something that was not there.

A twilight sadness had him in its grip. He took up his ukulele, an intrument to which, as I have said, he was greatly addicted, and played 'Ol' Man River' for awhile. But the melancholy still lingered. And now, it seemed to him, he had discovered its cause. What was wrong was the fact that he was not doing enough good in the world.

Look at it this way, he felt. The world is a sad, grey place, and we are put into it to promote as far as we can the happiness of others. If we concentrate on our own selfish pleasures, what do we find? We find that they speedily pall. We weary of gnawing knuckles of ham. The ukulele loses its fascination. Of course, if we could sit down and put our feet up and set a match to the good old pipe, that would be a different matter. But we no longer smoke, and so all that is left to us is the doing of good to others. By three o'clock, in short, Ignatius Mulliner had reached the third stage, the glutinously sentimental. It caused him to grab his hat, and sent him trotting round to Scantlebury Square.

But his object was not, as it usually was when he went to Scantlebury Square, to propose to Hermione Rossiter. He had a more unselfish motive. For some time past, by hints dropped and tentative remarks thrown out, he had been made aware that Mrs Rossiter greatly desired him to paint her daughter's portrait: and until now he had always turned to these remarks and hints a deaf ear. Mrs Rossiter's mother's heart wanted, he knew, to get the portrait for nothing: and, while love is love and all that, he had the artist's dislike for not collecting all that was coming to him. Ignatius Mulliner, the man, might entertain the idea of pleasing the girl he worshipped by painting her on the nod, but Ignatius Mulliner, the artist, had his schedule of prices. And until to-day it was the second Ignatius Mulliner who had said the deciding word.

This afternoon, however, everything was changed. In a short but moving speech he informed Hermione's mother that the one wish of his life was to paint her daughter's portrait; that for so great a privilege he would not dream of charging a fee; and that if she would call at the studio on the morrow, bringing Hermione with her, he would put the job in hand right away.

In fact, he very nearly offered to paint another portrait of Mrs Rossiter herself, in evening dress with her Belgian griffon.

He contrived, however, to hold the fatal words back: and it was perhaps the recollection of this belated prudence which gave him, as he stood on the pavement outside the house after the interview, a sense of having failed to be as altruistic as he might have been.

Stricken with remorse, he decided to look up good old Cyprian and ask him to come to the studio to-morrow and criticize his Academy picture. After that, he would find dear old George and press a little money on him. Ten minutes later, he was in Cyprian's sitting-room.

'One wishes what?' asked Cyprian incredulously.

'One wishes,' repeated Ignatius, 'that you would come round to-morrow morning and have a look at one's Academy picture and give one a hint or two about it.'

'Is one really serious?' cried Cyprian, his eyes beginning to gleam. It was seldom that he received invitations of this kind. He had, indeed, been thrown out of more studios for butting in and giving artists a hint or two about their pictures than any other art-critic in Chelsea.

'One is perfectly serious,' Ignatius assured him. 'One feels that an opinion from an expert will be invaluable.'

'Then one will be there at eleven sharp,' said Cyprian, 'without fail.'

Ignatius wrung his hand warmly, and hurried off to the Goat and Bottle to find George.

'George,' he said, 'George, my dear old chap; I passed a sleepless night last night, wondering if you had all the money you require. The fear that you might have run short seemed to go through me like a knife. Call on me for as much as you need.'

George's face was partially obscured by a tankard. At these words, his eyes, bulging above the pewter, took on a sudden expression of acute horror. He lowered the tankard, ashen to the lips, and raised his right hand.

'This,' he said in a shaking voice, 'is the end. From this moment I go off the stuff. Yes, you have seen George Plimsoll Rossiter drink his last mild-and-bitter. I am not a nervous man, but I know when I'm licked. And when it comes to a fellow's ears going...'

Ignatius patted his arm affectionately.

'Your ears have not gone, George,' he said. 'They are still there.'

And so, indeed, they were, as large and red as ever. But George was not to be comforted.

'I mean when a fellow thinks he hears things...I give you my honest word, old man – I solemnly assure you that I could have sworn I heard you voluntarily offer me money.'

'But I did.'

'You did?'

'Certainly.'

'You mean you definitely – literally – without any sort of prompting on my part – without my so much as saying a word to indicate that I could do with a small loan till Friday week – absolutely, positively offered to lend me money?'

'I did.'

George drew a deep breath and took up his tankard again.

'All this modern, advanced stuff you read about miracles not happening,' he said severely, 'is dashed poppycock. I disapprove of it. I resent it keenly. About how much?' he went on, pawing adoringly at Ignatius' sleeve. 'To about what, as it were, extent would you be prepared to go? A quid?'

Ignatius raised his eyebrows.

'A quid is not much, George,' he said with quiet reproach.

George made little gurgling noises.

'A fiver?'

Ignatius shook his head. The movement was a silent rebuke.

'Correct this petty, cheese-paring spirit, George,' he urged. 'Be big and broad. Think spaciously.'

'Not – a tenner?'

'I was about to suggest fifteen pounds,' said Ignatius. 'If you are sure that will be enough.'

'What ho!'

'You're positive you can manage with that? I know how many expenses you have.'

'What ho!'

'Very well, then. If you can get along with fifteen pounds, come round to my studio to-morrow morning and we'll fix it up.'

And, glowing with fervour, Ignatius slapped George's back in a hearty sort of way and withdrew.

'Something attempted, something done,' he said to himself, as he climbed into bed some hours later, 'has earned a night's repose.'

Like so many men who live intensely and work with their brains, my nephew Ignatius was a heavy sleeper. Generally, after waking to a new day, he spent a considerable time lying on his back in a sort of coma, not stirring till lured from his couch by the soft, appealing smell of frying bacon. On the following morning, however, he was conscious, directly he opened his eyes, of a strange alertness. He was keyed up to quite an extraordinary extent. He had, in short, reached the stage when the patient becomes a little nervous.

Yes, he felt, analysing his emotions, he was distinctly nervous. The noise of the cat stamping about in the passage outside

caused him exquisite discomfort. He was just about to shout
to Mrs Perkins, his charwoman, to stop the creature, when she
rapped suddenly on the panel to inform him that his shaving-
water lay without: and at the sound he immediately shot
straight up to the ceiling in a cocoon of sheets and blankets,
turned three complete somersaults in mid-air, and came down,
quivering like a frightened mustang, in the middle of the floor.
His heart was entangled with his tonsils, his eyes had worked
round to the back of their sockets, and he wondered dazedly
how many human souls besides himself had survived the
bomb-explosion.

Reason returning to her throne, his next impulse was to cry
quietly. Remembering after a while that he was a Mulliner, he
checked the unmanly tears and, creeping to the bathroom, took
a cold shower and felt a little better. A hearty breakfast assisted
the cure, and he was almost himself again, when the discovery
that there was not a pipe or a shred of tobacco in the place
plunged him once more into an inky gloom.

For a long time Ignatius Mulliner sat with his face in his
hands, while all the sorrows of the world seemed to rise before
him. And then, abruptly, his mood changed again. A moment
before, he had been pitying the human race with an intensity
that racked him almost unendurably. Now, the realization
surged over him that he didn't care a hoot about the human
race. The only emotion the human race evoked in him was an
intense dislike. He burned with an irritable loathing for all
created things. If the cat had been present, he would have
kicked it. If Mrs Perkins had entered, he would have struck her
with a mahl-stick. But the cat had gone off to restore its tissues
in the dust-bin, and Mrs Perkins was in the kitchen, singing
hymns. Ignatius Mulliner boiled with baffled fury. Here he was,

with all this concentrated hatred stored up within him, and not a living thing in sight on which to expend it. That, he told himself with a mirthless laugh, was the way things happened.

And just then the door opened, and there, looking like a camel arriving at an oasis, was Cyprian.

'Ah, my dear fellow,' said Cyprian. 'May one enter?'

'Come right in,' said Ignatius.

At the sight of this art-critic, who not only wore short side-whiskers but also one of those black stocks which go twice round the neck and add from forty to fifty per cent to the loathsomeness of the wearer's appearance, a strange, febrile excitement had gripped Ignatius Mulliner. He felt like a tiger at the Zoo who sees the keeper approaching with the luncheon-tray. He licked his lips slowly and gazed earnestly at the visitor. From a hook on the wall beside him there hung a richly inlaid Damascus dagger. He took it down and tested its point with the ball of his thumb.

Cyprian had turned his back, and was examining the Academy picture through a black-rimmed monocle. He moved his head about and peered between his fingers and made funny, art-critic noises.

'Ye-e-s,' said Cyprian. ''Myes. Ha! H'm. Hrrmph! The thing has rhythm, undoubted rhythm, and, to an extent, certain inevitable curves. And yet can one conscientiously say that one altogether likes it? One fears one cannot.'

'No?' said Ignatius.

'No,' said Cyprian. He toyed with his left whisker. He seemed to be massaging it for purposes of his own. 'One quite inevitably senses at a glance that the patine lacks vitality.'

'Yes?' said Ignatius.

'Yes,' said Cyprian. He toyed with the whisker again. It was too early to judge whether he was improving it at all. He shut his eyes, opened them, half closed them once more, drew back his head, fiddled with his fingers, and expelled his breath with a hissing sound, as if he were grooming a horse. 'Beyond a question one senses in the patine a lack of vitality. And vitality must never be sacrificed. The artist should use his palette as an orchestra. He should put on his colours as a great conductor uses his instruments. There must be significant form. The colour must have a flatness, a gravity, shall I say an aroma? The figure must be placed on the canvas in a manner not only harmonious but awake. Only so can a picture quite too exquisitely live. And, as regards the patine...'

He broke off. He had had more to say about the patine, but he had heard immediately behind him an odd, stealthy, shuffling sound not unlike that made by a leopard of the jungle when stalking its prey. Spinning round, he saw Ignatius Mulliner advancing upon him. The artist's lips were curled back over his teeth in a hideous set smile. His eyes glittered. And poised in his right hand he held a Damascus dagger, which, Cyprian noticed, was richly inlaid.

An art-critic who makes a habit of going round the studios of Chelsea and speaking his mind to men who are finishing their Academy pictures gets into the way of thinking swiftly. Otherwise, he would not quite too exquisitely live through a single visit. To cast a glance at the door and note that it was closed and that his host was between him and it was with Cyprian Rossiter the work of a moment; to dart behind the easel the work of another. And with the easel as a basis the two men for some tense minutes played a silent game of round-and-round-the-mulberry-bush. It was in the middle of the twelfth lap that Cyprian received a flesh wound in the upper arm.

On another man this might have had the effect of causing him to falter, lose his head, and become an easy prey to the pursuer. But Cyprian had the advantage of having been through this sort of thing before. Only a day or two ago, one of England's leading animal-painters had chivvied him for nearly an hour in a fruitless endeavour to get at him with a short bludgeon tipped with lead.

He kept cool. In the face of danger, his footwork, always impressive, took on a new agility. And finally, when Ignatius tripped over a loose mat, he seized his opportunity like the strategist which every art-critic has to be if he mixes with artists, and dodged nimbly into a small cupboard near the model-throne.

Ignatius recovered his balance just too late. By the time he had disentangled himself from the mat, leaped at the cupboard door and started to tug at the handle, Cyprian was tugging at it from the other side, and, strive though he might, Ignatius could not dislodge him.

Presently, he gave up the struggle and, moving moodily away, picked up his ukulele and played 'Ol' Man River' for awhile. He was just feeling his way cautiously through that rather tricky 'He don't say nuffin', He must know somefin'' bit, when the door opened once more and there stood George.

'What ho!' said George.

'Ah!' said Ignatius.

'What do you mean, Ah?'

'Just "Ah!",' said Ignatius.

'I've come for that money.'

'Ah?'

'That twenty quid or whatever it was that you very decently promised me yesterday. And, lying in bed this morning, the thought crossed my mind: Why not make it twenty-five? A nice, round sum,' argued George.

'Ah!'

'You keep saying "Ah!"' said George. 'Why do you say "Ah!"?'

Ignatius drew himself up haughtily.

'This is my studio, paid for with my own money, and I shall say "Ah!" in it just as often as I please.'

'Of course,' agreed George hurriedly. 'Of course, my dear old chap, of course, of course. Hullo!' He looked down. 'Shoelace undone. Dangerous. Might trip a fellow. Excuse me a moment.'

He stooped: and as Ignatius gazed at his spacious trouser-seat the thought came to him that in the special circumstances there was but one thing to be done. He waggled his right leg for a moment to limber it up, backed a pace or two and crept forward.

Mrs Rossiter, meanwhile, accompanied by her daughter Hermione, had left Scantlebury Square and, though a trifle short in the wind, had covered the distance between it and the studio in quite good time. But the effort had told upon her, and half-way up the stairs she was compelled to halt for a short rest. It was as she stood there, puffing slightly like a seal after diving for fish, that something seemed to shoot past her in the darkness.

'What was that?' she exclaimed.

'I thought I saw something, too,' said Hermione.

'Some heavy, moving object.'

'Yes,' said Hermione. 'Perhaps we had better go up and ask Mr Mulliner if he has been dropping things downstairs.'

They made their way to the studio. Ignatius was standing on one leg, rubbing the toes of his right foot. Your artist is proverbially a dreamy, absent-minded man, and he had realized too late that he was wearing bedroom slippers. Despite the fact, however, that he was in considerable pain, his expression was not unhappy. He had the air of a man who is conscious of having done the right thing.

'Good morning, Mr Mulliner,' said Mrs Rossiter.

'Good morning, Mr Mulliner,' said Hermione.

'Good morning,' said Ignatius, looking at them with deep loathing. It amazed him that he had ever felt attracted by this girl. Until this moment, his animosity had been directed wholly against the male members of her family: but now that she stood before him he realized that the real outstanding Rossiter gumboil was this Hermione. The brief flicker of *joie-de-vivre* which had followed his interview with George had died away, leaving his mood blacker than ever. One scarcely likes to think what might have happened, had Hermione selected that moment to tie her shoelace.

'Well, here we are,' said Mrs Rossiter.

At this point, unseen by them, the cupboard door began to open noiselessly. A pale face peeped out. The next instant, there was a cloud of dust, a whirring noise, and the sound of footsteps descending the stairs three at a time.

Mrs Rossiter put a hand to her heart and panted.

'What was that?'

'It was a little blurred,' said Hermione, 'but I think it was Cyprian.'

Ignatius uttered a passionate cry and dashed to the head of the stairs.

'Gone!'

He came back, his face contorted, muttering to himself. Mrs Rossiter looked at him keenly. It seemed plain to her that all that was wanted here was a couple of doctors with fountain-pens to sign the necessary certificate, but she was not dismayed. After all, as she reasoned with not a little shrewd sense, a gibbering artist is just as good as a sane artist, provided he makes no charge for painting portraits.

'Well, Mr Mulliner,' she said cheerily, dismissing from her mind the problem, which had been puzzling her a little, of why her son Cyprian had been in this studio behaving like the Scotch Express, 'Hermione has nothing to do this morning, so, if you are free, now would be a good time for the first sitting.'

Ignatius came out of his reverie.

'Sitting?'

'For the portrait.'

'What portrait?'

'Hermione's portrait.'

'You wish me to paint Miss Rossiter's portrait?'

'Why, you said you would – only last night.'

'Did I?' Ignatius passed a hand across his forehead. 'Perhaps I did. Very well. Kindly step to the desk and write out a cheque for fifty pounds. You have your book with you?'

'Fifty – what?'

'Guineas,' said Ignatius. 'A hundred guineas. I always require a deposit before I start work.'

'But last night you said you would paint her for nothing.'

'I said I would paint her for nothing?'

'Yes.'

A dim recollection of having behaved in the fatuous manner described came to Ignatius.

'Well, and suppose I did,' he said warmly. 'Can't you women ever understand when a man is kidding you? Have you no sense of humour? Must you always take every light quip literally?

If you want a portrait of Miss Rossiter, you will jolly well pay for it in the usual manner. The thing that beats me is why you do want a portrait of a girl who not only has most unattractive features but is also a dull yellow in colour. Furthermore, she flickers. As I look at her, she definitely flickers round the edges. Her face is sallow and unwholesome. Her eyes have no sparkle of intelligence. Her ears stick out and her chin goes in. To sum up, her whole appearance gives me an indefinable pain in the neck: and, if you hold me to my promise, I shall charge extra for moral and intellectual damage and wear and tear caused by having to sit opposite her and look at her.'

With these words, Ignatius Mulliner turned and began to rummage in a drawer for his pipe. But the drawer contained no pipe.

'What!' cried Mrs Rossiter.

'You heard,' said Ignatius.

'My smelling-salts!' gasped Mrs Rossiter.

Ignatius ran his hand along the mantelpiece. He opened two cupboards and looked under the settee. But he found no pipe.

The Mulliners are by nature a courteous family: and, seeing Mrs Rossiter sniffing and gulping there, a belated sense of having been less tactful than he might have been came to Ignatius.

'It is possible,' he said, 'that my recent remarks may have caused you pain. If so, I am sorry. My excuse must be that they came from a full heart. I am fed to the tonsils with the human race and look on the entire Rossiter family as perhaps its darkest blots. I cannot see the Rossiter family. There seems to me to be no market for them. All I require of the Rossiters is their blood. I nearly got Cyprian with a dagger, but he was too quick for me. If he fails as a critic, there is always a future for him as a Russian dancer. However, I had decidedly better luck with George. I gave him the juiciest kick I have ever administered to human frame. If he had been shot from a gun he couldn't have gone out quicker. Probably he passed you on the stairs?'

'So *that* was what passed us!' said Hermione, interested. 'I remember thinking at the time that there was a whiff of George.'

Mrs Rossiter was staring, aghast.

'You kicked my son!'

'As squarely in the seat of the pants, madam,' said Ignatius with modest pride, 'as if I had been practising for weeks.'

'My stricken child!' cried Mrs Rossiter. And, hastening from the room, she ran down the stairs in quest of the remains. A boy's best friend is his mother.

In the studio she had left, Hermione was gazing at Ignatius, in her eyes a look he had never seen there before.

'I had no idea you were so eloquent, Mr Mulliner,' she said, breaking the silence. 'What a vivid description that was that you gave of me. Quite a prose poem.'

Ignatius made a deprecating gesture.

'Oh, well,' he said.

'Do you really think I am like that?'

'I do.'

'Yellow?'

'Greeny yellow.'

'And my eyes . . . ?' She hesitated for a word.

'They are not unlike blue oysters,' said Ignatius, prompting her, 'which have been dead some time.'

'In fact, you don't admire my looks?'

'Far from it.'

She was saying something, but he had ceased to listen. Quite suddenly he had remembered that about a couple of weeks ago, at a little party which he had given in the studio, he had dropped a half-smoked cigar behind the bureau. And as no charwoman is allowed by the rules of her union to sweep under bureaux, it might – nay, must – still be there. With feverish haste he dragged the bureau out. It was.

Ignatius Mulliner sighed an ecstatic sigh. Chewed and mangled, covered with dust and bitten by mice, this object between his fingers was nevertheless a cigar – a genuine, smoke-able cigar, containing the regulation eight per cent of carbon monoxide. He struck a match and the next moment he had begun to puff.

And, as he did so, the milk of human kindness surged back into his soul like a vast tidal wave. As swiftly as a rabbit, handled by a competent conjurer, changes into a bouquet, a bowl of goldfish or the grand old flag, Ignatius Mulliner changed into a thing of sweetness and light, with charity towards all, with malice towards none. The pyridine played about his mucous surfaces, and he welcomed it like a long-lost brother. He felt gay, happy, exhilarated.

He looked at Hermione, standing there with her eyes sparkling and her beautiful face ashine, and he realized that he had been all wrong about her. So far from being a gumboil, she was the loveliest thing that had ever breathed the perfumed air of Kensington.

And then, chilling his ecstasy and stopping his heart in the middle of a beat, came the recollection of what he had said about her appearance. He felt pale and boneless. If ever a man had dished himself properly, that man, he felt, was Ignatius Mulliner. And he did not mean maybe.

She was looking at him, and the expression on her face

seemed somehow to suggest that she was waiting for something.

'Well?' she said.

'I beg your pardon?' said Ignatius.

She pouted.

'Well, aren't you going to – er – ?'

'What?'

'Well, fold me in your arms and all that sort of thing,' said Hermione, blushing prettily.

Ignatius tottered.

'Who, me?'

'Yes, you.'

'Fold you in my arms?'

'Yes.'

'But – er – do you want me to?'

'Certainly.'

'I mean... after all I said...'

She stared at him in amazement.

'Haven't you been listening to what I've been telling you?' she cried.

'I'm sorry.' Ignatius stammered. 'Good deal on my mind just now. Must have missed it. What did you say?'

'I said that, if you really think I look like that, you do not love me, as I had always supposed, for my beauty, but for my intellect. And if you knew how I have always longed to be loved for my intellect!'

Ignatius put down his cigar and breathed deeply.

'Let me get this right,' he said. 'Will you marry me?'

'Of course I will. You always attracted me strangely, Ignatius, but I thought you looked upon me as a mere doll.'

He picked up his cigar, took a puff, laid it down again, took a step forward, extended his arms, and folded her in them. And for a space they stood there, clasped together, murmuring those broken words that lovers know so well. Then, gently disengaging her, he went back to the cigar and took another invigorating puff.

'Besides,' she said, 'how could a girl help but love a man who could lift my brother George right down a whole flight of stairs with a single kick?'

Ignatius' face clouded.

'George! That reminds me. Cyprian said you said I was like George.'

'Oh! I didn't mean him to repeat that.'

'Well, he did,' said Ignatius moodily. 'And the thought was agony.'

'But I only meant that you and George were both always playing the ukulele. And I hate ukuleles.'

Ignatius' face cleared.

'I will give mine to the poor this afternoon. And, touching Cyprian . . . George said you said I reminded you of him.'

She hastened to soothe him.

'It's only the way you dress. You both wear such horrid sloppy clothes.'

Ignatius folded her in his arms once more.

'You shall take me this very instant to the best tailor in London,' he said. 'Give me a minute to put on my boots, and I'll be with you. You don't mind if I just step in at my tobacconist's for a moment on the way? I have a large order for him.'

I have heard it said that the cosy peace which envelops the bar-parlour of the Angler's Rest has a tendency to promote in the regular customers a certain callousness and indifference to human suffering. I fear there is something in the charge. We who have made the place our retreat sit sheltered in a backwater far removed from the rushing stream of Life. We may be dimly aware that out in the world there are hearts that ache and bleed: but we order another gin and ginger and forget about them. Tragedy, to us, has come to mean merely the occasional flatness of a bottle of beer.

Nevertheless, this crust of selfish detachment can be cracked. And when Mr Mulliner entered on this Sunday evening and announced that Miss Postlethwaite, our gifted and popular barmaid, had severed her engagement to Alfred Lukyn, the courteous assistant at the Bon Ton Drapery Stores in the High Street, it is not too much to say that we were stunned.

'But it's only half an hour ago,' we cried, 'that she went off to meet him in her best black satin with the lovelight in her eyes. They were going to church together.'

'They never reached the sacred edifice,' said Mr Mulliner, sighing and taking a grave sip of hot Scotch and lemon. 'The estrangement occurred directly they met. The rock on which the frail craft of Love split was the fact that Alfred Lukyn was wearing yellow shoes.'

'Yellow shoes?'

'Yellow shoes,' said Mr Mulliner, 'of a singular brightness. These came under immediate discussion. Miss Postlethwaite, a girl of exquisite sensibility and devoutness, argued that to attend evensong in shoes like that was disrespectful to the Vicar. The blood of the Lukyns is hot, and Alfred, stung, retorted that he had paid sixteen shillings and eightpence for them and that the Vicar could go and boil his head. The ring then changed hands and arrangements were put in train for the return of all gifts and correspondence.'

'Just a lovers' tiff.'

'Let us hope so.'

A thoughtful silence fell upon the bar-parlour. Mr Mulliner was the first to break it.

'Strange,' he said, coming out of his reverie, 'to what diverse ends Fate will employ the same instrument. Here we have two loving hearts parted by a pair of yellow shoes. Yet in the case of my cousin Cedric it was a pair of yellow shoes that brought him a bride. These things work both ways.'

To say that I ever genuinely liked my cousin Cedric (said Mr Mulliner) would be paltering with the truth. He was not a man of whom many men were fond. Even as a boy he gave evidence of being about to become what eventually he did become – one of those neat, prim, fussy, precise, middle-aged bachelors who are so numerous in the neighbourhood of St James Street. It is a type I have never liked, and Cedric, in addition to being neat, prim, fussy and precise, was also one of London's leading snobs.

For the rest, he lived in comfortable rooms at the Albany, where between the hours of nine-thirty and twelve in the morning he would sit closeted with his efficient secretary, Miss Myrtle Watling, busy on some task the nature of which remained wrapped in mystery. Some said he was writing a monumental history of Spats, others that he was engaged upon his Memoirs. My private belief is that he was not working at anything, but entertained Miss Watling during those hours simply because he lacked the nerve to dismiss her. She was one of those calm, strong young women who look steadily out upon the world through spectacles with tortoiseshell rims. Her mouth was firm, her chin resolute. Mussolini might have fired her, if at the top of his form, but I can think of nobody else capable of the feat.

So there you have my cousin Cedric. Forty-five years of age, forty-five inches round the waist, an established authority on the subject of dress, one of the six recognized bores at his club, and a man with the entrée into all the best houses in London. That the peace of such a one could ever be shattered, that anything could ever occur seriously to disturb the orderly routine of such a man's life, might seem incredible. And yet this happened. How true it is that in this world we can never tell behind what corner Fate may not be lurking with the brass knuckles.

The day which was to prove so devastating to Cedric Mulliner's bachelor calm began, ironically, on a note of bright happiness. It was a Sunday, and he was always at his best on Sundays, for that was the day on which Miss Watling did not come to the Albany. For some little time back he had been finding himself more than usually ill at ease in Miss Watling's presence. She had developed a habit of looking at him with an odd, speculative expression in her eyes. It was an expression whose meaning he could not read, but it had disturbed him. He was glad to be relieved of her society for a whole day.

Then, again, his new morning-clothes had just arrived from the tailor's and, looking at himself in the mirror, he found his appearance flawless. The tie – quiet and admirable. The trousers – perfect. The gleaming black boots – just right. In the matter of dress, he was a man with a position to keep up. Younger men looked to him for guidance. To-day, he felt, he would not fail them.

Finally, he was due at half-past one for luncheon at the house of Lord Knubble of Knopp in Grosvenor Square, and he knew that he could count on meeting there all that was best and fairest of England's aristocracy.

His anticipations were more than fulfilled. Except for a lout of a baronet who had managed to slip in somehow, there was nobody beside himself present at the luncheon table below the rank of Viscount: and, to complete his happiness, he found himself seated next to Lady Chloe Downblotton, the beautiful daughter of the seventh Earl of Choole, for whom he had long entertained a paternal and respectful fondness. And so capitally did they get on during the meal that, when the party broke up, she suggested that, if he were going in her direction, which was the Achilles statue in the Park, they might stroll together.

'The fact is,' said Lady Chloe, as they walked down Park Lane, 'I feel I must confide in somebody. I've just got engaged.'

'Engaged! Dear lady,' breathed Cedric reverently, 'I wish you every happiness. But I have seen no announcement in the *Morning Post*.'

'No. And I shouldn't think the betting is more than fifteen

to four that you ever will. It all depends on how the good old seventh Earl reacts when I bring Claude home this afternoon and lay him on the mat. I love Claude,' sighed Lady Chloe, 'with a passion too intense for words, but I'm quite aware that he isn't everybody's money. You see, he's an artist and, left to himself, he dresses more like a tramp cyclist than anything else on earth. Still, I'm hoping for the best. I dragged him off to Cohen Bros yesterday and made him buy morning-clothes and a top hat. Thank goodness, he looked positively respectable, so...'

Her voice died away in a strangled rattle. They had entered the Park and were drawing near to the Achilles statue, and coming towards them, his top hat raised in a debonair manner, was a young man of pleasing appearance, correctly clad in morning-coat, grey tie, stiff collar, and an unimpeachable pair of sponge-bag trousers, nicely creased from north to south.

But he was, alas, not one hundred per cent correct. From neck to ankles beyond criticism, below that he went all to pieces. What had caused Lady Chloe to lose the thread of her remarks and Cedric Mulliner to utter a horrified moan was the fact that this young man was wearing bright yellow shoes.

'Claude!' Lady Chloe covered her eyes with a shaking hand. 'Ye Gods!' she cried. 'The foot-joy! The banana specials! The yellow perils! Why? For what reason?'

The young man seemed taken aback.

'Don't you like them?' he said. 'I thought they were rather natty. Just what the rig-out needed, in my opinion, a touch of colour. It seemed to me to help the composition.'

'They're awful. Tell him how awful they are, Mr Mulliner.'

'Tan shoes are not worn with morning-clothes,' said Cedric in a low, grave voice. He was deeply shaken.

'Why not?'

'Never mind why not,' said Lady Chloe. 'They aren't. Look at Mr Mulliner's.'

The young man did so.

'Tame,' he said. 'Colourless. Lacking in spirit and that indefinable something. I don't like them.'

'Well, you've jolly well got to learn to like them,' said Lady Chloe, 'because you're going to change with Mr Mulliner this very minute.'

A shrill, bat-like, middle-aged bachelor squeak forced itself from Cedric's lips. He could hardly believe he had heard correctly.

'Come along, both of you,' said Lady Chloe briskly. 'You can do it over there behind those chairs. I'm sure you don't mind, Mr Mulliner, do you?'

Cedric was still shuddering strongly.

'You ask me to put on yellow shoes with morning-clothes?' he whispered, the face beneath his shining silk hat pale and drawn.

'Yes.'

'Here? In the Park? At the height of the Season?'

'Yes. Do hurry.'

'But...'

'Mr Mulliner! Surely? To oblige me?'

She was gazing at him with pleading eyes, and from the confused welter of Cedric's thoughts there emerged, clear and crystal-like, the recollection of the all-important fact that this girl was the daughter of an Earl and related on her mother's side not only to the Somersetshire Meophams, but to the Brashmarleys of Bucks, the Widringtons of Wilts, and the Hilsbury-Hepworths of Hants. Could he refuse any request, however monstrous, proceeding from one so extremely well-connected?

He stood palsied. All his life he had prided himself on the unassailable orthodoxy of his costume. As a young man he had never gone in for bright ties. His rigidity in the matter of turned-up trousers was a byword. And, though the fashion had been set by an Exalted Personage, he had always stood out against even such a venial lapse as the wearing of a white waistcoat with a dinner-jacket. How little this girl knew the magnitude of the thing she was asking of him. He blinked. His eyes watered and his ears twitched. Hyde Park seemed to whirl about him.

And then, like a voice from afar, something seemed to whisper in his ear that this girl's second cousin, Adelaide, had married Lord Slythe and Sayle and that among the branches of the family were the Sussex Booles and the ffrench-ffarmiloes – not the Kent ffrench-ffarmiloes but the Dorsetshire lot. It just turned the scale.

'So be it!' said Cedric Mulliner.

For a few moments after he found himself alone, my cousin Cedric had all the appearance of a man at a loss for his next move. He stood rooted to the spot, staring spellbound at the saffron horrors which had blossomed on his hitherto blameless feet. Then, pulling himself together with a strong effort, he slunk to Hyde Park Corner, stopped a passing cab, and, having directed the driver to take him to the Albany, leaped hastily in.

The relief of being under cover was at first so exquisite that his mind had no room for other thoughts. Soon, he told himself, he would be safe in his cosy apartment, with the choice of thirty-seven pairs of black boots to take the place of these ghastly objects. It was only when the cab reached the Albany that he realized the difficulties which lay in his path.

How could he walk through the lobby of the Albany looking like a ship with yellow fever on board – he, Cedric Mulliner, the man whose advice on the niceties of dress had frequently been sought by young men in the Brigade of Guards and once by the second son of a Marquis? The thing was inconceivable. All his better nature recoiled from it. Then what to do?

It is characteristic of the Mulliners as a family that, however sore the straits in which they find themselves, they never wholly lose their presence of mind. Cedric leaned out of the window and addressed the driver of the cab.

'My man,' he said, 'how much do you want for your boots?'

The driver was not one of London's lightning thinkers. For a full minute he sat, looking like a red-nosed sheep, allowing the idea to penetrate.

'My boots?' he said at length.

'Your boots!'

'How much do I want for my boots?'

'Precisely. I am anxious to obtain your boots. How much for the boots?'

'How much for the boots?'

'Exactly. The boots. How much for them?'

'You want to buy my boots?'

'Precisely.'

'Ah,' said the driver, 'but the whole thing is, you see, it's like this. I'm not wearing any boots. I suffer from corns, so I come out in a tennis shoe and a carpet slipper. I could do you them at ten bob the pair.'

Cedric Mulliner sank dumbly back. The disappointment had been numbing. But the old Mulliner resourcefulness stood him in good stead. A moment later, his head was out of the window again.

'Take me,' he said, 'to Seven, Nasturtium Villas, Marigold Road, Valley Fields.'

The driver thought this over for a while.

'Why?' he said.

'Never mind why.'

'The Albany you told me,' said the driver. 'Take me to the Albany was what you said. And this here is the Albany. Ask anyone.'

'Yes, yes, yes. But I now wish to go to Seven, Nasturtium Villas...'

'How do you spell it?'

'One "n". Seven, Nasturtium Villas, Marigold Road...'

'How do you spell *that*?'

'One "g".'

'And it's in Valley Fields, you say?'

'Precisely.'

'One "v"?'

'One "v" and one "f",' said Cedric.

The driver sat silent for awhile. The spelling-bee over, he seemed to be marshalling his thoughts.

'Now I'm beginning to get the whole thing,' he said. 'What you want to do is go to Seven, Nasturtium Villas, Marigold Road, Valley Fields.'

'Precisely.'

'Well, will you have the tennis shoe and the carpet slipper now, or wait till we get there?'

'I do not desire the tennis shoe. I have no wish for the carpet slipper. I am not in the market for them.'

'I could do you them at half-a-crown apiece.'

'No, thank you.'

'Couple of bob, then.'

'No, no, no. I do not want the tennis shoe. The carpet slipper makes no appeal to me.'

'You don't want the shoe?'

'No.'

'And you don't want the slipper?'

'No.'

'But you do want,' said the driver, assembling the facts and arranging them in an ordinary manner, 'to go to Seven, Nasturtium Villas, Marigold Road, Valley Fields?'

'Precisely.'

'Ah,' said the driver, slipping in his clutch with an air of quiet rebuke. 'Now we've got the thing straight. If you'd only told me that in the first place, we'd have been 'arf-way there by now.'

The urge which had come upon Cedric Mulliner to visit Seven, Nasturtium Villas, Marigold Road, Valley Fields, that picturesque suburb in the south-eastern postal division of London, had been due to no idle whim. Nor was it prompted by a mere passion for travel and sightseeing. It was at that address that his secretary, Miss Myrtle Watling, lived: and the plan which Cedric had now formed was, in his opinion, the best to date. What he proposed to do was to seek out Miss Watling, give her his latch-key, and dispatch her to the Albany in the cab to fetch him one of his thirty-seven pairs of black boots. When she returned with them he could put them on and look the world in the face again.

He could see no flaw in the scheme, nor did any present itself during the long ride to Valley Fields. It was only when the cab had stopped outside the front garden of the neat little red-brick house and he had alighted and told the driver to wait ('Wait?' said the driver. 'How do you mean, wait? Oh, you mean wait?') that doubts began to disturb him. Even as he raised his finger to press the door-bell, there crept over him a chilly feeling of mistrust, and he drew the finger back as sharply as if he had found it on the point of prodding a Dowager Duchess in the ribs.

Could he meet Miss Watling in morning-clothes and yellow shoes? Reluctantly he told himself that he could not. He remembered how often she had taken down at his dictation letters to the *Times* deploring modern laxity on matters of dress: and his brain reeled at the thought of how she would look if she saw him now. Those raised brows... those scornful lips... those clear, calm eyes registering disgust through their windshields...

No, he could not face Miss Watling.

A sort of dull resignation came over Cedric Mulliner. It was useless, he saw, to struggle any longer. He was on the point of moving from the door and going back to the cab and embarking on the laborious task of explaining to the driver that he wished to return to the Albany ('But I took you there once, and you didn't like it,' he could hear the man saying) when from somewhere close at hand there came to his ears a sudden, loud, gurgling noise, rather like that which might have proceeded from a pig suffocating in a vat of glue. It was the sound of someone snoring. He turned, and was aware of an open window at his elbow.

The afternoon, I should have mentioned before, was oppressively warm. It was the sort of afternoon when suburban householders, after keeping body and soul together with roast beef, Yorkshire pudding, mealy potatoes, apple tart, cheddar cheese and bottled beer, retire into sitting-rooms and take refreshing naps. Such a householder, enjoying such a nap, was the conspicuous feature of the room into which my cousin Cedric was now peering. He was a large, stout man, and he lay in an arm-chair with a handkerchief over his face and his feet on another chair. And those feet, Cedric saw, were clad merely in a pair of mauve socks. His boots lay beside him on the carpet.

With a sudden thrill as sharp as if he had backed into a hot radiator in his bathroom, Cedric perceived that they were black boots.

The next moment, as if impelled by some irresistible force, Cedric Mulliner had shot silently through the window and was crawling on all fours along the floor. His teeth were clenched, and his eyes gleamed with a strange light. If he had not been wearing a top hat, he would have been an almost exact replica of the hunting-cheetah of the Indian jungle stalking its prey.

Cedric crept stealthily on. For a man who had never done this sort of thing before, he showed astonishing proficiency and technique. Indeed, had the cheetah which he so closely resembled chanced to be present, it could undoubtedly have picked up a hint or two which it would have found useful in its business. Inch by inch he moved silently forward, and now his itching fingers were hovering over the nearer of the two boots. At this moment, however, the drowsy stillness of the summer afternoon was shattered by what sounded to his strained senses like G. K. Chesterton falling on a sheet of tin. It was, as a matter of fact, only his hat dropping to the floor, but in the highly nervous state of mind into which he had been plunged by recent events it nearly deafened him. With one noiseless, agile spring, remarkable in one of his waist-measurement, he dived for shelter behind the arm-chair.

A long moment passed. At first he thought that all was well. The sleeper had apparently not wakened. Then there was a gurgle, a heavy body sat up, and a large hand passed within an inch of Cedric's head and pressed the bell in the wall. And presently the door opened and a parlourmaid entered.

'Jane,' said the man in the chair.

'Sir?'

'Something woke me up.'

'Yes, sir?'

'I got the impression ... Jane!'

'Sir?'

'What is that top hat doing on the floor?'

'Top hat, sir?'

'Yes, top hat. This is a nice thing,' said the man, speaking querulously. 'I compose myself for a refreshing sleep, and almost before I can close my eyes the room becomes full of top hats. I come in here for a quiet rest, and without the slightest warning I find myself knee-deep in top hats. Why the top hat, Jane? I demand a categorical answer.'

'Perhaps Miss Myrtle put it there, sir.'

'Why would Miss Myrtle strew top hats about the place?'

'Yes, sir.'

'What do you mean, Yes, sir?'

'No, sir.'

'Very well. Another time, think before you speak. Remove the hat, Jane, and see to it that I am not disturbed again. It is imperative that I get my afternoon's rest.'

'Miss Myrtle said that you were to weed the front garden, sir.'

'I am aware of the fact, Jane,' said the man with dignity. 'In due course I shall proceed to the front garden and start weeding. But first I must have my afternoon's rest. This is a Sunday in June. The birds are sleeping in the trees. Master Willie is sleeping in his room, as ordered by the doctor. I, too, intend to sleep. Leave me, Jane, taking the top hat with you.'

The door closed. The man sank back in his chair with a satisfied grunt, and presently he had begun to snore again.

Cedric did not act hastily. Bitter experience was teaching him the caution which Boy Scouts learn in the cradle. For perhaps a quarter of an hour he remained where he was, crouching in his hiding place. Then the snoring rose in a crescendo. It had now become like something out of Wagner, and it seemed to Cedric that the moment had arrived when action could safely be taken. He removed his left boot and, creeping softly from his lair, seized one of the black boots and put it on. It was a nice fit, and for the first time something approaching contentment began to steal upon him. A minute more, one little minute, and all would be well.

This heartening thought had just crossed his mind when with an abruptness which caused his heart to loosen one of his front teeth the silence was again broken – this time by something that sounded like the Grand Fleet putting in a bit of gunnery-practice off the Nore. An instant later, he was back, quivering, in his niche behind the chair.

The sleeper sat up with a jerk.

'Save the women and children,' he said.

Then the hand came out and pressed the bell again.

'Jane!'

'Sir?'

'Jane, that beastly window-sash has got loose again. I never saw anything like the sashes in this house. A fly settles on them and down they come. Prop it up with a book or something.'

'Yes, sir.'

'And I'll tell you one thing, Jane, and you can quote me as having said so. Next time I want a quiet afternoon's rest, I shall go to a boiler-factory.'

The parlourmaid withdrew. The man heaved a sigh, and lowered himself into the chair again. And presently the room was echoing once more with the Ride of the Valkyries.

It was shortly after this that the bumps began on the ceiling.

They were good, hearty bumps. It sounded to Cedric as if a number of people with large feet were dancing Morris dances in the room above, and he chafed at the selfishness which could lead them to indulge in their pleasures at such a time. Already the man in the chair had begun to stir, and now he sat up and reached for the bell with the old familiar movement.

'Jane!'

'Sir?'

'Listen!'

'Yes, sir.'

'What is it?'

'It is Master Willie, I think, sir, taking his Sunday sleep.'

The man heaved himself out of the chair. It was plain that his emotions were too deep for speech. He yawned cavernously, and began to put on his boots.

'Jane!'

'Sir?'

'I have had enough of this. I shall now go and weed the front garden. Where is my hoe?'

'In the hall, sir.'

'Persecution,' said the man bitterly. 'That's what it is, persecution. Top hats . . . window-sashes . . . Master Willie . . . You can argue as much as you like, Jane, but I shall speak out fearlessly. I insist – and the facts support me – that it is persecution . . . Jane!'

A wordless gurgle proceeded from his lips. He seemed to be choking.

'Jane!'

'Yes, sir?'

'Look me in the face!'

'Yes, sir.'

'Now, answer me, Jane, and let us have no subterfuge or equivocation, Who turned this boot yellow?'

'Boot, sir?'

'Yes, boot.'

'Yellow, sir?'

'Yes, yellow. Look at that boot. Inspect it. Run your eye over it in an unprejudiced spirit. When I took this boot off it was black. I close my eyes for a few brief moments and when I open them it is yellow. I am not a man tamely to submit to this sort of thing. Who did this?'

'Not me, sir.'

'Somebody must have done it. Possibly it is the work of a gang. Sinister things are happening in this house. I tell you, Jane, that Seven, Nasturtium Villas has suddenly – on a Sunday, too, which makes it worse – become a house of mystery. I shall be vastly surprised if, before the day is out, clutching hands do not appear through the curtains and dead bodies drop out of the walls. I don't like it, Jane, and I tell you so frankly. Stand out of my way, woman, and let me get at those weeds.'

The door banged, and there was peace in the sitting-room. But not in the heart of Cedric Mulliner. All the Mulliners are clear thinkers, and it did not take Cedric long to recognize the fact that his position had changed considerably for the worse. Yes, he had lost ground. He had come into this room with a top hat and yellow boots. He would go out of it minus a top hat and wearing one yellow boot and one black one.

A severe set-back.

And now, to complete his discomfiture, his line of communications had been cut. Between him and the cab in which he could find at least temporary safety there stood the man with the hoe. It was a situation to intimidate even a man with a taste for adventure. Douglas Fairbanks would not have liked it. Cedric himself found it intolerable.

There seemed but one course to pursue. This ghastly house presumably possessed a back garden with a door leading out into it. The only thing to do was to flit noiselessly along the passage – if in such a house noiselessness were possible – and find that door and get out into the garden and climb over the wall into the next garden and sneak out into the road and gallop to the cab and so home. He had almost ceased to care what the hall-porter at the Albany would think of him. Perhaps he could pass his appearance off with a light laugh and some story of a bet. Possibly a handsome bribe would close the man's mouth. At any rate, whatever might be the issue, upshot or outcome, back to the Albany he must go, and that with all possible speed. His spirit was broken.

Tiptoeing over the carpet, Cedric opened the door and peeped out. The passage was empty. He crept along it, and had nearly reached its end when he heard the sound of footsteps descending the stairs. There was a door to his left. It was ajar.

He leaped through and found himself in a small room through the window of which he looked out onto a pleasant garden. The footsteps passed on and went down the kitchen stairs.

Cedric breathed again. It seemed to him that the danger was past and that he could now embark on the last portion of his perilous journey. The thought of the cab drew him like a magnet. Until this moment he had not been conscious of any marked fondness for the driver of the cab, but now he found himself yearning for his society. He panted for the driver as the hart pants after the water-brooks.

Cautiously, Cedric Mulliner opened the window. He put his head out to examine the terrain before proceeding farther. The sight encouraged him. The drop to the ground below was of the simplest. He had merely to wriggle through, and all would be well.

It was as he was preparing to do this that the window-sash descended on the back of his neck like a guillotine, and he found himself firmly pinned to the sill.

A thoughtful-looking ginger-coloured cat, which had risen from the mat at his entrance and had been scrutinizing him with a pale eye, now moved forward and sniffed speculatively at his left ankle. The proceedings seemed to the cat irregular but full of human interest. It sat down and gave itself up to meditation.

Cedric, meanwhile, had done the same. There is, if you come to think of it, little else that a man in his position can do but meditate. And so for some considerable space of time Cedric Mulliner looked down upon the smiling garden and busied himself with his thoughts.

These, as may readily be imagined, were not of the most

agreeable. In circumstances such as those in which he had been placed, it is but rarely that the sunny and genial side of a man's mind comes uppermost. He tends to be bitter, and it is inevitable that his rancour should be directed at those whom he considers responsible for his unpleasant situation.

In Cedric's case, there was no difficulty in fixing the responsibility. It was a woman – if one may apply the term to the only daughter of an Earl – who had caused his downfall. Nothing could be more significant of the revolution which circumstances had brought about in Cedric's mind than the fact that, regardless of her high position in Society, he now found himself thinking of Lady Chloe Downblotton in the harshest possible vein.

So moved, indeed, was he that, not content with thoroughly disliking Lady Chloe, he was soon extending his loathing – first to her nearer relations, and finally, incredible as it may seem, to the entire British aristocracy. Twenty-four hours ago – aye even a brief two hours ago – Cedric Mulliner had loved every occupant of Debrett's Peerage, from the premier Dukes right down to the people who scrape in at the bottom of the page under the heading 'Collateral Branches', with a respectful fervour which it had seemed that nothing would ever be able to quench. And now there ran riot in his soul something that was little short of Red Republicanism.

Drones, he considered them, and – it might be severe, but he stuck to it – mere popinjays. Yes, mere thriftless popinjays. It so happened that he had never actually seen a popinjay, but he was convinced by some strange instinct that this was what the typical aristocrat of his native country resembled.

'How long?' groaned Cedric. 'How long?'

He yearned for the day when the clean flame of Freedom, blazing from Moscow, should scorch these wastrels to a crisp, starting with Lady Chloe Downblotton and then taking the others in order of precedence.

It was at this point in his meditations that his attention was diverted from the Social Revolution by an agonizing pain in his right calf.

To the more meditative type of cat there comes at irregular intervals a strange, dreamy urge to stand on its hind legs and sharpen its claws on the nearest perpendicular object. This is usually a tree, but in the present case, there being no tree to hand, the ginger-coloured cat inside the room had made shift with Cedric's right calf. Absently, its mind revolving who knows what abstruse subjects, it blinked once or twice; then, rising, got its claws well into the flesh and pulled them down with a slow, lingering motion.

From Cedric's lips there came a cry like that of some Indian peasant who, wandering on the banks of the Ganges, suddenly finds himself being bitten in half by a crocodile. It rang through the garden like a clarion, and, as the echoes died away, a girl came up the path. The sun glinted on her tortoiseshell-rimmed spectacles, and Cedric recognized his secretary, Miss Myrtle Watling.

'Good afternoon, Mr Mulliner,' said Miss Watling.

She spoke in her usual calm, controlled voice. If she was surprised to see her employer and, seeing him, to behold nothing of him except his head, there was little to show it. A private secretary learns at the outset of their association never to be astonished at anything her employer may do.

Yet Myrtle Watling was not altogether devoid of feminine curiosity.

'What are you doing there, Mr Mulliner?' she asked.

'Something is biting me in the leg,' cried Cedric.

'It is probably Mortal Error,' said Miss Watling, who was a Christian Scientist. 'Why are you standing there in that rather constrained attitude?'

'The sash came down as I was looking out of the window.'

'Why were you looking out of the window?'

'To see how far there was to drop?'

'Why did you wish to drop?'

'I wanted to get away from here.'

'Why did you come here?'

It became plain to Cedric that he must tell his story. He was loath to do so, but to refrain meant that Myrtle Watling would stand there till sunset, saying sentences beginning with 'Why?' In a husky voice he told her all.

For some moment after he had finished, the girl remained silent. A pensive expression had come into her face.

'What you need,' she said, 'is someone to look after you.'

She paused.

'Well, it's not everybody's job,' she said reflectively, 'but I don't mind taking it on.'

A strange foreboding chilled Cedric.

'What do you mean?' he gasped.

'What you need,' said Myrtle Watling, 'is a wife. It is a matter which I have been turning over in my mind for some time, and now the thing is quite clear to me. You should be married. I will marry you, Mr Mulliner.'

Cedric uttered a low cry. This, then, was the meaning of that look which during the past few weeks he had happened to note from time to time in his secretary's glass-fringed eyes.

Footsteps sounded in the gravel path. A voice spoke, the voice of the man who had slept in the chair. He was plainly perturbed.

'Myrtle,' he said, 'I am not a man, as you know, to make a fuss about nothing. I take life as it comes, the rough with the smooth. But I feel it my duty to tell you that eerie influences are at work in this house. The atmosphere has become definitely sinister. Top hats appear from nowhere. Black boots turn yellow. And now this cabby here, this cab-driver fellow...I didn't get your name. Lanchester? Mr Lanchester, my daughter Myrtle...And now Mr Lanchester here tells me that a fare of his entered our front garden some time back and instantly vanished off the face of the earth, and has never been seen again. I am convinced that some little-known Secret Society is at work and that Seven, Nasturtium Villas, is one of those houses you see in the mystery-plays where shrieks are heard from dark corners and mysterious Chinamen flit to and fro making significant gestures and...' He broke off with a sharp howl of dismay, and stood staring. 'Good God! What's that?'

'What, father?'

'That. That bodiless head. That trunkless face. I give you my honest word that there is a severed head protruding from the side of the house. Come over where I'm standing. You can see it distinctly from here.'

'Oh, that?' said Myrtle. 'That is my fiancé.'

'Your fiancé?'

'My fiancé, Mr Cedric Mulliner.'

'Is that all there is of him?' asked the cabman, surprised.

'There is more inside the house,' said Myrtle.

Mr Watling, his composure somewhat restored, was scrutinizing Cedric narrowly.

'Mulliner? You're the fellow my daughter works for, aren't you?'

'I am,' said Cedric.

'And you want to marry her?'

'Certainly he wants to marry me,' said Myrtle, before Cedric could reply.

And suddenly something inside Cedric seemed to say 'Why not?' It was true that he had never contemplated matrimony, except with that shrinking horror which all middle-aged bachelors feel when the thought of it comes into their minds in moments of depression. It was true, also, that if he had been asked to submit specifications for a bride, he would have sketched out something differing from Myrtle Watling in not a few respects. But, after all, he felt as he looked at her strong, capable face, with a wife like this girl he would at least be shielded and sheltered from the world, and never again exposed to the sort of thing he had been going through that afternoon. It seemed good enough.

And there was another thing. And to a man of Cedric's strong Republican views it was perhaps the most important of all. Whatever you might say against Myrtle Watling, she was not a member of the gay and heartless aristocracy. No Sussex Booles, no Hants Hilsbury-Hepworths in *her* family. She came of good, solid suburban stock, related on the male side to the Higginsons of Tangerine Road, Wandsworth, and through the female branch connected with the Browns of Bickley, the Perkinses of Peckham, and the Wodgers, – the Winchmore Hill Wodgers, not the Ponder's End lot.

'It is my dearest wish,' said Cedric in a low, steady voice. 'And if somebody will kindly lift this window off my neck and kick this beastly cat or something which keeps clawing my leg, we can all get together and talk it over.'

The unwonted gravity of Mr Mulliner's demeanour had struck us all directly he entered the bar-parlour of the Angler's Rest: and the silent, moody way in which he sipped his hot Scotch and lemon convinced us that something was wrong. We hastened to make sympathetic inquiries.

Our solicitude seemed to please him. He brightened a little.

'Well, gentlemen,' he said, 'I had not intended to intrude my private troubles on this happy gathering, but, if you must know, a young second cousin of mine has left his wife and is filing papers of divorce. It has upset me very much.'

Miss Postlethwaite, our warm-hearted barmaid, who was polishing glasses, introduced a sort of bedside manner into her task.

'Some viper crept into his home?' she asked.

Mr Mulliner shook his head.

'No,' he said. 'No vipers. The whole trouble appears to have been that, whenever my second cousin spoke to his wife, she would open her eyes to their fullest extent, put her head on one side like a canary, and say "What?" He said he had stood it for eleven months and three days, which he believes to be a European record, and that the time had now come, in his opinion, to take steps.'

Mr Mulliner sighed.

'The fact of the matter is,' he said, 'marriage to-day is made much too simple for a man. He finds it so easy to go out and grab some sweet girl that when he has got her he does not value her. I am convinced that that is the real cause of this modern boom in divorce. What marriage needs, to make it a stable institution, is something in the nature of obstacles during the courtship period. I attribute the solid happiness of my nephew Osbert's union, to take but one instance, to the events which preceded it. If the thing had been a walk-over, he would have prized his wife far less highly.'

'It took him a long time to teach her his true worth?' we asked.

'Love burgeoned slowly?' hazarded Miss Postlethwaite.

'On the contrary,' said Mr Mulliner, 'she loved him at first sight. What made the wooing of Mabel Petherick-Soames so extraordinarily difficult for my nephew Osbert was not any coldness on her part, but the unfortunate mental attitude of J. Bashford Braddock. Does that name suggest anything to you, gentlemen?'

'No.'

'You do not think that a man with such a name would be likely to be a toughish sort of egg?'

'He might be, now you mention it.'

'He was. In Central Africa, where he spent a good deal of his time exploring, ostriches would bury their heads in the sand at Bashford Braddock's approach and even rhinoceroses, the most ferocious beasts in existence, frequently edged behind trees and hid till he had passed. And the moment he came into Osbert's life my nephew realized with a sickening clearness that those rhinoceroses had known their business.'

* * *

Until the advent of this man Braddock (said Mr Mulliner), Fortune seemed to have lavished her favours on my nephew Osbert in full and even overflowing measure. Handsome, like all the Mulliners, he possessed in addition to good looks the inestimable blessings of perfect health, a cheerful disposition, and so much money that Income-Tax assessors screamed with joy when forwarding Schedule D to his address. And, on top of all this, he had fallen deeply in love with a most charming girl and rather fancied that his passion was reciprocated.

For several peaceful, happy weeks all went well. Osbert advanced without a set-back of any description through the various stages of calling, sending flowers, asking after her father's lumbago, and patting her mother's Pomeranian to the point where he was able, with the family's full approval, to invite the girl out alone to dinner and a theatre. And it was on this night of nights, when all should have been joy and happiness, that the Braddock menace took shape.

Until Bashford Braddock made his appearance, no sort of hitch had occurred to mar the perfect tranquillity of the evening's proceedings. The dinner had been excellent, the play entertaining. Twice during the third act Osbert had ventured to squeeze the girl's hand in a warm, though of course gentlemanly, manner: and it seemed to him that the pressure had been returned. It is not surprising, therefore, that by the time they were parting on the steps of her house he had reached the conclusion that he was onto a good thing which should be pushed along.

Putting his fortune to the test, to win or lose it all, Osbert Mulliner reached forward, clasped Mabel Petherick-Soames to his bosom, and gave her a kiss so ardent that in the silent night it sounded like somebody letting off a Mills bomb.

And scarcely had the echoes died away, when he became aware that there was standing at his elbow a tall, broad-shouldered man in evening dress and an opera hat.

There was a pause. The girl was the first to speak.

'Hullo, Bashy,' she said, and there was annoyance in her voice. 'Where on earth did you spring from? I thought you were exploring on the Congo or somewhere.'

The man removed his opera hat, squashed it flat, popped it out again and spoke in a deep, rumbling voice.

'I returned from the Congo this morning. I have been dining with your father and mother. They informed me that you had gone to the theatre with this gentleman.'

'Mr Mulliner. My cousin, Bashford Braddock.'

'How do you do?' said Osbert.

There was another pause. Bashford Braddock removed his opera hat, squashed it flat, popped it out again and replaced it on his head. He seemed disappointed that he could not play a tune on it.

'Well, good night,' said Mabel.

'Good night,' said Osbert.

'Good night,' said Bashford Braddock.

The door closed, and Osbert, looking from it to his companion, found that the other was staring at him with a peculiar expression in his eyes. They were hard, glittering eyes. Osbert did not like them.

'Mr Mulliner,' said Bashford Braddock.

'Hullo?' said Osbert.

'A word with you. I saw all.'

'All?'

'All. Mr Mulliner, you love that girl.'

'I do.'

'So do I.'

'You do?'

'I do.'

Osbert felt a little embarrassed. All he could think of to say was that it made them seem like one great big family.

'I have loved her since she was so high.'

'How high?' asked Osbert, for the light was uncertain.

'About so high. And I have always sworn that if ever any man came between us; if ever any slinking, sneaking, pop-eyed, lop-eared son of a sea-cook attempted to rob me of that girl, I would . . .'

'Er – what?' asked Osbert.

Bashford Braddock laughed a short, metallic laugh.

'Did you ever hear what I did to the King of Mgumbo-Mgumbo?'

'I didn't even know there was a King of Mgumbo-Mgumbo.'

'There isn't – now,' said Bashford Braddock.

Osbert was conscious of a clammy, creeping sensation in the region of his spine.

'What did you do to him?'

'Don't ask.'

'But I want to know.'

'Far better not. You will find out quite soon enough if you continue to hang round Mabel Petherick-Soames. That is all, Mr Mulliner.' Bashford Braddock looked up at the twinkling stars. 'What delightful weather we are having,' he said. 'There was just the same quiet hush and peaceful starlight, I recollect, that time out in the Ngobi desert when I strangled the jaguar.'

Osbert's Adam's apple slipped a cog.

'W – what jaguar?'

'Oh, you wouldn't know it. Just one of the jaguars out there.

I had a rather tricky five minutes of it at first, because my right arm was in a sling and I could only use my left. Well, good night, Mr Mulliner, good night.'

And Bashford Braddock, having removed his opera hat, squashed it flat, popped it out again and replaced it on his head, stalked off into the darkness.

For several minutes after he had disappeared Osbert Mulliner stood motionless, staring after him with unseeing eyes. Then, tottering round the corner, he made his way to his residence in South Audley Street, and, contriving after three false starts to unlock the front door, climbed the stairs to his cosy library. There, having mixed himself a strong brandy-and-soda, he sat down and gave himself up to meditation: and eventually, after one quick drink and another taken rather slower, was able to marshal his thoughts with a certain measure of coherence. And those thoughts, I regret to say, when marshalled, were of a nature which I shrink from revealing to you.

It is never pleasant, gentlemen, to have to display a relative in an unsympathetic light, but the truth is the truth and must be told. I am compelled, therefore, to confess that my nephew Osbert, forgetting that he was a Mulliner, writhed at this moment in an agony of craven fear.

It would be possible, of course, to find excuses for him. The thing had come upon him very suddenly, and even the stoutest are sometimes disconcerted by sudden peril. Then, again, his circumstances and upbringing had fitted him ill for such a crisis. A man who has been pampered by Fortune from birth becomes highly civilized: and the more highly civilized we are, the less adroitly do we cope with bounders of the Braddock type who seem to belong to an earlier and rougher age. Osbert

Mulliner was simply unequal to the task of tackling cavemen. Apart from some slight skill at contract bridge, the only thing he was really good at was collecting old jade: and what a help that would be, he felt as he mixed himself a third brandy-and-soda, in a personal combat with a man who appeared to think it only sporting to give jaguars a chance by fighting them one-handed.

He could see but one way out of the delicate situation in which he had been placed. To give Mabel Petherick-Soames up would break his heart, but it seemed to be a straight issue between that and his neck, and in this black hour the voting in favour of the neck was a positive landslide. Trembling in every limb, my nephew Osbert went to the desk and began to compose a letter of farewell.

He was sorry, he wrote, that he would be unable to see Miss Petherick-Soames on the morrow, as they had planned, owing to his unfortunately being called away to Australia. He added that he was pleased to have made her acquaintance and that if, as seemed probable, they never saw each other again, he would always watch her future career with considerable interest.

Signing the letter 'Yrs truly, O. Mulliner,' Osbert addressed the envelope and, taking it up the street to the post-office, dropped it in the box. Then he returned home and went to bed.

The telephone, ringing by his bedside, woke Osbert at an early hour next morning. He did not answer it. A glance at his watch had told him that the time was half-past eight, when the first delivery of letters is made in London. It seemed only too likely that Mabel, having just received and read his communication, was endeavouring to discuss the matter with him over the wire. He rose, bathed, shaved and dressed, and had just finished a sombre breakfast when the door opened and Parker, his man, announced Major-General Sir Masterman Petherick-Soames.

An icy finger seemed to travel slowly down Osbert's backbone. He cursed the preoccupation which had made him omit to instruct Parker to inform all callers that he was not at home. With some difficulty, for the bones seemed to have been removed from his legs, he rose to receive the tall, upright, grizzled and formidable old man who entered, and rallied himself to play the host.

'Good morning,' he said. 'Will you have a poached egg?'

'I will not have a poached egg,' replied Sir Masterman. 'Poached egg, indeed! Poached egg, forsooth! Ha! Tchah! Bah!'

He spoke with such curt brusqueness that a stranger, had one been present, might have supposed him to belong to some league or society for the suppression of poached eggs. Osbert, however, with his special knowledge of the facts, was able to interpret this brusqueness correctly and was not surprised when his visitor, gazing at him keenly with a pair of steely blue eyes which must have got him very much disliked in military circles, plunged at once into the subject of the letter.

'Mr Mulliner, my niece Mabel has received a strange communication from you.'

'Oh, she got it all right?' said Osbert, with an attempt at ease.

'It arrived this morning. You had omitted to stamp it. There was threepence to pay.'

'Oh, I say, I'm fearfully sorry. I must...'

Major-General Sir Masterman Petherick-Soames waved down his apologies.

'It is not the monetary loss which has so distressed my niece, but the letter's contents. My niece is under the impression that last night she and you became engaged to be married, Mr Mulliner.'

Osbert coughed.

'Well – er – not exactly. Not altogether. Not, as it were ... I mean ... You see ...'

'I see very clearly. You have been trifling with my niece's affections, Mr Mulliner. And I have always sworn that if ever a man trifled with the affections of any of my nieces, I would ...' He broke off and, taking a lump of sugar from the bowl, balanced it absently on the edge of a slice of toast. 'Did you ever hear of a Captain Walkinshaw?'

'No.'

'Captain J. G. Walkinshaw? Dark man with an eyeglass. Used to play the saxophone.'

'No.'

'Ah? I thought you might have met him. He trifled with the affections of my niece, Hester. I horsewhipped him on the steps of the Drones Club. Is the name Blenkinsop-Bustard familiar to you?'

'No.'

'Rupert Blenkinsop-Bustard trifled with the affections of my niece Gertrude. He was one of the Somersetshire Blenkinsop-Bustards. Wore a fair moustache and kept pigeons. I horse-whipped him on the steps of the Junior Bird-Fanciers. By the way, Mr Mulliner, what is your club?'

'The United Jade-Collectors,' quavered Osbert.

'Has it steps?'

'I – I believe so.'

'Good. Good.' A dreamy look came into the General's eyes. 'Well, the announcement of your engagement to my niece Mabel will appear in to-morrow's *Morning Post*. If it is contradicted...Well, good morning, Mr Mulliner, good morning.'

And, replacing in the dish the piece of bacon which he had been poising on a teaspoon, Major-General Sir Masterman Petherick-Soames left the room.

The meditation to which my nephew Osbert had given himself up on the previous night was as nothing to the meditation to which he gave himself up now. For fully an hour he must have sat, his head supported by his hands, frowning despairingly at the remains of the marmalade on the plate before him. Though, like all the Mulliners, a clear thinker, he had to confess himself completely non-plussed. The situation had become so complicated that after awhile he went up to the library and tried to work it out on paper, letting X equal himself. But even this brought no solution, and he was still pondering deeply when Parker came up to announce lunch.

'Lunch?' said Osbert, amazed. 'Is it lunch-time already?'

'Yes, sir. And might I be permitted to offer my respectful congratulations and good wishes, sir?'

'Eh?'

'On your engagement, sir. The General happened to mention to me as I let him out that a marriage had been arranged and would shortly take place between yourself and Miss Mabel Petherick-Soames. It was fortunate that he did so, as I was thus enabled to give the gentleman the information he required.'

'Gentleman?'

'A Mr Bashford Braddock, sir. He rang up about an hour after the General had left and said he had been informed of your engagement and wished to know if the news was well-founded. I assured him that it was, and he said he would be calling to see you later. He was very anxious to know when you would be at home. He seemed a nice, friendly gentleman, sir.'

Osbert rose as if the chair in which he sat had suddenly become incandescent.

'Parker!'

'Sir?'

'I am unexpectedly obliged to leave London, Parker. I don't know where I am going – probably the Zambesi or Greenland – but I shall be away a long time. I shall close the house and give the staff an indefinite holiday. They will receive three months' wages in advance, and at the end of that period will communicate with my lawyers, Messrs Peabody, Thrupp, Thrupp, Thrupp, Thrupp and Peabody of Lincoln's Inn. Inform them of this.'

'Very good, sir.'

'And, Parker.'

'Sir?'

'I am thinking of appearing shortly in some amateur theatricals. Kindly step round the corner and get me a false wig, a false nose, some false whiskers and a good stout pair of blue spectacles.'

Osbert's plans when, after a cautious glance up and down the street, he left the house an hour later and directed a taxi-cab to take him to an obscure hotel in the wildest and least-known part of the Cromwell Road were of the vaguest. It was only when he reached that haven and had thoroughly wigged, nosed, whiskered and blue-spectacled himself that he began to formulate a definite plan of campaign. He spent the rest of the day in his room, and shortly before lunch next morning set out for the Second-Hand Clothing establishment of the Bros Cohen, near Covent Garden, to purchase a complete traveller's outfit. It was his intention to board the boat sailing on the morrow for India and to potter awhile about the world, taking in *en route* Japan, South Africa, Peru, Mexico, China, Venezuela, the Fiji Islands and other beauty-spots.

All the Cohens seemed glad to see him when he arrived at the shop. They clustered about him in a body, as if guessing by instinct that here came one of those big orders. At this excellent emporium one may buy, in addition to second-hand clothing, practically anything that exists: and the difficulty – for the brothers are all thrustful salesmen – is to avoid doing so. At the end of five minutes, Osbert was mildly surprised to find himself in possession of a smoking-cap, three boxes of poker-chips, some polo sticks, a fishing-rod, a concertina, a ukulele, and a bowl of goldfish.

He clicked his tongue in annoyance. These men appeared to him to have got quite a wrong angle on the situation. They seemed to think that he proposed to make his travels one long round of pleasure. As clearly as he was able, he tried to tell them that in the few broken years that remained to him before a shark or jungle-fever put an end to his sorrows he would have little heart for polo, for poker, or for playing the concertina while watching the gambols of goldfish. They might just as well offer him, he said querulously, a cocked hat or a sewing-machine.

Instant activity prevailed among the brothers.

'Fetch the gentleman his sewing-machine, Isadore.'

'And, while you're getting him the cocked hat, Lou,' said Irving, 'ask the customer in the shoe department if he'll be kind enough to step this way. You're in luck,' he assured Osbert. 'If you're going travelling in foreign parts, he's the very man to advise you. You've heard of Mr Braddock?'

There was very little of Osbert's face visible behind his whiskers, but that little paled beneath its tan.

'Mr B – b – b...?'

'That's right. Mr Braddock, the explorer.'

'Air!' said Osbert. 'Give me air!'

He made rapidly for the door, and was about to charge through when it opened to admit a tall, distinguished-looking man of military appearance.

'Shop!' cried the newcomer in a clear, patrician voice, and Osbert reeled back against a pile of trousers. It was Major-General Sir Masterman Petherick-Soames.

A platoon of Cohens advanced upon him, Isadore hastily snatching up a fireman's helmet and Irving a microscope and a couple of jig-saw puzzles. The General waved them aside.

'Do you,' he asked, 'keep horsewhips?'

'Yes, sir. Plenty of horsewhips.'

'I want a nice strong one with a medium-sized handle and lots of spring,' said Major-General Sir Masterman Petherick-Soames.

And at this moment Lou returned, followed by Bashford Braddock.

'Is this the gentleman?' said Bashford Braddock genially. 'You're going abroad, sir, I understand. Delighted if I can be of any service.'

'Bless my soul,' said Major-General Sir Masterman Petherick-Soames. 'Bashford? It's so confoundedly dark in here, I didn't recognize you.'

'Switch on the light, Irving,' said Isadore.

'No, don't,' said Osbert. 'My eyes are weak.'

'If your eyes are weak you ought not to be going to the Tropics,' said Bashford Braddock.

'This gentleman a friend of yours?' asked the General.

'Oh, no. I'm just going to help him to buy an outfit.'

'The gentleman's already got a smoking-cap, poker-chips, polo sticks, a fishing-rod, a concertina, a ukulele, a bowl of goldfish, a cocked hat and a sewing-machine,' said Isadore.

'Ah?' said Bashford Braddock. 'Then all he will require now is a sun helmet, a pair of puttees, and a pot of ointment for relieving alligator-bites.'

With the rapid decision of an explorer who is buying things for which somebody else is going to pay, he completed the selection of Osbert's outfit.

'And what brings you here, Bashford?' asked the General.

'Me? Oh, I looked in to buy a pair of spiked boots. I want to trample on a snake.'

'An odd coincidence. I came here to buy a horsewhip to horsewhip a snake.'

'A bad week-end for snakes,' said Bashford Braddock.

The General nodded gravely.

'Of course, my snake,' he said, 'may prove not to be a snake. In classifying him as a snake I may have misjudged him. In that case I shall not require this horsewhip. Still, they're always useful to have about the house.'

'Undoubtedly. Lunch with me, General?'

'Delighted, my dear fellow.'

'Goodbye, sir,' said Bashford Braddock, giving Osbert a friendly nod. 'Glad I was able to be of some use. When do you sail?'

'Gentleman's sailing to-morrow morning on the *Rajputana*,' said Isadore.

'What!' cried Major-General Sir Masterman Petherick-Soames. 'Bless my soul! I didn't realize you were going to *India*.

I was out there for years and can give you all sorts of useful hints. The old *Rajputana*? Why, I know the purser well. I'll come and see you off and have a chat with him. No doubt I shall be able to get you a number of little extra attentions. No, no, my dear fellow, don't thank me. I have a good deal on my mind at the moment, and it will be a relief to do somebody a kindness.'

It seemed to Osbert, as he crawled back to the shelter of his Cromwell Road bedroom, that Fate was being altogether too rough with him. Obviously, if Sir Masterman Petherick-Soames intended to come down to the boat to see him off, it would be madness to attempt to sail. On the deck of a liner under the noon-day sun the General must inevitably penetrate his disguise. His whole scheme of escape must be cancelled and another substituted. Osbert ordered two pots of black coffee, tied a wet handkerchief round his forehead, and plunged once more into thought.

It has been frequently said of the Mulliners that you may perplex but you cannot baffle them. It was getting on for dinner-time before Osbert finally decided upon a plan of action: but this plan, he perceived as he examined it, was far superior to the first one.

He had been wrong, he saw, in thinking of flying to foreign climes. For one who desired as fervently as he did never to see Major-General Sir Masterman Petherick-Soames again in this world, the only real refuge was a London suburb. Any momentary whim might lead Sir Masterman to pack a suitcase and take the next boat to the Far East, but nothing would ever cause him to take a tram for Dulwich, Cricklewood, Winchmore Hill, Brixton, Balham or Surbiton. In those trackless wastes Osbert would be safe.

Osbert decided to wait till late at night; then go back to his house in South Audley Street, pack his collection of old jade and a few other necessaries, and vanish into the unknown.

It was getting on for midnight when, creeping warily to the familiar steps, he inserted his latch-key in the familiar keyhole. He had feared that Bashford Braddock might be watching the house, but there were no signs of him. He slipped swiftly into the dark hall and closed the front door softly behind him.

It was at this moment that he became aware that from under the door of the dining-room at the other end of the hall there was stealing a thin stream of light.

For an instant, this evidence that the house was not, as he had supposed, unoccupied startled Osbert considerably. Then, recovering himself, he understood what must have happened. Parker, his man, instead of leaving as he had been told to do, was taking advantage of his employer's presumed absence from London to stay on and do some informal entertaining. Osbert, thoroughly incensed, hurried to the dining-room and felt that his suspicion had been confirmed. On the table were set out all the materials, except food and drink, of a cosy little supper for two. The absence of food and drink was accounted for, no doubt, by the fact that Parker and – Osbert saw only too good reason to fear – his lady-friend were down in the larder, fetching them.

Osbert boiled from his false wig to the soles of his feet with a passionate fury. So this was the sort of thing that went on the moment his back was turned, was it? There were heavy curtains hiding the window, and behind these he crept. It was his intention to permit the feast to begin and then, stepping forth like some avenging Nemesis, to confront his erring man-servant and put it across him in no uncertain manner. Bashford Braddock and Major-General Sir Masterman Petherick-Soames, with their towering stature and whipcord muscles, might intimidate him, but with a shrimp like Parker he felt that he could do himself justice. Osbert had been through much in the last forty-eight hours, and unpleasantness with a man who, like Parker, stood a mere five feet five in his socks appeared to him rather in the nature of a tonic.

He had not been waiting long when there came to his ears the sound of footsteps outside. He softly removed his wig, his nose, his whiskers and his blue spectacles. There must be no disguise to soften the shock when Parker found himself confronted. Then, peeping through the curtains, he prepared to spring.

Osbert did not spring. Instead, he shrank back like a more than ordinarily diffident tortoise into its shell, and tried to achieve the maximum of silence by breathing through his ears. For it was no Parker who had entered, no frivolous lady-friend, but a couple of plug-uglies of such outstanding physique that Bashford Braddock might have been the little brother of either of them.

Osbert stood petrified. He had never seen a burglar before, and he wished, now that he was seeing these, that it could have been arranged for him to do so through a telescope. At this close range, they gave him much the same feeling the prophet Daniel must have had on entering the lions' den, before his relations with the animals had been established on their subsequent basis of easy camaraderie. He was thankful that when the breath which he had been holding for some eighty seconds at length forced itself out in a loud gasp, the noise was drowned by the popping of a cork.

It was from a bottle of Osbert's best Bollinger that this cork had been removed. The marauders, he was able to see, were men who believed in doing themselves well. In these days when almost everybody is on some sort of diet it is rarely that one comes across the old-fashioned type of diner who does not worry about balanced meals and calories but just squares his shoulders and goes at it till his eyes bubble. Osbert's two guests plainly belonged to this nearly obsolete species. They were drinking out of tankards and eating three varieties of meat simultaneously, as if no such thing as a high blood-pressure had ever been invented. A second pop announced the opening of another quart of champagne.

At the outset of the proceedings, there had been little or nothing in the way of supper-table conversation. But now, the first keen edge of his appetite satisfied by about three pounds of ham, beef and mutton, the burglar who sat nearest to Osbert was able to relax. He looked about him approvingly.

'Nice little crib, this, Ernest,' he said.

'R!' replied his companion – a man of few words, and those somewhat impeded by cold potatoes and bread.

'Must have been some real swells in here one time and another.'

'R!'

'Baronets and such, I wouldn't be surprised.'

'R!' said the second burglar, helping himself to more champagne and mixing in a little port, sherry, Italian vermouth, old brandy and green Chartreuse to give it body.

The first burglar looked thoughtful.

'Talking of baronets,' he said, 'a thing I've often wondered is – well, suppose you're having a dinner, see?'

'R!'

'As it might be in this very room.'

'R!'

'Well, would a baronet's sister go in before the daughter of the younger son of a peer? I've often wondered about that.'

The second burglar finished his champagne, port, sherry, Italian vermouth, old brandy and green Chartreuse, and mixed himself another.

'Go in?'

'Go in to dinner.'

'If she was quicker on her feet, she would,' said the second burglar. 'She'd get to the door first. Stands to reason.'

The first burglar raised his eyebrows.

'Ernest,' he said coldly, 'you talk like an uneducated son of a what-not. Haven't you never been taught nothing about the rules and manners of good Society?'

The second burglar flushed. It was plain that the rebuke had touched a tender spot. There was a strained silence. The first burglar resumed his meal. The second burglar watched him with a hostile eye. He had the air of a man who is waiting for his chance, and it was not long before he found it.

'Harold,' he said.

'Well?' said the first burglar.

'Don't gollup your food, Harold,' said the second burglar.

The first burglar started. His eyes gleamed with sudden fury. His armour, like his companion's, had been pierced.

'Who's golluping his food?'

'You are.'

'I am?'

'Yes, you.'

'Who, me?'

'R!'

'Golluping my food?'

'R! Like a pig or something.'

It was evident to Osbert, peeping warily through the curtains, that the generous fluids which these two men had been drinking so lavishly had begun to have their effect. They spoke thickly, and their eyes had become red and swollen.

'I may not know all about baronets' younger sisters,' said the burglar Ernest, 'but I don't gollup my food like pigs or something.'

And, as if to drive home the reproach, he picked up the leg of mutton and began to gnaw it with an affected daintiness.

The next moment the battle had been joined. The spectacle of the other's priggish object-lesson was too much for the burglar Harold. He plainly resented tuition in the amenities from one on whom he had always looked as a social inferior. With a swift movement of the hand he grasped the bottle before him and bounced it smartly on his colleague's head.

Osbert Mulliner cowered behind the curtain. The sportsman in him whispered that he was missing something good, for ring-seats to view which many men would have paid large sums, but he could not nerve himself to look out. However, there was plenty of interest in the thing, even if you merely listened. The bumps and crashes seemed to indicate that the two principals were hitting one another with virtually everything in the room except the wall-paper and the large sideboard. Now they appeared to be grappling on the floor, anon fighting at long range with bottles. Words and combinations of whose existence he had till then been unaware, floated to Osbert's ears: and more and more he asked himself, as the combat proceeded: What would the harvest be?

And then, with one titanic crash, the battle ceased as suddenly as it had begun.

* * *

It was some moments before Osbert Mulliner could bring himself to peep from behind the curtains. When he did so, he seemed to be gazing upon one of those Orgy scenes which have done so much to popularize the motion-pictures. Scenically, the thing was perfect. All that was needed to complete the resemblance was a few attractive-looking girls with hardly any clothes on.

He came out and gaped down at the ruins. The burglar Harold was lying with his head in the fireplace: the burglar Ernest was doubled up under the table: and it seemed to Osbert almost absurd to think that these were the same hearty fellows who had come into the room to take pot-luck so short a while before. Harold had the appearance of a man who has been passed through a wringer. Ernest gave the illusion of having recently become entangled in some powerful machinery. If, as was probable, they were known to the police, it would take a singularly keen-eyed constable to recognize them now.

The thought of the police reminded Osbert of his duty as a citizen. He went to the telephone and called up the nearest station and was informed that representatives of the Law would be round immediately to scoop up the remains. He went back to the dining-room to wait, but its atmosphere jarred upon him. He felt the need of fresh air: and, going to the front door, he opened it and stood upon the steps, breathing deeply.

And, as he stood there, a form loomed through the darkness and a heavy hand fell on his arm.

'Mr Mulliner, I think? Mr Mulliner, if I mistake not? Good evening, Mr Mulliner,' said the voice of Bashford Braddock. 'A word with you, Mr Mulliner.'

Osbert returned his gaze without flinching. He was conscious of a strange, almost uncanny calm. The fact was that, everything in this world being relative, he was regarding Bashford Braddock at this moment as rather an undersized little pipsqueak, and wondering why he had ever worried about the man. To one who had come so recently from the society of Harold and Ernest, Bashford Braddock seemed like one of Singer's Midgets.

'Ah, Braddock?' said Osbert.

At this moment, with a grinding of brakes, a van stopped before the door and policemen began to emerge.

'Mr Mulliner?' asked the sergeant.

Osbert greeted him affably.

'Come in,' he said. 'Come in. Go straight through. You will find them in the dining-room. I'm afraid I had to handle them a little roughly. You had better 'phone for a doctor.'

'Bad are they?'

'A little the worse for wear.'

'Well, they asked for it,' said the sergeant.

'Exactly, sergeant,' said Osbert. '*Rem acŭ tetigisti.*'

Bashford Braddock had been standing listening to this exchange of remarks with a somewhat perplexed air.

'What's all this?' he said.

Osbert came out of his thoughts with a start.

'You still here, my dear chap?'

'I am.'

'Want to see me about anything, dear boy? Something on your mind?'

'I just want a quiet five minutes alone with you, Mr Mulliner.'

'Certainly, my dear old fellow,' said Osbert. 'Certainly, certainly, certainly. Just wait till these policemen have gone and I will be at your disposal. We have had a little burglary.'

'Burg—,' Bashford Braddock was beginning, when there

came out onto the steps a couple of policemen. They were supporting the burglar Harold, and were followed by others assisting the burglar Ernest. The sergeant, coming last, shook his head at Osbert a little gravely.

'You ought to be careful, sir,' he said. 'I don't say these fellows didn't deserve all you gave them, but you want to watch yourself. One of these days . . .'

'Perhaps I did overdo it a little,' admitted Osbert. 'But I am rather apt to see red on these occasions. One's fighting blood, you know. Well, good night, sergeant, good night. And now,' he said, taking Bashford Braddock's arm in a genial grip, 'what was it you wanted to talk to me about? Come into the house. We shall be all alone there. I gave the staff a holiday. There won't be a soul except ourselves.'

Bashford Braddock released his arm. He seemed embarrassed. His face, as the light of the street lamp shone upon it, was strangely pale.

'Did you—' He gulped a little. 'Was that really you?'

'Really me? Oh, you mean those two fellows. Oh, yes, I found them in my dining-room, eating my food and drinking my wine as cool as you please, and naturally I set about them. But the sergeant was quite right. I *do* get too rough when I lose my temper. I must remember,' he said, taking out his handkerchief and tying a knot in it, 'to cure myself of that. The fact is, I sometimes don't know my own strength. But you haven't told me what it is you want to see me about?'

Bashford Braddock swallowed twice in quick succession. He edged past Osbert to the foot of the steps. He seemed oddly uneasy. His face had now taken on a greenish tinge.

'Oh, nothing, nothing.'

'But, my dear fellow,' protested Osbert, 'it must have been

something important to bring you round at this time of night.'

Bashford Braddock gulped.

'Well, it was like this. I – er – saw the announcement of your engagement in the paper this morning, and I thought— I – er – just thought I would look in and ask you what you would like for a wedding-present.'

'My dear chap! Much too kind of you.'

'So – er – so silly if I gave a fish-slice and found that everybody else had given fish-slices.'

'That's true. Well, why not come inside and talk it over?'

'No, I won't come in, thanks. I'd rather not come in. Perhaps you will write and let me know. *Poste Restante*, Bongo on the Congo, will find me. I am returning there immediately.'

'Certainly,' said Osbert. He looked down at his companion's feet. 'My dear old lad, what on earth are you wearing those extraordinary boots for?'

'Corns,' said Bashford Braddock.

'Why the spikes?'

'They relieve the pressure on the feet.'

'I see, well, good night, Mr Braddock.'

'Good night, Mr Mulliner.'

'Good night,' said Osbert.

'Good night,' said Bashford Braddock.

The poet who was spending the summer at the Angler's Rest had just begun to read us his new sonnet-sequence when the door of the bar-parlour opened and there entered a young man in gaiters. He came quickly in and ordered beer. In one hand he was carrying a double-barrelled gun, in the other a posy of dead rabbits. These he dropped squashily to the floor: and the poet, stopping in mid-sentence, took one long, earnest look at the remains. Then, wincing painfully, he turned a light green and closed his eyes. It was not until the banging of the door announced the visitor's departure that he came to life again.

Mr Mulliner regarded him sympathetically over his hot Scotch and lemon.

'You appear upset,' he said.

'A little,' admitted the poet. 'A momentary malaise. It may be a purely personal prejudice, but I confess to preferring rabbits with rather more of their contents inside them.'

'Many sensitive souls in your line of business hold similar views,' Mr Mulliner assured him. 'My niece Charlotte did.'

'It is my temperament,' said the poet. 'I dislike all dead things – particularly when, as in the case of the above rabbits, they have so obviously, so – shall I say? – blatantly made the Great

Change. Give me,' he went on, the greenish tinge fading from his face, 'life and joy and beauty.'

'Just what my niece Charlotte used to say.'

'Oddly enough, that thought forms the theme of the second sonnet in my sequence – which, now that the young gentleman with the portable Morgue has left us, I will...'

'My niece Charlotte,' said Mr Mulliner, with quiet firmness, 'was one of those gentle, dreamy, wistful girls who take what I have sometimes felt to be a mean advantage of having an ample private income to write Vignettes in Verse for the artistic weeklies. Charlotte's Vignettes in Verse had a wide vogue among the editors of London's higher-browed but less prosperous periodicals. Directly these frugal men realized that she was willing to supply unstinted Vignettes gratis, for the mere pleasure of seeing herself in print, they were all over her. The consequence was that before long she had begun to move freely in the most refined literary circles: and one day, at a little luncheon at the Crushed Pansy (The Restaurant With A Soul), she found herself seated next to a godlike young man at the sight of whom something seemed to go off inside her like a spring.'

'Talking of Spring...' said the poet.

Cupid (proceeded Mr Mulliner), has always found the family to which I belong a ready mark for his bow. Our hearts are warm, our passions quick. It is not too much to say that my niece Charlotte was in love with this young man before she had finished spearing the first anchovy out of the hors-d'œuvres dish. He was intensely spiritual-looking, with a broad, white forehead and eyes that seemed to Charlotte not so much eyes as a couple of holes punched in the surface of a beautiful soul. He wrote, she learned, Pastels in Prose: and his name, if she had caught it correctly at the moment of their introduction, was Aubrey Trefusis.

Friendship ripens quickly at the Crushed Pansy. The *poulet rôti au cresson* had scarcely been distributed before the young man was telling Charlotte his hopes, his fears, and the story of his boyhood. And she was amazed to find that he sprang – not from a long line of artists but from an ordinary, conventional county family of the type that cares for nothing except hunting and shooting.

'You can readily imagine,' he said, helping her to Brussels sprouts, 'how intensely such an environment jarred upon my unfolding spirit. My family are greatly respected in the neighbourhood, but I personally have always looked upon them as a gang of blood-imbrued plug-uglies. My views on kindness to animals are rigid. My impulse, on encountering a rabbit, is to offer it lettuce. To my family, on the other hand, a rabbit seems incomplete without a deposit of small shot in it. My father, I believe, has cut off more assorted birds in their prime than any other man in the Midlands. A whole morning was spoiled for me last week by the sight of a photograph of him in the *Tatler*, looking rather severely at a dying duck. My elder brother Reginald spreads destruction in every branch of the animal kingdom. And my younger brother Wilfred is, I understand, working his way up to the larger fauna by killing sparrows with an air-gun. Spiritually, one might just as well live in Chicago as at Bludleigh Court.'

'Bludleigh Court?' cried Charlotte.

'The moment I was twenty-one and came into a modest but sufficient inheritance, I left the place and went to London to lead the life literary. The family, of course, were appalled. My uncle Francis, I remember, tried to reason with me for hours.

Uncle Francis, you see, used to be a famous big-game hunter. They tell me he has shot more gnus than any other man who ever went to Africa. In fact, until recently he virtually never stopped shooting gnus. Now, I hear, he has developed lumbago and is down at Bludleigh treating it with Riggs's Super-fine Emulsion and sun-baths.'

'But is Bludleigh Court your home?'

'That's right. Bludleigh Court, Lesser Bludleigh, near Goresby-on-the-Ouse, Bedfordshire.'

'But Bludleigh Court belongs to Sir Alexander Bassinger.'

'My name is really Bassinger. I adopted the pen-name of Trefusis to spare the family's feelings. But how do you come to know of the place?'

'I'm going down there next week for a visit. My mother was an old friend of Lady Bassinger.'

Aubrey was astonished. And, being, like all writers of Pastels in Prose, a neat phrase-maker, he said what a small world it was, after all.

'Well, well, well!' he said.

'From what you tell me,' said Charlotte, 'I'm afraid I shall not enjoy my visit. If there's one thing I loathe, it's anything connected with sport.'

'Two minds with but a single thought,' said Aubrey. 'Look here, I'll tell you what. I haven't been near Bludleigh for years, but if you're going there, why, dash it, I'll come too – aye, even though it means meeting my uncle Francis.'

'You will?'

'I certainly will. I don't consider it safe that a girl of your exquisite refinement and sensibility should be dumped down at an abattoir like Bludleigh Court without a kindred spirit to lend her moral stability.'

'What do you mean?'

'I'll tell you.' His voice was grave. 'That house exercises a spell.'

'A what?'

'A spell. A ghastly spell that saps the strongest humanitarian principles. Who knows what effect it might have upon you, should you go there without someone like me to stand by you and guide you in your hour of need?'

'What nonsense!'

'Well, all I can tell you is that once, when I was a boy, a high official of Our Dumb Brothers' League of Mercy arrived there latish on a Friday night, and at two-fifteen on the Saturday afternoon he was the life and soul of an informal party got up for the purpose of drawing one of the local badgers out of an upturned barrel.'

Charlotte laughed merrily.

'The spell will not affect me,' she said.

'Nor me, of course,' said Aubrey. 'But all the same, I would prefer to be by your side, if you don't mind.'

'Mind, Mr Bassinger!' breathed Charlotte softly, and was thrilled to note that at the words and the look with which she accompanied them this man to whom – for, as I say, we Mulliners are quick workers – she had already given her heart, quivered violently. It seemed to her that in those soulful eyes of his she had seen the love-light.

Bludleigh Court, when Charlotte reached it some days later, proved to be a noble old pile of Tudor architecture, situated in rolling parkland and flanked by pleasant gardens leading to a lake with a tree-fringed boathouse. Inside, it was comfortably furnished and decorated throughout with groves of glass cases containing the goggle-eyed remnants of birds and beasts assassinated at one time or another by Sir Alexander Bassinger and his son, Reginald. From every wall there peered down with an air of mild reproach selected portions of the gnus, moose, elks, zebus, antelopes, giraffes, mountain goats and wapiti which had had the misfortune to meet Colonel Sir Francis Pashley-Drake before lumbago spoiled him for the chase. The cemetery also included a few stuffed sparrows, which showed that little Wilfred was doing his bit.

The first two days of her visit Charlotte passed mostly in the society of Colonel Pashley-Drake, the uncle Francis to whom Aubrey had alluded. He seemed to have taken a paternal fancy to her: and, lithely though she dodged down back-stairs and passages, she generally found him breathing heavily at her side. He was a red-faced, almost circular man, with eyes like a prawn's, and he spoke to her freely of lumbago, gnus and Aubrey.

'So you're a friend of my young nephew?' he said, snorting twice in a rather unpleasant manner. It was plain that he disapproved of the pastel-artist. 'Shouldn't see too much of him, if I were you. Not the sort of fellow I'd like any daughter of mine to get friendly with.'

'You are quite wrong,' said Charlotte warmly. 'You have only to gaze into Mr Bassinger's eyes to see that his morals are above reproach.'

'I never gaze into his eyes,' replied Colonel Pashley-Drake. 'Don't like his eyes. Wouldn't gaze into them if you paid me. I maintain his whole outlook on life is morbid and unwholesome. I like a man to be a clean, strong, upstanding Englishman who can look his gnu in the face and put an ounce of lead in it.'

'Life,' said Charlotte coldly, 'is not all gnus.'

'You imply that there are also wapiti, moose, zebus and

mountain goats?' said Sir Francis. 'Well, maybe you're right. All the same, I'd give the fellow a wide berth, if I were you.'

'So far from doing so,' replied Charlotte proudly, 'I am about to go for a stroll with him by the lake at this very moment.'

And, turning away with a petulant toss of her head, she moved off to meet Aubrey, who was hurrying towards her across the terrace.

'I am so glad you came, Mr Bassinger,' she said to him as they walked together in the direction of the lake. 'I was beginning to find your uncle Francis a little excessive.'

Aubrey nodded sympathetically. He had observed her in conversation with his relative and his heart had gone out to her.

'Two minutes of my uncle Francis,' he said, 'is considered by the best judges a good medium dose for an adult. So you find him trying, eh? I was wondering what impression my family had made on you.'

Charlotte was silent for a moment.

'How relative everything is in this world,' she said pensively. 'When I first met your father, I thought I had never seen anybody more completely loathsome. Then I was introduced to your brother Reginald, and I realized that, after all, your father might have been considerably worse. And, just as I was thinking that Reginald was the furthest point possible, along came your uncle Francis, and Reginald's quiet charm seemed to leap out at me like a beacon on a dark night. Tell me,' she said, 'has no one ever thought of doing anything about your uncle Francis?'

Aubrey shook his head gently.

'It is pretty generally recognized now that he is beyond the reach of human science. The only thing to do seems to be to let him go on till he eventually runs down.'

They sat together on a rustic bench overlooking the water. It was a lovely morning. The sun shone on the little wavelets which the sighing breeze drove gently to the shore. A dreamy stillness had fallen on the world, broken only by the distant sound of Sir Alexander Bassinger murdering magpies, of Reginald Bassinger encouraging dogs to eviscerate a rabbit, of Wilfred busy among the sparrows, and a monotonous droning noise from the upper terrace, which was Colonel Sir Francis Pashley-Drake telling Lady Bassinger what to do with the dead gnu.

Aubrey was the first to break the silence.

'How lovely the world is, Miss Mulliner.'

'Yes, isn't it!'

'How softly the breeze caresses yonder water.'

'Yes, doesn't it!'

'How fragrant a scent of wild flowers it has.'

'Yes, hasn't it!'

They were silent again.

'On such a day,' said Aubrey, 'the mind seems to turn irresistibly to Love.'

'Love?' said Charlotte, her heart beginning to flutter.

'Love,' said Aubrey. 'Tell me, Miss Mulliner, have you ever thought of Love?'

He took her hand. Her head was bent, and with the toe of her dainty shoe she toyed with a passing snail.

'Life, Miss Mulliner,' said Aubrey, 'is a Sahara through which we all must pass. We start at the Cairo of the cradle and we travel on to the – er – well, we go travelling on.'

'Yes, don't we!' said Charlotte.

'Afar we can see the distant goal . . .'

'Yes, can't we!'

'... and would fain reach it.'

'Yes, wouldn't we!'

'But the way is rough and weary. We have to battle through the sand-storms of Destiny, face with what courage we may the howling simoons of Fate. And very unpleasant it all is. But sometimes in the Sahara of Life, if we are fortunate, we come upon the Oasis of Love. That oasis, when I had all but lost hope, I reached at one-fifteen on the afternoon of Tuesday, the twenty-second of last month. There comes a time in the life of every man when he sees Happiness beckoning to him and must grasp it. Miss Mulliner, I have something to ask you which I have been trying to ask ever since the day when we two first met. Miss Mulliner ... Charlotte ... Will you be my ... Gosh! Look at that whacking great rat! Loo-loo-loo-loo-loo-loo-loo-loo!' said Aubrey, changing the subject.

Once, in her childhood, a sportive playmate had secretly withdrawn the chair on which Charlotte Mulliner was preparing to seat herself. Years had passed, but the recollection of the incident remained green in her memory. In frosty weather she could still feel the old wound. And now, as Aubrey Bassinger suddenly behaved in this remarkable manner, she experienced the same sensation again. It was as though something blunt and heavy had hit her on the head at the exact moment when she was slipping on a banana-skin.

She stared round-eyed at Aubrey. He had released her hand, sprung to his feet, and now, armed with her parasol, was beating furiously in the lush grass at the waterside. And every little while his mouth would open, his head would go back, and uncouth sounds would proceed from his slavering jaws.

'Yoicks! Yoicks! Yoicks!' cried Aubrey.

And again,

'Tally-ho! Hard For'ard! Tally-ho!'

Presently the fever seemed to pass. He straightened himself and came back to where she stood.

'It must have got away into a hole or something,' he said, removing a bead of perspiration from his forehead with the ferrule of the parasol. 'The fact of the matter is, it's silly ever to go out in the country without a good dog. If only I'd had a nice, nippy terrier with me, I might have obtained some solid results. As it is, a fine rat – gone – just like that! Oh, well, that's Life, I suppose.' He paused. 'Let me see,' he said. 'Where was I?'

And then it was as though he waked from a trance. His flushed face paled.

'I say,' he stammered, 'I'm afraid you must think me most awfully rude.'

'Pray do not mention it,' said Charlotte coldly.

'Oh, but you must. Dashing off like that.'

'Not at all.'

'What I was going to say, when I was interrupted, was, will you be my wife?'

'Oh?'

'Yes.'

'Well, I won't.'

'You won't?'

'No. Never.' Charlotte's voice was tense with a scorn which she did not attempt to conceal. 'So this is what you were all the time, Mr Bassinger – a secret sportsman!'

Aubrey quivered from head to foot.

'I'm not! I'm not! It was the hideous spell of this ghastly house that overcame me.'

'Pah!'

'What did you say?'

'I said "Pah!".'

'Why did you say "Pah!"?'

'Because,' said Charlotte, with flashing eyes, 'I do not believe you. Your story is thin and fishy.'

'But it's the truth. It was as if some hypnotic influence had gripped me, forcing me to act against all my higher inclinations. Can't you understand? Would you condemn me for a moment's passing weakness? Do you think,' he cried passionately, 'that the real Aubrey Bassinger would raise a hand to touch a rat, save in the way of kindness? I love rats, I tell you – love them. I used to keep them as a boy. White ones with pink eyes.'

Charlotte shook her head. Her face was cold and hard.

'Good-bye, Mr Bassinger,' she said. 'From this instant we meet as strangers.'

She turned and was gone. And Aubrey Bassinger, covering his face with his hands, sank on the bench, feeling like a sand-bagged leper.

The mind of Charlotte Mulliner, in the days which followed the painful scene which I have just described, was torn, as you may well imagine, with conflicting emotions. For a time, as was natural, anger predominated. But after awhile sadness overcame indignation. She mourned for her lost happiness.

And yet, she asked herself, how else could she have acted? She had worshipped Aubrey Bassinger. She had set him upon a pedestal, looked up to him as a great white soul. She had supposed him one who lived, far above this world's coarseness and grime, on a rarefied plane of his own, thinking beautiful thoughts. Instead of which, it now appeared, he went about the place chasing rats with parasols. What could she have done but spurn him?

That there lurked in the atmosphere of Bludleigh Court

a sinister influence that sapped the principles of the most humanitarian and sent them ravening to and fro, seeking for prey, she declined to believe. The theory was pure banana-oil. If such an influence was in operation at Bludleigh, why had it not affected her?

No, if Aubrey Bassinger chased rats with parasols, it could only mean that he was one of Nature's rat-chasers. And to such a one, cost what it might to refuse, she could never confide her heart.

Few things are more embarrassing to a highly-strung girl than to be for any length of time in the same house with a man whose love she has been compelled to decline, and Charlotte would have given much to be able to leave Bludleigh Court. But there was, it seemed, to be a garden-party on the following Tuesday, and Lady Bassinger had urged her so strongly to stay on for it that departure was out of the question.

To fill the leaden moments, she immersed herself in her work. She had a long-standing commission to supply the *Animal-Lovers' Gazette* with a poem for its Christmas number, and to the task of writing this she proceeded to devote herself. And gradually the ecstasy of literary composition eased her pain.

The days crept by. Old Sir Alexander continued to maltreat magpies. Reginald and the local rabbits fought a never-ceasing battle, they striving to keep up the birthrate, he to reduce it. Colonel Pashley-Drake maundered on about gnus he had met. And Aubrey dragged himself about the house, looking licked to a splinter. Eventually Tuesday came, and with it the garden-party.

Lady Bassinger's annual garden-party was one of the big events of the countryside. By four o'clock all that was bravest and fairest for miles around had assembled on the big lawn. But Charlotte, though she had stayed on specially to be present, was not one of the gay throng. At about the time when the first strawberry was being dipped in its cream, she was up in her room, staring with bewildered eyes at a letter which had arrived by the second post.

The *Animal-Lovers' Gazette* had turned her poem down!

Yes, turned it down flat, in spite of the fact that it had been commissioned and that she was not asking a penny for it. Accompanying the rejected manuscript was a curt note from the editor, in which he said that he feared its tone might offend his readers.

Charlotte was stunned. She was not accustomed to having her efforts rejected. This one, moreover, had seemed to her so particularly good. A hard judge of her own work, she had said to herself, as she licked the envelope, that this time, if never before, she had delivered the goods.

She unfolded the manuscript and re-read it.

It ran as follows:

GOOD GNUS

(*A Vignette in Verse*)

BY

CHARLOTTE MULLINER

When cares attack and life seems black,
How sweet it is to pot a yak,
　　Or puncture hares and grizzly bears,
　　　　And others I could mention:
But in my Animals' 'Who's Who'
No name stands higher than the Gnu:
　　And each new gnu that comes in view
　　　　Receives my prompt attention.

When Afric's sun is sinking low,
And shadows wander to and fro,
   And everywhere there's in the air
     A hush that's deep and solemn;
Then is the time good men and true
With View Halloo pursue the gnu:
   (The safest spot to put your shot
     Is through the spinal column).

To take the creature by surprise
We must adopt some rude disguise,
   Although deceit is never sweet,
     And falsehoods don't attract us:
So, as with gun in hand you wait,
Remember to impersonate
   A tuft of grass, a mountain-pass,
     A kopje or a cactus.

A brief suspense, and then at last
The waiting's o'er, the vigil past:
   A careful aim. A spurt of flame.
     It's done. You've pulled the trigger,
And one more gnu, so fair and frail,
Has handed in its dinner-pail:
   (The females all are rather small,
     The males are somewhat bigger).

Charlotte laid the manuscript down, frowning. She chafed
at the imbecility of editors. Less than ever was she able to understand what anyone could find in it to cavil at. Tone likely to
offend? What did the man mean about the tone being likely
to offend? She had never heard such nonsense in her life. How
could the tone possibly offend? It was unexceptionable. The
whole poem breathed that clean, wholesome, healthy spirit of

Sport which has made England what it is. And the thing was not only lyrically perfect, but educational as well. It told the young reader, anxious to shoot gnus but uncertain of the correct procedure, exactly what he wanted to know.

She bit her lip. Well, if this *Animal-Lovers'* bird didn't know a red-hot contribution when he saw one, she would jolly well find somebody else who did – and quick, too. She...

At this moment, something occurred to distract her thoughts. Down on the terrace below, little Wilfred, complete with air-gun, had come into her line of vision. The boy was creeping along in a quiet, purposeful manner, obviously intent on the chase: and it suddenly came over Charlotte Mulliner in a wave that here she had been in this house all this time and never once had thought of borrowing the child's weapon and having a plug at something with it.

The sky was blue. The sun was shining. All Nature seemed to call to her to come out and kill things.

She left the room and ran quickly down the stairs.

And what of Aubrey, meanwhile? Grief having slowed him up on his feet, he had been cornered by his mother and marched off to hand cucumber sandwiches at the garden-party. After a brief spell of servitude, however, he had contrived to escape and was wandering on the terrace, musing mournfully, when he observed his brother Wilfred approaching. And at the same moment Charlotte Mulliner emerged from the house and came hurrying in their direction. In a flash, Aubrey perceived that here was a situation which, shrewdly handled, could be turned greatly to his advantage. Affecting to be unaware of Charlotte's approach, he stopped his brother and eyed the young thug sternly.

'Wilfred,' he said, 'where are you going with that gun?'

The boy appeared embarrassed.

'Just shooting.'

Aubrey took the weapon from him and raised his voice slightly. Out of the corner of his eye he had seen that Charlotte was now well within hearing.

'Shooting, eh?' he said. 'Shooting? I see. And have you never been taught, wretched child, that you should be kind to the animals that crave your compassion? Has no one ever told you that he prayeth best who loveth best all things both great and small? For shame, Wilfred, for shame!'

Charlotte had come up, and was standing there, looking at them inquiringly.

'What's all this about?' she asked.

Aubrey started dramatically.

'Miss Mulliner! I was not aware that you were there. All this? Oh, nothing. I found this lad here on his way to shoot sparrows with his air-gun, and I am taking the thing from him. It may seem to you a high-handed action on my part. You may consider me hyper-sensitive. You may ask, Why all this fuss about a few birds? But that is Aubrey Bassinger. Aubrey Bassinger will not lightly allow even the merest sparrow to be placed in jeopardy. Tut, Wilfred,' he said. 'Tut! Cannot you see now how wrong it is to shoot the poor sparrows?'

'But I wasn't going to shoot sparrows,' said the boy. 'I was going to shoot uncle Francis while he is having his sun-bath.'

'It is also wrong,' said Aubrey, after a slight hesitation, 'to shoot uncle Francis while he is having his sun-bath.'

Charlotte Mulliner uttered an impatient exclamation. And Aubrey, looking at her, saw that her eyes were glittering with a strange light. She breathed quickly through her delicately-chiselled nose. She seemed feverish, and a medical man would have been concerned about her blood-pressure.

'Why?' she demanded vehemently. 'Why is it wrong? Why shouldn't he shoot his uncle Francis while he is having his sun-bath?'

Aubrey stood for a moment, pondering. Her razor-like feminine intelligence had cut cleanly to the core of the matter. After all, now that she put it like that, why not?

'Think how it would tickle him up.'

'True,' said Aubrey, nodding. 'True.'

'And his uncle Francis is precisely the sort of man who ought to have been shot at with air-guns incessantly for the last thirty years. The moment I met him, I said to myself, "That man ought to be shot at with air-guns."'

Aubrey nodded again. Her girlish enthusiasm had begun to infect him.

'There is much in what you say,' he admitted.

'Where is he?' asked Charlotte, turning to the boy.

'On the roof of the boathouse.'

Charlotte's face clouded.

'H'm!' she said. 'That's awkward. How is one to get at him?'

'I remember uncle Francis telling me once,' said Aubrey, 'that, when you went shooting tigers, you climbed a tree. There are plenty of trees by the boathouse.'

'Admirable!'

For an instant there came to disturb Aubrey's hearty joy in the chase a brief, faint flicker of prudence.

'But ... I say ... Do you really think ... Ought we ...?'

Charlotte's eyes flashed scornfully.

'Infirm of purpose,' she said. 'Give me the air-gun!'

'I was only thinking...'

'Well?'

'I suppose you know he'll have practically nothing on?'

Charlotte Mulliner laughed lightly.

'He can't intimidate *me*,' she said. 'Come! Let us be going.'

Up on the roof of the boathouse, the beneficent ultra-violet rays of the afternoon sun pouring down on his globular surface, Colonel Sir Francis Pashley-Drake lay in that pleasant half-waking, half-dreaming state that accompanies this particular form of lumbago-treatment. His mind flitted lightly from one soothing subject to another. He thought of elks he had shot in Canada, of moufflon he had shot in the Grecian Archipelago, of giraffes he had shot in Nigeria. He was just on the point of thinking of a hippopotamus which he had shot in Egypt, when the train of his meditations was interrupted by a soft popping sound not far away. He smiled affectionately. So little Wilfred was out with his air-gun, eh?

A thrill of quiet pride passed through Colonel Pashley-Drake. He had trained the lad well, he felt. With a garden-party in progress, with all the opportunities it offered for quiet gorging, how many boys of Wilfred's age would have neglected their shooting to hang round the tea-table and stuff themselves with cakes. But this fine lad...

Ping! There it was again. The boy must be somewhere quite close at hand. He wished he could be at his side, giving him kindly advice. Wilfred, he felt, was a young fellow after his own heart. What destruction he would spread among the really worthwhile animals when he grew up and put aside childish things and exchanged his air-gun for a Winchester repeater.

Sir Francis Pashley-Drake started. Two inches from where

he lay a splinter of wood had sprung from the boathouse roof.
He sat up, feeling a little less affectionate.

'Wilfred!'

There was no reply.

'Be careful, Wilfred, my boy. You nearly...'

A sharp, agonizing twinge caused him to break off abruptly.
He sprang to his feet and began to address the surrounding
landscape passionately in one of the lesser-known dialects of
the Congo basin. He no longer thought of Wilfred with quiet
pride. Few things so speedily modify an uncle's love as a
nephew's air-gun bullet in the fleshy part of the leg. Sir Francis
Pashley-Drake's plans for this boy's future had undergone in
one brief instant a complete change. He no longer desired to
stand beside him through his formative years, teaching him the
secrets of shikar. All he wanted to do was to get close enough
to him to teach him with the flat of his right hand to be a bit
more careful where he pointed his gun.

He was expressing a synopsis of these views in a mixture of
Urdu and Cape Dutch, when the words were swept from his
lips by the sight of a woman's face, peering from the branches
of a near-by tree.

Colonel Pashley-Drake reeled where he stood. Like so many
out-door men, he was the soul of modesty. Once, in Bechuana-
land, he had left a native witch-dance in a marked manner
because he considered the chief's third supplementary wife
insufficiently clad. An acute consciousness of the sketchiness
of his costume overcame him. He blushed brightly.

'My dear young lady...' he stammered.

He had got thus far when he perceived that the young woman
was aiming at him something that looked remarkably like an
air-gun. Her tongue protruded thoughtfully from the corner of

her mouth, she had closed one eye and with the other was squinting tensely along the barrel.

Colonel Sir Francis Pashley-Drake did not linger. In all England there was probably no man more enthusiastic about shooting: but the fascination of shooting as a sport depends almost wholly on whether you are at the right or wrong end of the gun. With an agility which no gnu, unless in the very pink of condition, could have surpassed, he sprang to the side of the roof and leaped off. There was a clump of reeds not far from the boathouse. He galloped across the turf and dived into them.

Charlotte descended from her tree. Her expression was petulant. Girls nowadays are spoiled, and only too readily become peevish when baulked of their pleasures.

'I had no idea he was so nippy,' she said.

'A quick mover,' agreed Aubrey. 'I imagine he got that way from dodging rhinoceroses.'

'Why can't they make these silly guns with two barrels? A single barrel doesn't give a girl a chance.'

Nestling among the reeds, Colonel Sir Francis Pashley-Drake, in spite of the indignation natural to a man in his position, could not help feeling a certain complacency. The old woodcraft of the hunter had stood him, he felt, in good stead. Not many men, he told himself, would have had the initiative and swift intelligence to act so promptly in the face of peril.

He was aware of voices close by.

'What do we do now?' he heard Charlotte Mulliner say.

'We must think,' said the voice of his nephew Aubrey.

'He's in there somewhere.'

'Yes.'

'I hate to see a fine head like that get away,' said Charlotte, and her voice was still querulous. 'Especially after I winged him. The very next poem I write is going to be an appeal to air-gun manufacturers to use their intelligence, if they have any, and turn out a line with two barrels.'

'I shall write a Pastel in Prose on the same subject,' agreed Aubrey.

'Well, what shall we do?'

There was a short silence. An insect of unknown species crept up Colonel Pashley-Drake and bit him in the small of the back.

'I'll tell you what,' said Aubrey. 'I remember uncle Francis mentioning to me once that when wounded zebus take cover by the reaches of the Lower Zambesi, the sportsman despatches a native assistant to set fire to . . .'

Sir Francis Pashley-Drake emitted a hollow groan. It was drowned by Charlotte's cry of delight.

'Why, of course! How clever you are, Mr Bassinger.'

'Oh no,' said Aubrey modestly.

'Have you matches?'

'I have a cigarette-lighter.'

'Then would it be bothering you too much to go and set light to those reeds – about there would be a good place – and I'll wait here with the gun.'

'I should be charmed.'

'I hate to trouble you.'

'No trouble, I assure you,' said Aubrey. 'A pleasure.'

Three minutes later the revellers on the lawn were interested to observe a sight rare at the better class of English garden-party. Out of a clump of laurel-bushes that bordered the smoothly mown turf there came charging a stout, pink gentleman of middle age who hopped from side to side as he ran. He was wearing a loin-cloth, and seemed in a hurry. They had just time to recognize in this newcomer their hostess's brother, Colonel Sir Francis Pashley-Drake, when he snatched a cloth from the nearest table, draped it round him, and with a quick leap took refuge behind the portly form of the Bishop of Stortford, who was talking to the local Master of Hounds about the difficulty he had in keeping his vicars off the incense.

Charlotte and Aubrey had paused in the shelter of the laurels. Aubrey, peering through this zareba, clicked his tongue regretfully.

'He's taken cover again,' he said. 'I'm afraid we shall find it difficult to dig him out of there. He's gone to earth behind a bishop.'

Receiving no reply, he turned.

'Miss Mulliner!' he exclaimed. 'Charlotte! What is the matter?'

A strange change had come over the girl's beautiful face since he had last gazed at it. The fire had died out of those lovely eyes, leaving them looking like those of a newly awakened somnambulist. She was pale, and the tip of her nose quivered.

'Where am I?' she murmured.

'Bludleigh Manor, Lesser Bludleigh, Goresby-on-the-Ouse, Bedfordshire. Telephone 28 Goresby,' said Aubrey quickly.

'Have I been dreaming? Or did I really . . . Ah, yes, yes!' she moaned, shuddering violently. 'It all comes back to me. I shot Sir Francis with the air-gun!'

'You certainly did,' said Aubrey, and would have gone on to comment with warm approbation on the skill she had shown, a skill which – in an untrained novice – had struck him as really remarkable. But he checked himself. 'Surely,' he said, 'you are not letting the fact disturb you? It's the sort of thing that might have happened to anyone.'

She interrupted him.

'How right you were, Mr Bassinger, to warn me against the spell of Bludleigh. And how wrong I was to blame you for borrowing my parasol to chase a rat. Can you ever forgive me?'

'Charlotte!'

'Aubrey!'

'Charlotte!'

'Hush!' she said. 'Listen.'

On the lawn, Sir Francis Pashley-Drake was telling his story to an enthralled audience. The sympathy of the meeting, it was only too plain, was entirely with him. This shooting of a sitting sun-bather had stirred the feelings of his hearers deeply. Indignant exclamations came faintly to the ears of the young couple in the laurels.

'Most irregular!'

'Not done!'

'Scarcely cricket!'

And then, from Sir Alexander Bassinger, a stern 'I shall require a full explanation.'

Charlotte turned to Aubrey.

'What shall we do?'

'Well,' said Aubrey, reflecting, 'I don't think we had better just go and join the party and behave as if nothing had happened. The atmosphere doesn't seem right. What I would propose is that we take a short cut through the fields to the station, hook up with the five-fifty express at Goresby, go to London, have a bit of dinner, get married and . . .'

'Yes, yes,' cried Charlotte. 'Take me away from this awful house.'

'To the ends of the world,' said Aubrey fervently. He paused. 'Look here,' he said suddenly, 'if you move over to where I'm standing, you get the old boy plumb spang against the sky-line. You wouldn't care for just one last...'

'No, no!'

'Merely a suggestion,' said Aubrey. 'Ah well, perhaps you're right. Then let's be shifting.'

6 THOSE IN PERIL ON THE TEE

I think the two young men in the chessboard knickerbockers were a little surprised when they looked up and perceived Mr Mulliner brooding over their table like an affable Slave of the Lamp. Absorbed in their conversation, they had not noticed his approach. It was their first visit to the Angler's Rest, and their first meeting with the Sage of its bar-parlour: and they were not yet aware that to Mr Mulliner any assemblage of his fellow-men over and above the number of one constitutes an audience.

'Good evening, gentlemen,' said Mr Mulliner. 'You have been playing golf, I see.'

They said they had.

'You enjoy the game?'

They said they did.

'Perhaps you will allow me to request Miss Postlethwaite, princess of barmaids, to re-fill your glasses?'

They said they would.

'Golf,' said Mr Mulliner, drawing up a chair and sinking smoothly into it, 'is a game which I myself have not played for some years. I was always an indifferent performer, and I gradually gave it up for the simpler and more straightforward pastime of fishing. It is a curious fact that, gifted though the

Mulliners have been in virtually every branch of life and sport, few of us have ever taken kindly to golf. Indeed, the only member of the family I can think of who attained to any real proficiency with the clubs was the daughter of a distant cousin of mine – one of the Devonshire Mulliners who married a man named Flack. Agnes was the girl's name. Perhaps you have run across her? She is always playing in tournaments and competitions, I believe.'

The young men said No, they didn't seem to know the name.

'Ah?' said Mr Mulliner. 'A pity. It would have made the story more interesting to you.'

The two young men exchanged glances.

'Story?' said the one in the slightly more prismatic knicker-bockers, speaking in a voice that betrayed agitation.

'Story?' said his companion, blenching a little.

'The story,' said Mr Mulliner, 'of John Gooch, Frederick Pilcher, Sidney McMurdo and Agnes Flack.'

The first young man said he didn't know it was so late. The second young man said it was extraordinary how time went. They began to talk confusedly about trains.

'The story,' repeated Mr Mulliner, holding them with the effortless ease which makes this sort of thing such child's play to him, 'of Agnes Flack, Sidney McMurdo, Frederick Pilcher and John Gooch.'

It is an odd thing (said Mr Mulliner) how often one finds that those who practise the Arts are quiet, timid little men, shy in company and unable to express themselves except through the medium of the pencil or the pen. I have noticed it again and again. John Gooch was like that. So was Frederick Pilcher. Gooch was a writer and Pilcher was an artist, and they used to meet a good deal at Agnes Flack's house, where they were constant callers. And every time they met John Gooch would say to himself, as he watched Pilcher balancing a cup of tea and smiling his weak, propitiatory smile, 'I am fond of Frederick, but his best friend could not deny that he is a pretty dumb brick.' And Pilcher, as he saw Gooch sitting on the edge of his chair and fingering his tie, would reflect, 'Nice fellow as John is, he is certainly a total loss in mixed society.'

Mark you, if ever men had an excuse for being ill at ease in the presence of the opposite sex, these two had. They were both eighteen-handicap men, and Agnes was exuberantly and dynamically scratch. Her physique was an asset to her, especially at the long game. She stood about five feet ten in her stockings, and had shoulders and forearms which would have excited the envious admiration of one of those muscular women on the music-halls, who good-naturedly allow six brothers, three sisters, and a cousin by marriage to pile themselves on her collar-bone while the orchestra plays a long-drawn chord and the audience hurries out to the bar. Her eye resembled the eye of one of the more imperious queens of history: and when she laughed, strong men clutched at their temples to keep the tops of their heads from breaking loose.

Even Sidney McMurdo was as a piece of damp blotting-paper in her presence. And he was a man who weighed two hundred and eleven pounds and had once been a semi-finalist in the Amateur Championship. He loved Agnes Flack with an ox-like devotion. And yet – and this will show you what life is – when she laughed, it was nearly always at him. I am told by those in a position to know that, on the occasion when he first proposed to her – on the sixth green – distant rumblings of her mirth were plainly heard in the club-house locker-room, causing two men who were afraid of thunderstorms to scratch their match.

Such, then, was Agnes Flack. Such, also, was Sidney McMurdo. And such were Frederick Pilcher and John Gooch.

Now John Gooch, though, of course, they had exchanged a word from time to time, was in no sense an intimate of Sidney McMurdo. It was consequently a surprise to him when one night, as he sat polishing up the rough draft of a detective story – for his was the talent that found expression largely in blood, shots in the night, and millionaires who are found murdered in locked rooms with no possible means of access except a window forty feet above the ground – the vast bulk of McMurdo lumbered across his threshold and deposited itself in a chair.

The chair creaked. Gooch stared. McMurdo groaned.

'Are you ill?' said John Gooch.

'Ha!' said Sidney McMurdo.

He had been sitting with his face buried in his hands, but now he looked up; and there was a red glare in his eyes which sent a thrill of horror through John Gooch. The visitor reminded him of the Human Gorilla in his novel, *The Mystery of the Severed Ear.*

'For two pins,' said Sidney McMurdo, displaying a more mercenary spirit than the Human Gorilla, who had required no cash payment for his crimes, 'I would tear you to shreds.'

'Me?' said John Gooch, blankly.

'Yes, you. And that fellow Pilcher, too.' He rose; and, striding to the mantelpiece, broke off a corner of it and crumbled it in his fingers. 'You have stolen her from me.'

'Stolen? Whom?'

'My Agnes.'

John Gooch stared at him, thoroughly bewildered. The idea

of stealing Agnes Flack was rather like the notion of sneaking off with the Albert Hall. He could make nothing of it.

'She is going to marry you.'

'What!' cried John Gooch, aghast.

'Either you or Pilcher.' McMurdo paused. 'Shall I tear you into little strips and tread you into the carpet?' he murmured, meditatively.

'No,' said John Gooch. His mind was blurred, but he was clear on that point.

'Why did you come butting in?' groaned Sidney McMurdo, absently taking up the poker and tying it into a lover's knot. 'I was getting along splendidly until you two pimples broke out. Slowly but surely I was teaching her to love me, and now it can never be. I have a message for you. From her. I proposed to her for the eleventh time to-night; and when she had finished laughing she told me that she could never marry a mere mass of brawn. She said she wanted brain. And she told me to tell you and the pest Pilcher that she had watched you closely and realized that you both loved her, but were too shy to speak, and that she understood and would marry one of you.'

There was a long silence.

'Pilcher is a splendid fellow,' said John Gooch. 'She must marry Pilcher.'

'She will, if he wins the match.'

'What match?'

'The golf match. She read a story in a magazine the other day where two men played a match at golf to decide which was to win the heroine; and about a week later she read another story in another magazine where two men played a match at golf to decide which was to win the heroine. And a couple of days ago she read three more stories in three more magazines where exactly the same thing happened; and she has decided to accept it as an omen. So you and the hound Pilcher are to play eighteen holes, and the winner marries Agnes.'

'The winner?'

'Certainly.'

'I should have thought – I forget what I was going to say.'

McMurdo eyed him keenly.

'Gooch,' he said, 'you are not one of those thoughtless butterflies, I hope, who go about breaking girls' hearts?'

'No, no,' said John Gooch, learning for the first time that this was what butterflies did.

'You are not one of those men who win a good girl's love and then ride away with a light laugh?'

John Gooch said he certainly was not. He would not dream of laughing, even lightly, at any girl. Besides, he added, he could not ride. He had once had three lessons in the Park, but had not seemed to be able to get the knack.

'So much the better for you,' said Sidney McMurdo heavily. 'Because, if I thought that, I should know what steps to take. Even now...' He paused, and looked at the poker in a rather yearning sort of way. 'No, no,' he said, with a sigh, 'better not, better not.' He flung the thing down with a gesture of resignation. 'Better, perhaps, on the whole not.' He rose, frowning. 'Well, good night, weed,' he said. 'The match will be played on Friday morning. And may the better – or, rather, the less impossibly foul – man win.'

He banged the door, and John Gooch was alone.

But not for long. Scarcely half an hour had passed when the door opened once more to admit Frederick Pilcher. The artist's face was pale, and he was breathing heavily. He sat down, and after a brief interval contrived to summon up a smile. He rose and patted John Gooch on the shoulder.

'John,' he said, 'I am a man who as a general rule hides his feelings. I mask my affections. But I want to say, straight out, here and now, that I like you, John.'

'Yes?' said John Gooch.

Frederick Pilcher patted his other shoulder. 'I like you so much, John, old man, that I can read your thoughts, strive to conceal them though you may. I have been watching you closely of late, John, and I know your secret. You love Agnes Flack.'

'I don't!'

'Yes, you do. Ah, John, John,' said Frederick Pilcher, with a gentle smile, 'why try to deceive an old friend? You love her, John. You love that girl. And I have good news for you, John – tidings of great joy. I happen to know that she will look favourably on your suit. Go in and win, my boy, go in and win. Take my advice and dash round and propose without a moment's delay.'

John Gooch shook his head. He, too, smiled a gentle smile.

'Frederick,' he said, 'this is like you. Noble. That's what I call it. Noble. It's the sort of thing the hero does in act two. But it must not be, Frederick. It must not, shall not be. I also can read a friend's heart, and I know that you, too, love Agnes Flack. And I yield my claim. I am excessively fond of you, Frederick, and I give her up to you. God bless you, old fellow. God, in fact, bless both of you.'

'Look here,' said Frederick Pilcher, 'have you been having a visit from Sidney McMurdo?'

'He did drop in for a minute.'

There was a tense pause.

'What I can't understand,' said Frederick Pilcher, at length, peevishly, 'is why, if you don't love this infernal girl, you kept calling at her house practically every night and sitting goggling at her with obvious devotion.'

'It wasn't devotion.'

'It looked like it.'

'Well, it wasn't. And, if it comes to that, why did you call on her practically every night and goggle just as much as I did?'

'I had a very good reason,' said Frederick Pilcher. 'I was studying her face. I am planning a series of humorous drawings on the lines of Felix the Cat, and I wanted her as a model. To goggle at a girl in the interests of one's Art, as I did, is a very different thing from goggling wantonly at her, like you.'

'Is that so?' said John Gooch. 'Well, let me tell you that I wasn't goggling wantonly. I was studying her psychology for a series of stories which I am preparing, entitled *Madeline Monk, Murderess*.'

Frederick Pilcher held out his hand.

'I wronged you, John,' he said. 'However, be that as it may, the point is that we both appear to be up against it very hard. An extraordinarily well-developed man, that fellow McMurdo.'

'A mass of muscle.'

'And of a violent disposition.'

'Dangerously so.'

Frederick Pilcher drew out his handkerchief and dabbed at his forehead.

'You don't think, John, that you might ultimately come to love Agnes Flack?'

'I do not.'

'Love frequently comes after marriage, I believe.'

'So does suicide.'

'Then it looks to me,' said Frederick Pilcher, 'as if one of us was for it. I see no way out of playing that match.'

'Nor I.'

'The growing tendency on the part of the modern girl to read trashy magazine stories,' said Frederick Pilcher severely, 'is one that I deplore. I view it with alarm. And I wish to goodness that you authors wouldn't write tales about men who play golf matches for the hand of a woman.'

'Authors must live,' said John Gooch. 'How is your game these days, Frederick?'

'Improved, unfortunately. I am putting better.'

'I am steadier off the tee.' John Gooch laughed bitterly. 'When I think of the hours of practice I have put in, little knowing that a thing of this sort was in store for me, I appreciate the irony of life. If I had not bought Sandy McHoots' book last spring I might now be in a position to be beaten five and four.'

'Instead of which, you will probably win the match on the twelfth.'

John Gooch started.

'You can't be as bad as that!'

'I shall be on Friday.'

'You mean to say you aren't going to try?'

'I do.'

'You have sunk to such depths that you would deliberately play below your proper form?'

'I have.'

'Pilcher,' said John Gooch, coldly, 'you are a hound, and I never liked you from the start.'

* * *

You would have thought that, after the conversation which I have just related, no depth of low cunning on the part of Frederick Pilcher would have had the power to surprise John Gooch. And yet, as he saw the other come out of the clubhouse to join him on the first tee on the Friday morning, I am not exaggerating when I say that he was stunned.

John Gooch had arrived at the links early, wishing to get in a little practice. One of his outstanding defects as a golfer was a pronounced slice; and it seemed to him that, if he drove off a few balls before the match began, he might be able to analyse this slice and see just what was the best stance to take up in order that it might have full scope. He was teeing his third ball when Frederick Pilcher appeared.

'What – what – what—!' gasped John Gooch.

For Frederick Pilcher, discarding the baggy, mustard-coloured plus-fours in which it was his usual custom to infest the links, was dressed in a perfectly-fitting morning-coat, yellow waistcoat, striped trousers, spats, and patent-leather shoes. He wore a high stiff collar, and on his head was the glossiest top hat ever seen off the Stock Exchange. He looked intensely uncomfortable; and yet there was on his face a smirk which he made no attempt to conceal.

'What's the matter?' he asked.

'Why are you dressed like that?' John Gooch uttered an exclamation. 'I see it all. You think it will put you off your game.'

'Some idea of the kind did occur to me,' replied Frederick Pilcher, airily.

'You fiend!'

'Tut, tut, John. These are hard words to use to a friend.'

'You are no friend of mine.'

'A pity,' said Frederick Pilcher, 'for I was hoping that you would ask me to be your best man at the wedding.' He took a club from his bag and swung it. 'Amazing what a difference clothes make. You would hardly believe how this coat cramps the shoulders. I feel as if I were a sardine trying to wriggle in its tin.'

The world seemed to swim before John Gooch's eyes. Then the mist cleared, and he fixed Frederick Pilcher with a hypnotic gaze.

'You are going to play well,' he said, speaking very slowly and distinctly. 'You are going to play well. You are going to play well. You—'

'Stop it!' cried Frederick Pilcher.

'You are going to play well. You are going—'

A heavy hand descended on his shoulder. Sidney McMurdo was regarding him with a black scowl.

'We don't want any of your confounded chivalry,' said Sidney McMurdo. 'This match is going to be played in the strictest spirit of— What the devil are you dressed like that for?' he demanded, wheeling on Frederick Pilcher.

'I – I have to go into the City immediately after the match,' said Pilcher. 'I shan't have time to change.'

'H'm. Well, it's your own affair. Come along,' said Sidney McMurdo, gritting his teeth. 'I've been told to referee this match, and I don't want to stay here all day. Toss for the honour, worms.'

John Gooch spun a coin. Frederick Pilcher called tails. The coin fell heads up.

'Drive off, reptile,' said Sidney McMurdo.

As John Gooch addressed his ball, he was aware of a strange sensation which he could not immediately analyse. It was only

when, after waggling two or three times, he started to draw his
club back that it flashed upon him that this strange sensation
was confidence. For the first time in his life he seemed to have
no doubt that the ball, well and truly struck, would travel
sweetly down the middle of the fairway. And then the hideous
truth dawned on him. His subconscious self had totally misunderstood the purport of his recent remarks and had got the
whole thing nicely muddled up.

Much has been written of the subconscious self, and all that
has been written goes to show that of all the thick-headed,
blundering chumps who take everything they hear literally, it
is the worst. Anybody of any intelligence would have realized
that when John Gooch said, 'You are going to play well,' he
was speaking to Frederick Pilcher; but his subconscious self
had missed the point completely. It had heard John Gooch say,
'You are going to play well,' and it was seeing that he did so.

The unfortunate man did what he could. Realizing what had
happened, he tried with a despairing jerk to throw his swing
out of gear just as the club came above his shoulder. It was a
fatal move. You may recall that when Arnaud Massy won the
British Open Championship one of the features of his play was
a sort of wiggly twiggle at the top of the swing, which seemed
to have the effect of adding yards to his drive. This wiggly
twiggle John Gooch, in his effort to wreck his shot, achieved
to a nicety. The ball soared over the bunker in which he had
hoped to waste at least three strokes; and fell so near the
green that it was plain that only a miracle could save him from
getting a four.

There was a sardonic smile on Frederick Pilcher's face as he
stepped on to the tee. In a few moments he would be one
down, and it would not be his fault if he failed to maintain the

advantage. He drew back the head of his club. His coat, cut by a fashionable tailor who, like all fashionable tailors, resented it if the clothes he made permitted his customers to breathe, was so tight that he could not get the club-head more than half-way up. He brought it to this point, then brought it down in a lifeless semi-circle.

'Nice!' said Sidney McMurdo, involuntarily. He despised and disliked Frederick Pilcher, but he was a golfer. And a golfer cannot refrain from giving a good shot its meed of praise.

For the ball, instead of trickling down the hill as Frederick Pilcher had expected, was singing through the air like a shell. It fell near John Gooch's ball and, bounding past it, ran on to the green.

The explanation was, of course, simple. Frederick Pilcher was a man who, in his normal golfing costume, habitually over-swung. This fault the tightness of his coat had now rendered impossible. And his other pet failing, the raising of the head, had been checked by the fact that he was wearing a top hat. It had been Pilcher's intention to jerk his head till his spine cracked; but the unseen influence of generations of ancestors who had devoted the whole of their intellect to the balancing of top hats on windy days was too much for him.

A minute later the two men had halved the hole in four.

The next hole, the water-hole, they halved in three. The third, long and over the hill, they halved in five.

And it was as they moved to the fourth tee that a sort of madness came upon both Frederick Pilcher and John Gooch simultaneously.

* * *

These two, you must remember, were eighteen-handicap men. That is to say, they thought well of themselves if they could get sixes on the first, sevens on the third, and anything from fours to elevens on the second – according to the number of balls they sank in the water. And they had done these three holes in twelve. John Gooch looked at Frederick Pilcher and Frederick Pilcher looked at John Gooch. Their eyes were gleaming, and they breathed a little stertorously through their noses.

'Pretty work,' said John Gooch.

'Nice stuff,' said Frederick Pilcher.

'Get a move on, blisters,' growled Sidney McMurdo.

It was at this point that the madness came upon these two men.

Picture to yourself their position. Each felt that by continuing to play in this form he was running a deadly risk of having to marry Agnes Flack. Each felt that his opponent could not possibly keep up so hot a pace much longer, and the prudent course, therefore, was for himself to ease off a bit before the crash came. And each, though fully aware of all this, felt that he was dashed if he wasn't going to have a stab at doing the round of his life. It might well be that, having started off at such a clip, he would find himself finishing somewhere in the eighties. And that, surely, would compensate for everything.

After all, felt John Gooch, suppose he did marry Agnes Flack, what of it? He had faith in his star, and it seemed to him that she might quite easily get run over by a truck or fall off a cliff during the honeymoon. Besides, with all the facilities for divorce which modern civilization so beneficently provides, what was there to be afraid of in marriage, even with an Agnes Flack?

Frederick Pilcher's thoughts were equally optimistic. Agnes Flack, he reflected, was undeniably a pot of poison; but so much the better. Just the wife to keep an artist up to the mark. Hitherto he had had a tendency to be a little lazy. He had avoided his studio and loafed about the house. Married to Agnes Flack, his studio would see a lot more of him. He would spend all day in it – probably have a truckle bed put in and never leave it at all. A sensible man, felt Frederick Pilcher, can always make a success of marriage if he goes about it in the right spirit.

John Gooch's eyes gleamed. Frederick Pilcher's jaw protruded. And neck and neck, fighting grimly for their sixes and sometimes even achieving fives, they came to the ninth green, halved the hole, and were all square at the turn.

It was at this point that they perceived Agnes Flack standing on the club-house terrace.

'Yoo-hoo!' cried Agnes in a voice of thunder.

And John Gooch and Frederick Pilcher stopped dead in their tracks, blinking like abruptly-awakened somnambulists.

She made a singularly impressive picture, standing there with her tweed-clad form outlined against the white of the club-house wall. She had the appearance of one who is about to play Boadicea in a pageant; and John Gooch, as he gazed at her, was conscious of a chill that ran right down his back and oozed out at the soles of his feet.

'How's the match coming along?' she yelled, cheerily.

'All square,' replied Sidney McMurdo, with a sullen scowl. 'Wait where you are for a minute, germs,' he said. 'I wish to have a word with Miss Flack.'

He drew Agnes aside and began to speak to her in a low rumbling voice. And presently it was made apparent to all within a radius of half a mile that he had been proposing to her once again, for suddenly she threw her head back and there went reverberating over the countryside that old familiar laugh.

'Ha, ha, ha, ha, ha, ha, HA!' laughed Agnes Flack.

John Gooch shot a glance at his opponent. The artist, pale to the lips, was removing his coat and hat and handing them to his caddie. And, even as John Gooch looked, he unfastened his braces and tied them round his waist. It was plain that from now on Frederick Pilcher intended to run no risk of not overswinging.

John Gooch could appreciate his feelings. The thought of how that laugh would sound across the bacon and eggs on a rainy Monday morning turned the marrow in his spine to ice and curdled every red corpuscle in his veins. Gone was the exhilarating ferment which had caused him to skip like a young ram when a long putt had given him a forty-six for the first nine. How bitterly he regretted now those raking drives, those crisp flicks of the mashie-niblick of which he had been so proud ten minutes ago. If only he had not played such an infernally good game going out, he reflected, he might at this moment be eight or nine down and without a care in the world.

A shadow fell between him and the sun; and he turned to see Sidney McMurdo standing by his side, glaring with a singular intensity.

'Bah!' said Sidney McMurdo, having regarded him in silence for some moments.

He turned on his heel and made for the club-house.

'Where are you going, Sidney?' asked Agnes Flack.

'I am going home,' replied Sidney McMurdo, 'before I murder these two miserable harvest-bugs. I am only flesh and blood, and the temptation to grind them into powder and scatter them to the four winds will shortly become too strong. Good morning.'

Agnes emitted another laugh like a steam-riveter at work.

'Isn't he funny?' she said, addressing John Gooch, who had clutched at his scalp and was holding it down as the vibrations died away. 'Well, I suppose I shall have to referee the rest of the match myself. Whose honour? Yours? Then drive off and let's get at it.'

The demoralizing effects of his form on the first nine holes had not completely left John Gooch. He drove long and straight, and stepped back appalled. Only a similar blunder on the part of his opponent could undo the damage.

But Frederick Pilcher had his wits well about him. He overswung as he had never overswung before. His ball shot off into the the long grass on the right of the course, and he uttered a pleased cry.

'Lost ball, I fancy,' he said. 'Too bad!'

'I marked it,' said John Gooch, grimly. 'I will come and help you find it.'

'Don't trouble.'

'It is no trouble.'

'But it's your hole, anyway. It will take me three or four to get out of there.'

'It will take me four or five to get a yard from where I am.'

'Gooch,' said Frederick Pilcher, in a cautious whisper, 'you are a cad.'

'Pilcher,' said John Gooch, in tones equally hushed, 'you are a low bounder. And if I find you kicking that ball under a bush, there will be blood shed – and in large quantities.'

'Ha, ha!'

'Ha, ha to you!' said John Gooch.

The ball was lying in a leathery tuft, and, as Pilcher had predicted, it took three strokes to move it back to the fairway. By the time Frederick Pilcher had reached the spot where John Gooch's drive had finished, he had played seven.

But there was good stuff in John Gooch. It is often in times of great peril that the artistic temperament shows up best. Missing the ball altogether with his next three swings, he topped it with his fourth, topped it again with his fifth, and, playing the like, sent a low, skimming shot well over the green into the bunker beyond. Frederick Pilcher, aiming for the same bunker, sliced and landed on the green. The six strokes which it took John Gooch to get out of the sand decided the issue. Frederick Pilcher was one up at the tenth.

But John Gooch's advantage was short-lived. On the right, as you approach the eleventh green there is a deep chasm, spanned by a wooden bridge. Frederick Pilcher, playing twelve, just failed to put his ball into this, and it rolled on to within a few feet of the hole. It seemed to John Gooch that the day was his. An easy mashie-shot would take him well into the chasm, from which no eighteen-handicap player had ever emerged within the memory of man. This would put him two down – a winning lead. He swung jubilantly, and brought off a nicely-lofted shot which seemed to be making for the very centre of the pit.

And so, indeed, it was; and it was this fact that undid John Gooch's schemes. The ball, with all the rest of the chasm to choose from, capriciously decided to strike the one spot on the left-hand rail of the wooden bridge which would deflect it towards the flag. It bounded high in the air, fell on the green, and the next moment, while John Gooch stood watching with fallen jaw and starting eyes, it had trickled into the hole.

There was a throbbing silence. Then Agnes Flack spoke.

'Important, if true,' she said. 'All square again. I will say one thing for you two – you make this game very interesting.'

And once more she sent the birds shooting out of the tree-tops with that hearty laugh of hers. John Gooch, coming slowly to after the shattering impact of it, found that he was clutching Frederick Pilcher's arm. He flung it from him as if it had been a loathsome snake.

A grimmer struggle than that which took place over the next six holes has probably never been seen on any links. First one, then the other seemed to be about to lose the hole, but always a well-judged slice or a timely top enabled his opponent to rally. At the eighteenth tee the game was still square; and John Gooch, taking advantage of the fact that Agnes had stopped to tie her shoe-lace, endeavoured to appeal to his one-time friend's better nature.

'Frederick,' he said, 'this is not like you.'

'What isn't like me?'

'Playing this low-down game. It is not like the old Frederick Pilcher.'

'Well, what sort of a game do you think you are playing?'

'A little below my usual, it is true,' admitted John Gooch. 'But that is due to nervousness. You are deliberately trying to foozle, which is not only painting the lily but very dishonest. And I can't see what motive you have, either.'

'You can't, can't you?'

John Gooch laid a hand persuasively on the other's shoulder. 'Agnes Flack is a most delightful girl.'

'Who is?'

'Agnes Flack.'

'A delightful girl?'

'Most delightful.'

'Agnes Flack is a delightful girl?'

'Yes.'

'Oh?'

'She would make you very happy.'

'Who would?'

'Agnes Flack.'

'Make me happy?'

'Very happy.'

'Agnes Flack would make me happy?'

'Yes.'

'Oh?'

John Gooch was conscious of a slight discouragement. He did not seem to be making headway.

'Well, then, look here,' he said, 'what we had better do is to have a gentleman's agreement.'

'Who are the gentlemen?'

'You and I.'

'Oh?'

John Gooch did not like the other's manner, nor did he like the tone of voice in which he had spoken. But then there were so many things about Frederick Pilcher that he did not like that it seemed useless to try to do anything about it. Moreover, Agnes Flack had finished tying her shoe-lace, and was making for them across the turf like a mastodon striding over some prehistoric plain. It was no time for wasting words.

'A gentleman's agreement to halve the match,' he said hurriedly.

'What's the good of that? She would only make us play extra holes.'

'We would halve those, too.'

'Then we should have to play it off another day.'

'But before that we could leave the neighbourhood.'

'Sidney McMurdo would follow us to the ends of the earth.'

'Ah, but suppose we didn't go there? Suppose we simply lay low in the city and grew beards?'

'There's something in it,' said Frederick Pilcher, reflectively.

'You agree?'

'Very well.'

'Splendid!'

'What's splendid?' asked Agnes Flack, thudding up.

'Oh – er – the match,' said John Gooch. 'I was saying to Pilcher that this was a splendid match.'

Agnes Flack sniffed. She seemed quieter than she had been at the outset, as though something were on her mind.

'I'm glad you think so,' she said. 'Do you two always play like this?'

'Oh, yes. Yes. This is about our usual form.'

'H'm! Well, push on.'

It was with a light heart that John Gooch addressed his ball for the last drive of the match. A great weight had been lifted from his mind, and he told himself that now there was no objection to bringing off a real sweet one. He swung lustily; and the ball, struck on its extreme left side, shot off at right angles, hit the ladies' tee-box, and, whizzing back at a high rate of speed, would have mown Agnes Flack's ankles from under her, had she not at the psychological moment skipped in a manner extraordinarily reminiscent of the high hills mentioned in Sacred Writ.

'Sorry, old man,' said John Gooch, hastily, flushing as he encountered Frederick Pilcher's cold look of suspicion. 'Frightfully sorry, Frederick, old man. Absolutely unintentional.'

'What are you apologizing to *him* for?' demanded Agnes Flack with a good deal of heat. It had been a near thing, and the girl was ruffled.

Frederick Pilcher's suspicions had plainly not been allayed by John Gooch's words. He drove a cautious thirty yards, and waited with the air of one suspending judgement for his opponent to play his second. It was with a feeling of relief that John Gooch, smiting vigorously with his brassie, was enabled to establish his *bona fides* with a shot that rolled to within mashie-niblick distance of the green.

Frederick Pilcher seemed satisfied that all was well. He played his second to the edge of the green. John Gooch ran his third up into the neighbourhood of the pin.

Frederick Pilcher stooped and picked his ball up.

'Here!' cried Agnes Flack.

'Hey!' ejaculated John Gooch.

'What on earth do you think you're doing?' said Agnes Flack.

Frederick Pilcher looked at them with mild surprise.

'What's the matter?' he said. 'There's a blob of mud on my ball. I just wanted to brush it off.'

'Oh, my heavens!' thundered Agnes Flack. 'Haven't you ever read the rules? You're disqualified.'

'Disqualified?'

'Dis-jolly-well-qualified,' said Agnes Flack, her eyes flashing scorn. 'This cripple here wins the match.'

Frederick Pilcher heaved a sigh.

'So be it,' he said. 'So be it.'

'What do you mean, so be it? Of course it is.'

'Exactly. Exactly. I quite understand. I have lost the match. So be it.'

And, with drooping shoulders, Frederick Pilcher shuffled off in the direction of the bar.

John Gooch watched him go with a seething fury which for the moment robbed him of speech. He might, he told himself, have expected something like this. Frederick Pilcher, lost to every sense of good feeling and fair play, had double-crossed him. He shuddered as he realized how inky must be the hue of Frederick Pilcher's soul; and he wished in a frenzy of regret that he had thought of picking his own ball up. Too late! Too late!

For an instant the world had been blotted out for John Gooch by a sort of red mist. This mist clearing, he now saw Agnes Flack standing looking at him in a speculative sort of way, an odd expression in her eyes. And beyond her, leaning darkly against the club-house wall, his bulging muscles swelling beneath his coat and his powerful fingers tearing to pieces what appeared to be a section of lead piping, stood Sidney McMurdo.

John Gooch did not hesitate. Although McMurdo was some distance away, he could see him quite clearly; and with equal clearness he could remember every detail of that recent interview with him. He drew a step nearer to Agnes Flack, and having gulped once or twice, began to speak.

'Agnes,' he said huskily, 'there is something I want to say to you. Oh, Agnes, have you not guessed—'

'One moment,' said Agnes Flack. 'If you're trying to propose to me, sign off. There is nothing doing. The idea is all wet.'

'All wet?'

'All absolutely wet. I admit that there was a time when I toyed with the idea of marrying a man with brains, but there are limits. I wouldn't marry a man who played golf as badly as you do if he were the last man in the world. Sid-nee!' she roared, turning and cupping her mouth with her hands; and a nervous golfer down by the lake-hole leaped three feet and got his mashie entangled between his legs.

'Hullo?'

'I'm going to marry you, after all.'

'Me?'

'Yes, you.'

'Three rousing cheers!' bellowed McMurdo.

Agnes Flack turned to John Gooch. There was something like commiseration in her eyes, for she was a woman. Rather on the large side, but still a woman.

'I'm sorry,' she said.

'Don't mention it,' said John Gooch.

'I hope this won't ruin your life.'

'No, no.'

'You still have your Art.'

'Yes, I still have my Art.'

'Are you working on anything just now?' asked Agnes Flack.

'I'm starting a new story to-night,' said John Gooch. 'It will be called *Saved from the Scaffold.*'

There had been a gap for a week or so in our little circle at the Angler's Rest, and that gap the most serious that could have occurred. Mr Mulliner's had been the vacant chair, and we had felt his absence acutely. Inquiry on his welcome return elicited the fact that he had been down in Hertfordshire, paying a visit to his cousin Lady Wickham, at her historic residence, Skeldings Hall. He had left her well, he informed us, but somewhat worried.

'About her daughter Roberta,' said Mr Mulliner.

'Delicate girl?' we asked sympathetically.

'Not at all. Physically, most robust. What is troubling my cousin is the fact that she does not get married.'

A tactless Mild-and-Bitter, who was a newcomer to the bar-parlour and so should not have spoken at all, said that that was often the way with these plain girls. The modern young man, he said, valued mere looks too highly, and instead of being patient, and carrying on pluckily till he was able to penetrate the unsightly exterior to the good womanly heart within . . .

'My cousin's daughter Roberta,' said Mr Mulliner with some asperity, 'is not plain. Like all the Mulliners on the female side, however distantly removed from the main branch, she is remarkably beautiful. And yet she does not get married.'

'A mystery,' we mused.

'One,' said Mr Mulliner, 'that I have been able to solve. I was privileged to enjoy a good deal of Roberta's confidence during my visit, and I also met a young man named Algernon Crufts who appears to enjoy still more and also to be friendly with some of those of the male sex in whose society she has been moving lately. I am afraid that, like so many spirited girls of to-day, she is inclined to treat her suitors badly. They get discouraged, and I think with some excuse. There was young Attwater, for instance...'

Mr Mulliner broke off and sipped his hot Scotch and lemon. He appeared to have fallen into a reverie. From time to time, as he paused in his sipping, a chuckle escaped him.

'Attwater?' we said.

'Yes, that was the name.'

'What happened to him?'

'Oh, you wish to hear the story? Certainly, certainly, by all means.'

He rapped gently on the table, eyed his re-charged glass with quiet satisfaction, and proceeded.

In the demeanour of Roland Moresby Attwater, that rising young essayist and literary critic, there appeared (said Mr Mulliner) as he stood holding the door open to allow the ladies to leave his uncle Joseph's dining-room, no outward and visible sign of the irritation that seethed beneath his mud-stained shirt-front. Well-bred and highly civilized, he knew how to wear the mask. The lofty forehead that shone above his rimless pince-nez was smooth and unruffled, and if he bared his teeth it was only in a polite smile. Nevertheless, Roland Attwater was fed to the eyebrows.

In the first place, he hated these family dinners. In the second place, he had been longing all the evening for a chance to explain that muddy shirt, and everybody had treated it with a silent tact which was simply maddening. In the third place, he knew that his uncle Joseph was only waiting for the women to go to bring up once again the infuriating topic of Lucy.

After a preliminary fluttering, not unlike that of hens disturbed in a barnyard, the female members of the party rustled past him in single file – his aunt Emily; his aunt Emily's friend, Mrs Hughes Higham; his aunt Emily's companion and secretary, Miss Partlett; and his aunt Emily's adopted daughter, Lucy. The last-named brought up the rear of the procession. She was a gentle-looking girl with spaniel eyes and freckles, and as she passed she gave Roland a swift, shy glance of admiration and gratitude. It was the sort of look Ariadne might have given Theseus immediately after his turn-up with the Minotaur: and a casual observer, not knowing the facts, would have supposed that, instead of merely opening a door for her, Roland had rescued her at considerable bodily risk from some frightful doom.

Roland closed the door and returned to the table. His uncle, having pushed port towards him, coughed significantly and opened fire.

'How did you think Lucy was looking to-night, Roland?'

The young man winced, but the fine courtly spirit which is such a characteristic of the younger members of the intelligentsia did not fail him. Instead of banging the speaker over the head with the decanter, he replied with quiet civility:

'Splendid.'

'Nice girl.'

'Very.'

'Wonderful disposition.'

'Quite.'

'And so sensible.'

'Precisely.'

'Very different from these shingled, cigarette-smoking young women who infest the place nowadays.'

'Decidedly.'

'Had one of 'em up before me this morning,' said uncle Joseph, frowning austerely over his port. Sir Joseph Moresby was by profession a metropolitan magistrate. 'Charged with speeding. That's their idea of life.'

'Girls,' argued Roland, 'will be girls.'

'Not while I'm sitting at Bosher Street police-court, they won't,' said his uncle, with decision. 'Unless they want to pay five-pound fines and have their licences endorsed.' He sipped thoughtfully. 'Look here, Roland,' he said, as one struck by a novel idea, 'why the devil don't you marry Lucy?'

'Well, uncle—'

'You've got a bit of money, she's got a bit of money. Ideal. Besides, you want somebody to look after you.'

'Do you suggest,' inquired Roland, his eyebrows rising coldly, 'that I am incapable of looking after myself?'

'Yes, I do. Why, dammit, you can't even dress for dinner, apparently, without getting mud all over your shirt-front.'

Roland's cue had been long in coming, but it had arrived at a very acceptable moment.

'If you really want to know how that mud came to be on my shirt-front, uncle Joseph,' he said, with quiet dignity, 'I got it saving a man's life.'

'Eh? What? How?'

'A man slipped on the pavement as I was passing through

Grosvenor Square on my way here. It was raining, you know, and I—'

'You walked here?'

'Yes. And just as I reached the corner of Duke Street—'

'Walked here in the rain? There you are! Lucy would never let you do a foolish thing like that.'

'It began to rain after I had started.'

'Lucy would never have let you start.'

'Are you interested in my story, uncle,' said Roland, stiffly, 'or shall we go upstairs?'

'Eh? My dear boy, of course, of course. Most interested. Want to hear the whole thing from beginning to end. You say it was raining and this fellow slipped off the pavement. And then I suppose a car or a taxi or something came along suddenly and you pulled him out of danger. Yes, go on, my boy.'

'How do you mean, go on?' said Roland morosely. He felt like a public speaker whose chairman has appropriated the cream of his speech and inserted it in his own introductory remarks. 'That's all there is.'

'Well, who was the man? Did he ask you for your name and address?'

'He did.'

'Good! A young fellow once did something very similar to what you did, and the man turned out to be a millionaire and left him his entire fortune. I remember reading about it.'

'In the *Family Herald*, no doubt?'

'Did your man look like a millionaire?'

'He did not. He looked like what he actually was – the proprietor of a small bird-and-snake shop in the Seven Dials.'

'Oh!' said Sir Joseph, a trifle dashed. 'Well, I must tell Lucy about this,' he said, brightening. 'She will be tremendously excited. Just the sort of thing to appeal to a warm-hearted girl like her. Look here, Roland, why don't you marry Lucy?'

Roland came to a swift decision. It had not been his intention to lay bare his secret dreams to this pertinacious old blighter, but there seemed no other way of stopping him. He drained a glass of port and spoke crisply.

'Uncle Joseph, I love somebody else.'

'Eh? What's that? Who?'

'This is, of course, strictly between ourselves.'

'Of course.'

'Her name is Wickham. I expect you know the family? The Hertfordshire Wickhams.'

'Hertfordshire Wickhams!' Sir Joseph snorted with extra-ordinary violence. 'Bosher Street Wickhams, you mean. If it's Roberta Wickham, a red-headed hussy who ought to be smacked and sent to bed without her supper, that's the girl I fined this morning.'

'You fined her!' gasped Roland.

'Five pounds,' said his uncle, complacently. 'Wish I could have given her five years. Menace to the public safety. How on earth did you get to know a girl like that?'

'I met her at a dance. I happened to mention that I was a critic of some small standing, and she told me that her mother wrote novels. I chanced to receive one of Lady Wickham's books for review shortly afterwards, and the – er – favourable tone of my notice apparently gave her some pleasure.' Roland's voice trembled slightly, and he blushed. Only he knew what it had cost him to write eulogistically of that terrible book. 'She has invited me down to Skeldings, their place in Hertfordshire, for the week-end to-morrow.'

'Send her a telegram.'

'Saying what?'

'That you can't go.'

'But I am going.' It is a pretty tough thing if a man of letters who has sold his critical soul is not to receive the reward of his crime. 'I wouldn't miss it for anything.'

'Don't you be a fool, my boy,' said Sir Joseph. 'I've known you all your life – know you better than you know yourself – and I tell you it's sheer insanity for a man like you to dream of marrying a girl like that. Forty miles an hour she was going, right down the middle of Piccadilly. The constable proved it up to the hilt. You're a quiet, sensible fellow, and you ought to marry a quiet, sensible girl. You're what I call a rabbit.'

'A rabbit!'

'There is no stigma attached to being a rabbit,' said Sir Joseph, pacifically. 'Every man with a grain of sense is one. It simply means that you prefer a normal, wholesome life to gadding about like a – like a non-rabbit. You're going out of your class, my boy. You're trying to change your zoological species, and it can't be done. Half the divorces to-day are due to the fact that rabbits won't believe they're rabbits till it's too late. It is the peculiar nature of the rabbit—'

'I think we had better join the ladies, uncle Joseph,' said Roland, frostily. 'Aunt Emily will be wondering what has become of us.'

In spite of the innate modesty of all heroes, it was with something closely resembling chagrin that Roland discovered, on going to his club in the morning, that the Press of London was unanimously silent on the subject of his last night's exploit. Not that one expected anything in the nature of publicity, of course, or even desired it. Still, if there had happened to be some small paragraph under some such title as 'Gallant Behaviour of an Author' or 'Critical Moment for a Critic,' it would have done no harm to the sale of that little book of thoughtful essays which Blenkinsop's had just put on the market.

And the fellow had seemed so touchingly grateful at the time.

Pawing at Roland's chest with muddy hands he had told him that he would never forget this moment as long as he lived. And he had not bothered even to go and call at a newspaper office.

Well, well! He swallowed his disappointment and a light lunch and returned to his flat, where he found Bryce, his man-servant, completing the packing of his suit-case.

'Packing?' said Roland. 'That's right. Did those socks arrive?'

'Yes, sir.'

'Good!' said Roland. They were some rather special gents' half-hose from the Burlington Arcade, subtly passionate, and he was hoping much from them. He wandered to the table, and became aware that on it lay a large cardboard box. 'Hullo, what's this?'

'A man left it a short while ago, sir. A somewhat shabbily-dressed person. The note accompanying it is on the mantel-piece, sir.'

Roland went to the mantelpiece; and, having inspected the dirty envelope for a moment with fastidious distaste, opened it in a gingerly manner.

'The box appears to me, sir,' continued Bryce, 'to contain something alive. It seemed to me that I received the impression of something squirming.'

'Good Lord!' exclaimed Roland, staring at the letter.

'Sir?'

'It's a snake. That fool has sent me a snake. Of all the—'

A hearty ringing at the front door-bell interrupted him. Bryce, rising from the suit-case, vanished silently. Roland continued to regard the unwelcome gift with a peevish frown.

'Miss Wickham, sir,' said Bryce at the door.

The visitor, who walked springily into the room, was a girl of remarkable beauty. She resembled a particularly good-looking schoolboy who had dressed up in his sister's clothes.

'Ah!' she said, cocking a bright eye at the suit-case. 'I'm glad you're bustling about. We ought to be starting soon. I'm going to drive you down in the two-seater.' She began a restless tour of the room. 'Hullo!' she said, arriving at the box. 'What might this be?' She shook it experimentally. 'I say! There's something squishy inside!'

'Yes, it's—'

'Roland,' said Miss Wickham, having conducted further experiments, 'immediate investigation is called for. Inside this box there is most certainly some living organism. When you shake it it definitely squishes.'

'It's all right. It's only a snake.'

'Snake!'

'Perfectly harmless,' he hastened to assure her. 'The fool expressly states that. Not that it matters, because I'm going to send it straight back, unopened.'

Miss Wickham squeaked with pleased excitement.

'Who's been sending you snakes?'

Roland coughed diffidently.

'I happened to – er – save a man's life last night. I was coming along at the corner of Duke Street—'

'Now, isn't that an extraordinary thing?' said Miss Wickham, meditatively. 'Here have I lived all these years and never thought of getting a snake!'

'—when a man—'

'The one thing every young girl should have.'

'—slipped off the pavement—'

'There are the most tremendous possibilities in a snake. The diner-out's best friend. Pop it on the table after the soup and be Society's pet.'

Roland, though nothing, of course, could shake his great love, was conscious of a passing feeling of annoyance.

'I'll tell Bryce to take the thing back to the man,' he said, abandoning his story as a total loss.

'Take it back?' said Miss Wickham, amazed. 'But, Roland, what frightful waste! Why, there are moments in life when knowing where to lay your hand on a snake means more than words can tell.' She started. 'Golly! Didn't you once say that old Sir Joseph What's-his-name – the beak, you know – was your uncle? He fined me five of the best yesterday for absolutely crawling along Piccadilly. He needs a sharp lesson. He must be taught that he can't go about the place persecuting the innocent like that. I'll tell you what. Ask him to lunch here and hide the thing in his napkin! That'll make him think a bit!'

'No, no!' cried Roland, shuddering strongly.

'Roland! For my sake!'

'No, no, really!'

'And you said dozens of times that you would do anything in the world for me!' She mused. 'Well, at least let me tie a string to it and dangle it out of the window in front of the next old lady that comes along.'

'No, no, please! I must send it back to the man.'

Miss Wickham's discontent was plain, but she seemed to accept defeat.

'Oh, all right, if you're going to refuse me every little thing! But let me tell you, my lad, that you're throwing away the laugh of a lifetime. Wantonly and callously chucking it away. Where is Bryce? Gone to earth in the kitchen, I suppose. I'll go and give him the thing while you strap the suit-case. We ought to be starting, or we shan't get there by tea-time.'

'Let me do it.'

'No, I'll do it.'

'You mustn't trouble.'

'No trouble,' said Miss Wickham, amiably.

In this world, as has been pointed out in various ways by a great many sages and philosophers, it is wiser for the man who shrinks from being disappointed not to look forward too keenly to moments that promise pleasure. Roland Attwater, who had anticipated considerable enjoyment from his drive down to Skeldings Hall, soon discovered, when the car had threaded its way through the London traffic and was out in the open country, that the conditions were not right for enjoyment. Miss Wickham did not appear to share the modern girl's distaste for her home. She plainly wanted to get there as quickly as possible. It seemed to Roland that from the time they left High Barnet to the moment when, with a grinding of brakes, they drew up at the door of Skeldings Hall the two-seater had only touched Hertfordshire at odd spots.

Yet, as they alighted, Roberta Wickham voiced a certain dissatisfaction with her work.

'Forty-three minutes,' she said, frowning at her watch. 'I can do better than that.'

'Can you?' gulped Roland. 'Can you, indeed?'

'Well, we're in time for tea, anyhow. Come in and meet the

mater. Forgotten Sports of the Past – Number Three, Meeting the Mater.'

Roland met the mater. The phrase, however, is too mild and inexpressive and does not give a true picture of the facts. He not merely met the mater; he was engulfed and swallowed up by the mater. Lady Wickham, that popular novelist ('Strikes a singularly fresh note.' – R. Moresby Attwater in the *New Examiner*), was delighted to see her guest. Welcoming Roland to her side, she proceeded to strike so many singularly fresh notes that he was unable to tear himself away till it was time to dress for dinner. She was still talking with unimpaired volubility on the subject of her books, of which Roland had been kind enough to write so appreciatively, when the gong went.

'Is it as late as that?' she said, surprised, releasing Roland, who had thought it later. 'We shall have to go on with our little talk after dinner. You know your room? No? Oh, well, Claude will show you. Claude, will you take Mr Attwater up with you? His room is at the end of your corridor. By the way, you don't know each other, do you? Sir Claude Lynn – Mr Attwater.'

The two men bowed; but in Roland's bow there was not that heartiness which we like to see in our friends when we introduce them to fellow-guests. A considerable part of the agony which he had been enduring for the last two hours had been caused not so much by Lady Wickham's eloquence, though that had afflicted him sorely, as by the spectacle of this man Lynn, whoever he might be, monopolizing the society of Bobbie Wickham in a distant corner. There had been to him something intolerably possessive about the back of Sir Claude's neck as he bent toward Miss Wickham. It was the neck of a man who is being much more intimate and devotional than a jealous rival cares about.

The close-up which he now received of this person did nothing to allay Roland's apprehension. The man was handsome, sickeningly handsome, with just that dark, dignified, clean-cut handsomeness which attracts impressionable girls. It was, indeed, his dignity that so oppressed Roland now. There was something about Sir Claude Lynn's calm and supercilious eye that made a fellow feel that he belonged to entirely the wrong set in London and that his trousers were bagging at the knees.

'A most delightful man,' whispered Lady Wickham, as Sir Claude moved away to open the door for Bobbie. 'Between ourselves, the original of Captain Mauleverer, D.S.O., in my *Blood Will Tell*. Very old family, ever so much money. Plays polo splendidly. And tennis. And golf. A superb shot. Member for East Bittlesham, and I hear on all sides that he may be in the Cabinet any day.'

'Indeed?' said Roland, coldly.

It seemed to Lady Wickham, as she sat with him in her study after dinner – she had stated authoritatively that he would much prefer a quiet chat in that shrine of literature to any shallow revelry that might be going on elsewhere – that Roland was a trifle distrait. Nobody could have worked harder to entertain him than she. She read him the first seven chapters of the new novel on which she was engaged, and told him in gratifying detail the plot of the rest of it, but somehow all did not seem well. The young man, she noticed, had developed a habit of plucking at his hair and once he gave a sharp, gulping cry which startled her. Lady Wickham began to feel disappointed in Roland, and was not sorry when he excused himself.

'I wonder,' he said, in a rather overwrought sort of way, 'if you would mind if I just went and had a word with Miss Wickham? I – I – there's something I wanted to ask her.'

'Certainly,' said Lady Wickham, without warmth. 'You will probably find her in the billiard-room. She said something about having a game with Claude. Sir Claude is wonderful at billiards. Almost like a professional.'

Bobbie was not in the billiard-room, but Sir Claude was, practising dignified cannons which never failed to come off. At Roland's entrance he looked up like an inquiring statue.

'Miss Wickham?' he said. 'She left half an hour ago. I think she went to bed.'

He surveyed Roland's flushed dishevelment for a moment with a touch of disapproval, then resumed his cannons. Roland, though he had that on his mind concerning which he desired Miss Wickham's counsel and sympathy, felt that it would have to stand over till the morning. Meanwhile, lest his hostess should pop out of the study and recapture him, he decided to go to bed himself.

He had just reached the passage where his haven lay, when a door which had apparently been standing ajar opened and Bobbie appeared, draped in a sea-green négligée of such a calibre that Roland's heart leaped convulsively and he clutched at the wall for support.

'Oh, there you are,' she said, a little petulantly. 'What a time you've been!'

'Your mother was—'

'Yes, I suppose she would be,' said Miss Wickham, understandingly. 'Well, I only wanted to tell you about Sidney.'

'Sidney? Do you mean Claude?'

No. Sidney. The snake. I was in your room just after dinner, to see if you had everything you wanted, and I noticed the box on your dressing-table.'

'I've been trying to get hold of you all the evening to ask you what to do about that,' said Roland, feverishly. 'I was most awfully upset when I saw the beastly thing. How Bryce came to be such an idiot as to put it in the car—'

'He must have misunderstood me,' said Bobbie, with a clear and childlike light shining in her hazel eyes. 'I suppose he thought I said, "Put this in the back" instead of "Take this back." But what I wanted to say was that it's all right.'

'All right?'

'Yes. That's why I've been waiting up to see you. I thought that, when you went to your room and found the box open, you might be a bit worried.'

'The box open!'

'Yes. But it's all right. It was I who opened it.'

'Oh, but I say – you – you oughtn't to have done that. The snake may be roaming about all over the house.'

'Oh, no, it's all right. I know where it is.'

'That's good.'

'Yes, it's all right. I put it in Claude's bed.'

Roland Attwater clutched at his hair as violently as if he had been listening to chapter six of Lady Wickham's new novel.

'You – you – you – what?'

'I put it in Claude's bed.'

Roland uttered a little whinnying sound, like a very old horse a very long way away.

'Put it in Claude's bed!'

'Put it in Claude's bed.'

'But – but – but why?'

'Why not?' asked Miss Wickham, reasonably.

'But – oh, my heavens!'

'Something on your mind?' inquired Miss Wickham, solicitously.

'It will give him an awful fright.'

'Jolly good for him. I was reading an article in the evening paper about it. Did you know that fear increases the secretory activity of the thyroid, suprarenal, and pituitary glands? Well, it does. Bucks you up, you know. Regular tonic. It'll be like a day at the seaside for old Claude when he puts his bare foot on Sidney. Well, I must be turning in. Got that schoolgirl complexion to think about. Good night.'

For some minutes after he had tottered to his room, Roland sat on the edge of the bed in deep meditation. At one time it seemed as if his reverie was going to take a pleasant turn. This was when the thought presented itself to him that he must have overestimated the power of Sir Claude's fascination. A girl could not, he felt, have fallen very deeply under a man's spell if she started filling his bed with snakes the moment she left him.

For an instant, as he toyed with this heartening reflection, something remotely resembling a smile played about Roland's sensitive mouth. Then another thought came to wipe the smile away – the realization that, while the broad general principle of putting snakes in Sir Claude's bed was entirely admirable, the flaw in the present situation lay in the fact that this particular snake could be so easily traced to its source. The butler, or whoever had taken his luggage upstairs, would be sure to remember carrying up a mysterious box. Probably it had squished as he carried it and was already the subject of comment in the servants' hall. Discovery was practically certain.

Roland rose jerkily from his bed. There was only one thing to be done, and he must do it immediately. He must go to Sir Claude's room and retrieve his lost pet. He crept to the door and listened carefully. No sound came to disturb the stillness of the house. He stole out into the corridor.

It was at this precise moment that Sir Claude Lynn, surfeited with cannons, put on his coat, replaced his cue in the rack, and came out of the billiard-room.

If there is one thing in this world that should be done quickly or not at all, it is the removal of one's personal snake from the bed of a comparative stranger. Yet Roland, brooding over the snowy coverlet, hesitated. All his life he had had a horror of crawling and slippery things. At his private school, while other boys had fondled frogs and achieved terms of intimacy with slow-worms, he had not been able to bring himself even to keep white mice. The thought of plunging his hand between those sheets and groping for an object of such recognized squishiness as Sidney appalled him. And, even as he hesitated, there came from the corridor outside the sound of advancing footsteps.

Roland was not by nature a resourceful young man, but even a child would have known what to do in this crisis. There was a large cupboard on the other side of the room, and its door had been left invitingly open. In the rapidity with which he bolted into this his uncle Joseph would no doubt have seen further convincing evidence of his rabbit-hood. He reached it and burrowed behind a mass of hanging clothes just as Sir Claude entered the room.

* * *

It was some small comfort to Roland – and at the moment he needed what comfort he could get, however small – to find that there was plenty of space in the cupboard. And what was even better, seeing that he had had no time to close the door, it was generously filled with coats, overcoats, raincoats, and trousers. Sir Claude Lynn was evidently a man who believed in taking an extensive wardrobe with him on country-house visits; and, while he deplored the dandyism which this implied, Roland would not have had it otherwise. Nestling in the undergrowth, he peered out between a raincoat and a pair of golfing knickerbockers. A strange silence had fallen, and he was curious to know what his host was doing with himself.

At first he could not sight him; but, shifting slightly to the left, he brought him into focus, and discovered that in the interval that had passed Sir Claude had removed nearly all his clothes and was now standing before the open window, doing exercises.

It was not prudery that caused this spectacle to give Roland a sharp shock. What made him start so convulsively was the man's horrifying aspect as revealed in the nude. Downstairs, in the conventional dinner-costume of the well-dressed man, Sir Claude Lynn had seemed robust and soldierly, but nothing in his appearance then had prepared Roland for the ghastly physique which he exhibited now. He seemed twice his previous size, as if the removal of constricting garments had caused him to bulge in every direction. When he inflated his chest, it looked like a barrel. And, though Roland in the circumstances would have preferred any other simile, there was only one thing to which his rippling muscles could be compared. They were like snakes, and nothing but snakes. They heaved and twisted beneath his skin just as Sidney was presumably even now heaving and twisting beneath the sheets.

If ever there was a man, in short, in whose bedroom one would rather not have been concealed in circumstances which might only too easily lead to a physical encounter, that man was Sir Claude Lynn; and Roland, seeing him, winced away with a shudder so violent that a coat-hanger which had been trembling on the edge of its peg fell with a disintegrating clatter.

There was a moment of complete silence: then the trousers behind which he cowered were snatched away, and a huge hand, groping like the tentacle of some dreadful marine monster, seized him painfully by the hair and started pulling.

'Ouch!' said Roland, and came out like a winkle at the end of a pin.

A modesty which Roland, who was modest himself, should have been the first to applaud had led the other to clothe himself hastily for this interview in a suit of pyjamas of a stupefying mauve. In all his life Roland had never seen such a colour-scheme; and in some curious way the brilliance of them seemed to complete his confusion. The result was that, instead of plunging at once into apologies and explanations, he remained staring with fallen jaw; and his expression, taken in conjunction with the fact that his hair, rumpled by the coats, appeared to be standing on end, supplied Sir Claude with a theory which seemed to cover the case. He remembered that Roland had had much the same cock-eyed look when he had come into the billiard-room. He recalled that immediately after dinner Roland had disappeared and had not joined the rest of the party in the drawing-room. Obviously the fellow must have been drinking like a fish in some secret part of the house for hours.

'Get out!' he said curtly, taking Roland by the arm with a look of disgust and leading him sternly to the door. An abstemious man himself, Sir Claude Lynn had a correct horror of excess in others. 'Go and sleep it off. I suppose you can find your way to your room? It's the one at the end of the corridor, as you seem to have forgotten.'

'But listen—'

'I cannot understand how a man of any decent upbringing can make such a beast of himself.'

'Do listen!'

'Don't shout like that,' snapped Sir Claude, severely. 'Good heavens, man, do you want to wake the whole house? If you dare to open your mouth again, I'll break you into little bits.'

Roland found himself out in the passage, staring at a closed door. Even as he stared it opened sharply, and the upper half of the mauve-clad Sir Claude popped out.

'No drunken singing in the corridor, mind!' said Sir Claude, sternly, and disappeared.

It was a little difficult to know what to do. Sir Claude had counselled slumber, but the suggestion was scarcely a practical one. On the other hand there seemed nothing to be gained by hanging about in the passage. With slow and lingering steps Roland moved towards his room, and had just reached it when the silence of the night was rent by a shattering scream; and the next moment there shot through the door he had left a large body. And, as Roland gazed dumbly, a voice was raised in deafening appeal.

'Shot-gun!' vociferated Sir Claude. 'Help! Shot-gun! Bring a shot-gun, somebody!'

There was not the smallest room for doubt that the secretory activity of his thyroid, suprarenal, and pituitary glands had been increased to an almost painful extent.

It is only in the most modern and lively country houses that this sort of thing can happen without attracting attention. So quickly did the corridor fill that it seemed to Roland as if dressing-gowned figures had shot up through the carpet. Among those present he noticed Lady Wickham in blue, her daughter Roberta in green, three male guests in bath-robes, the under-housemaid in curl-papers, and Simmons, the butler, completely and correctly clad in full afternoon costume. They were all asking what was the matter, but, as Lady Wickham's penetrating voice o'ertopped the rest, it was to her that Sir Claude turned to tell his story.

'A snake?' said Lady Wickham, interested.

'A snake.'

'In your bed?'

'In my bed.'

'Most unusual,' said Lady Wickham, with a touch of displeasure.

Sir Claude's rolling eye, wandering along the corridor, picked out Roland as he shrank among the shadows. He pointed at him with such swift suddenness that his hostess only saved herself from a nasty blow by means of some shifty footwork.

'That's the man!' he cried.

Lady Wickham, already ruffled, showed signs of peevishness.

'My dear Claude,' she said, with a certain asperity, 'do come to some definite decision. A moment ago you said there was a snake in your room; now you say it was a man. Besides, can't you see that that is Mr Attwater? What would he be doing in your room?'

'I'll tell you what he was doing. He was putting that infernal snake in my bed. I found him there.'

'Found him there? In your bed?'

'In my cupboard. Hiding. I hauled him out.'

All eyes were turned upon Roland. His own he turned with

a look of wistful entreaty upon Roberta Wickham. A cavalier of the nicest gallantry, nothing, of course, would induce him to betray the girl; but surely she would appreciate that the moment had come for her to step forward and clear a good man's name with a full explanation.

He had been too sanguine. A pretty astonishment lit up Miss Wickham's lovely eyes. But her equally lovely mouth did not open.

'But Mr Attwater has no snake,' argued Lady Wickham. 'He is a well-known man-of-letters. Well-known men-of-letters,' she said, stating a pretty generally recognized fact, 'do not take snakes with them when they go on visits.'

A new voice joined in the discussion.

'Begging your pardon, your ladyship.'

It was the voice of Simmons, grave and respectful.

'Begging your pardon, your ladyship, it is my belief that Mr Attwater did have a serpent in his possession. Thomas, who conveyed his baggage to his room, mentioned a cardboard box that seemed to contain something alive.'

From the expression of the eyes that once more raked him in his retirement, it was plain that the assembled company were of the opinion that it was Roland's turn to speak. But speech was beyond him. He had been backing slowly for some little time, and now, as he backed another step, the handle of his bedroom door insinuated itself into the small of his back. It was almost as if the thing were hinting to him that refuge lay beyond.

He did not resist the kindly suggestion. With one quick, emotional movement he turned, plunged into his room, and slammed the door behind him.

From the corridor without came the sound of voices in

debate. He was unable to distinguish words, but the general trend of them was clear. Then silence fell.

Roland sat on his bed, staring before him. He was roused from his trance by a tap on the door.

'Who's that?' he cried, bounding up. His eye was wild. He was prepared to sell his life dearly.

'It is I, sir. Simmons.'

'What do you want?'

The door opened a few inches. Through the gap there came a hand. In the hand was a silver salver. On the salver lay something squishy that writhed and wriggled.

'Your serpent, sir,' said the voice of Simmons.

It was the opinion of Roland Attwater that he was now entitled to the remainder of the night in peace. The hostile forces outside must now, he felt, have fired their last shot. He sat on his bed, thinking deeply, if incoherently. From time to time the clock on the stables struck the quarters, but he did not move. And then into the silence it seemed to him that some sound intruded – a small tapping sound that might have been the first tentative efforts of a very young woodpecker just starting out in business for itself. It was only after this small noise had continued for some moments that he recognized it for what it was. Somebody was knocking softly on his door.

There are moods in which even the mildest man will turn to bay, and there gleamed in Roland Attwater's eyes as he strode to the door and flung it open a baleful light. And such was his militant condition that, even when he glared out and beheld Roberta Wickham, still in that green négligée, the light did not fade away. He regarded her malevolently.

'I thought I'd better come and have a word with you,' whispered Miss Wickham.

'Indeed?' said Roland.

'I wanted to explain.'

'Explain!'

'Well,' said Miss Wickham, 'you may not think there's any explanation due to you, but I really feel there is. Oh, yes, I do. You see, it was this way. Claude had asked me to marry him.'

'And so you put a snake in his bed? Of course! Quite natural!'

'Well, you see, he was so frightfully perfect and immaculate and dignified and – oh, well, you've seen him for yourself, so you know what I mean. He was too darned overpowering – that's what I'm driving at – and it seemed to me that if I could only see him really human and undignified – just once – I might – well, you see what I mean?'

'And the experiment, I take it, was successful?'

Miss Wickham wriggled her small toes inside her slippers.

'It depends which way you look at it. I'm not going to marry him, if that's what you mean.'

'I should have thought,' said Roland, coldly, 'that Sir Claude behaved in a manner sufficiently – shall I say human? – to satisfy even you.'

Miss Wickham giggled reminiscently.

'He did leap, didn't he? But it's all off, just the same.'

'Might I ask why?'

'Those pyjamas,' said Miss Wickham, firmly. 'The moment I caught a glimpse of them, I said to myself, "No wedding bells for me!" No! I've seen too much of life to be optimistic about a man who wears mauve pyjamas.' She plunged for a space into maiden meditation. When she spoke again, it was on another aspect of the affair. 'I'm afraid mother is rather cross with you, Roland.'

'You surprise me!'

'Never mind. You can slate her next novel.'

'I intend to,' said Roland, grimly, remembering what he had suffered in the study from chapters one to seven of it.

'But meanwhile I don't think you had better meet her again just yet. Do you know, I really think the best plan would be for you to go away to-night without saying good-bye. There is a very good milk-train which gets you into London at six-forty-five.'

'When does it start?'

'At three-fifteen.'

'I'll take it,' said Roland.

There was a pause. Roberta Wickham drew a step closer.

'Roland,' she said, softly, 'you were a dear not to give me away. I do appreciate it so much.'

'Not at all!'

'There would have been an awful row. I expect mother would have taken away my car.'

'Ghastly!'

'I want to see you again quite soon, Roland. I'm coming up to London next week. Will you give me lunch? And then we might go and sit in Kensington Gardens or somewhere where it's quiet.'

Roland eyed her fixedly.

'I'll drop you a line,' he said.

Sir Joseph Moresby was an early breakfaster. The hands of the clock pointed to five minutes past eight as he entered his dining-room with a jaunty and hopeful step. There were, his senses told him, kidneys and bacon beyond that door. To his surprise he found that there was also his nephew Roland. The young man was pacing the carpet restlessly. He had a rumpled look, as if he had slept poorly, and his eyes were pink about the rims.

'Roland!' exclaimed Sir Joseph. 'Good gracious! What are you doing here? Didn't you go to Skeldings after all?'

'Yes, I went,' said Roland, in a strange, toneless voice.

'Then what—?'

'Uncle Joseph,' said Roland, 'you remember what we were talking about at dinner? Do you really think Lucy would have me if I asked her to marry me?'

'What! My dear boy, she's been in love with you for years.'

'Is she up yet?'

'No. She doesn't breakfast till nine.'

'I'll wait.'

Sir Joseph grasped his hand.

'Roland, my boy—' he began.

But there was that on Roland's mind that made him unwilling to listen to set speeches.

'Uncle Joseph,' he said, 'do you mind if I join you for a bite of breakfast?'

'My dear boy, of course—'

'Then I wish you would ask them to be frying two or three eggs and another rasher or so. While I'm waiting I'll be starting on a few kidneys.'

It was ten minutes past nine when Sir Joseph happened to go into the morning-room. He had supposed it empty, but he perceived that the large arm-chair by the window was occupied by his nephew Roland. He was leaning back with the air of one whom the world is treating well. On the floor beside him sat Lucy, her eyes fixed adoringly on the young man's face.

'Yes, yes,' she was saying. 'How wonderful! Do go on, darling.'

Sir Joseph tiptoed out, unnoticed. Roland was speaking as he softly closed the door.

'Well,' Sir Joseph heard him say, 'it was raining, you know, and just as I reached the corner of Duke Street—'

'And then,' said Mr Mulliner, 'there was the case of Dudley Finch.'

He looked inquiringly at his glass, found that it was three-parts full, and immediately proceeded to resume the Saga of his cousin's daughter, Roberta.

'At the moment at which I would introduce Dudley Finch to you,' said Mr Mulliner, 'we find him sitting in the lobby of Claridge's Hotel, looking at his watch with the glazing eye of a starving man. Five minutes past two was the time it registered, and Roberta Wickham had promised to meet him for lunch at one-thirty sharp. He heaved a plaintive sigh, and a faint sense of grievance began to steal over him. Impious though it was to feel that that angelic girl had any faults, there was no denying, he told himself, that this tendency of hers to keep a fellow waiting for his grub amounted to something very like a flaw in an otherwise perfect nature. He rose from his chair and, having dragged his emaciated form to the door, tottered out into Brook Street and stood gazing up and down it like a male Lady of Shalott.

Standing there in the weak sunlight (said Mr Mulliner), Dudley Finch made a singularly impressive picture. He was – sartorially – so absolutely right in every respect. From his brilliantined hair to his gleaming shoes, from his fawn-coloured spats to his Old Etonian tie, he left no loophole to the sternest critic. You felt as you saw him that if this was the sort of chap who lunched at Claridge's, old man Claridge was in luck.

It was not admiration, however, that caused the earnest-looking young man in the soft hat to stop as he hurried by. It was surprise. He stared wide-eyed at Dudley.

'Good heavens!' he exclaimed. 'I thought you were on your way to Australia.'

'No,' said Dudley Finch, 'not on my way to Australia.' His smooth forehead wrinkled in a frown. 'Rolie, old thing,' he said, with gentle reproach, 'you oughtn't to go about London in a hat like that.' Roland Attwater was his cousin, and a man does not like to see his relatives careering all over the Metropolis looking as if cats had brought them in. 'And your tie doesn't match your socks.'

He shook his head sorrowfully. Roland was a literary man, and, worse, had been educated at an inferior school – Harrow, or some such name, Dudley understood that it was called; but even so he ought to have more proper feeling about the vital things of life.

'Never mind my hat,' said Roland. 'Why aren't you on your way to Australia?'

'Oh, that's all right. Broadhurst had a cable, and isn't sailing till the fifteenth.'

Roland Attwater looked relieved. Like all the more serious-minded members of the family, he was deeply concerned about his cousin's future. With regard to this there had been for some time past a little friction, a little difficulty in reconciling two sharply conflicting points of view. The family had wanted Dudley to go into his uncle John's business in the City; whereas what Dudley desired was that some broad-minded sportsman should slip him a few hundred quid and enable him to start a new dance-club. A compromise had been effected when his godfather, Mr Sampson Broadhurst, arriving suddenly from Australia, had offered to take the young man back with him and teach him sheep-farming. It fortunately happening that he was a great reader of the type of novel in which everyone who goes to Australia automatically amasses a large fortune and leaves it to the hero, Dudley had formally announced at a family council that – taking it by and large – Australia seemed to him a pretty good egg, and that he had no objection to having a pop at it.

'Thank goodness,' said Roland. 'I thought you might have backed out of going at the last moment.'

Dudley smiled.

'Funny you should have said that, old man. A coincidence, I mean. Because that's just exactly what I've half made up my mind to do.'

'What!'

'Absolutely. The fact is, Rolie,' said Dudley, confidentially, 'I've just met the most topping girl. And sometimes, when I think of buzzing off on the fifteenth and being separated from her by all those leagues of water, I could howl like a dog. I've a jolly good mind to let the old man sail by himself, and stick here on my native heath.'

'This is appalling! You mustn't dream—'

'She's the most wonderful girl. Knows you, too. Roberta Wickham's her name. She lets me call her Bobbie. She—'

He broke off abruptly. His eyes, gazing past Roland, were shining with a holy light of devotion. His lips had parted in a brilliant smile.

'Yo-ho!' he cried.

Roland turned. A girl was crossing the road; a slim, boyish-looking girl, with shingled hair of a glorious red. She came tripping along with all the gay abandon of a woman who is forty minutes late for lunch and doesn't give a hoot.

'Yo-ho!' yowled young Mr Finch. 'Yo frightfully ho!'

The girl came up, smiling and debonair.

'I'm not late, am I?' she said.

'Rather not,' cooed the love-sick Dudley. 'Not a bit. Only just got here myself.'

'That's good,' said Miss Wickham. 'How are you, Roland?'

'Very well, thanks,' replied Roland Attwater, stiffly.

'I must congratulate you, mustn't I?'

'What on?' asked Dudley, puzzled.

'His engagement, of course.'

'Oh, that!' said Dudley. He knew that his cousin had recently become engaged to Lucy Moresby, and he had frequently marvelled at the lack of soul which could have led one acquainted with the divine Roberta to go and tack himself on to any inferior female. He put it down to Roland having been at Harrow.

'I hope you will be very happy.'

'Thank you,' said Roland, sedately. 'Well, I must be going. Good-bye. Glad to have seen you.'

He stalked off towards Grosvenor Square. It seemed to Dudley that his manner was peculiar.

'Not a very cordial bird, old Rolie,' he said, returning to the point at the luncheon-table. 'Biffed off a trifle abruptly, didn't it strike you?'

Miss Wickham sighed.

'I'm afraid Roland doesn't like me.'

'Not like you!' Dudley swallowed a potato which, in a calmer moment, he would have realized was some eighty degrees Fahrenheit too warm for mastication. 'Not like you!' he repeated, with watering eyes. 'The man must be an ass.'

'We were great friends at one time,' said Roberta, sadly. 'But ever since that snake business—'

'Snake business?'

'Roland had a snake, and I took it with me when he came down to Hertfordshire for the week-end. And I put it in a man's bed, and the mater got the impression that Roland had done it, and he had to sneak away on a milk-train. He's never quite forgiven me, I'm afraid.'

'But what else could you have done?' demanded Dudley, warmly. 'I mean to say, if a fellow's got a snake, naturally you put it in some other fellow's bed.'

'That's just what I felt.'

'Only once in a blue moon, I mean, you get hold of a snake. When you do, you can't be expected to waste it.'

'Exactly. Roland couldn't see that, though. Nor, for the matter of that,' continued Miss Wickham, dreamily, 'could mother.'

'I say,' said Dudley, 'that reminds me. I'd like to meet your mother.'

'Well, I'm going down there this evening. Why don't you come, too?'

'No, I say, really? May I?'

'Of course.'

'Rather short notice, though, isn't it?'

'Oh, that's all right. I'll send the mater a wire. She'll be awfully glad to see you.'

'You're sure?'

'Oh, rather! Awfully glad.'

'Well, that's fine. Thanks ever so much.'

'I'll motor you down.'

Dudley hesitated. Something of the brightness died out of his fair young face. He had had experience of Miss Wickham as a chauffeuse and had died half-a-dozen deaths in the extremely brief space of time which it had taken her to thread her way through half a mile of traffic.

'If it's all the same,' he said, nervously, 'I think I'll pop down by train.'

'Just as you like. The best one's the six-fifteen. Gets you there in time for dinner.'

'Six-fifteen? Right. Liverpool Street, of course? Just bring a suit-case, I suppose? Fine! I say, you're really sure your mother won't think I'm butting in?'

'Of course not. She'll be awfully glad to see you.'

'Splendid!' said Dudley.

The six-fifteen train was just about to draw out of Liverpool Street Station when Dudley flung himself and suit-case into it that evening. He had rather imprudently stepped in at the Drones Club on his way and, while having a brief refresher at the bar, had got into an interesting argument with a couple of the lads. There had only just been time for him to race to the cloak-room, retrieve his suit-case, and make a dash for the train. Fortunately, he had chanced upon an excellent taxi, and here he was, a little out of breath from the final sprint down the platform, but in every other respect absolutely all-righto. He leaned back against the cushions and gave himself up to thought.

From thinking of Bobbie he drifted shortly into meditation on her mother. If all went well, he felt this up-to-the-present-unmet mater was destined to be an important figure in his life. It was to her that he would have to go after Bobbie, hiding her face shyly on his waistcoat, had whispered that she had loved him from the moment they had met.

'Lady Wickham,' he would say. 'No, not Lady Wickham – mother!'

Yes, that was undoubtedly the way to start. After that it would be easy. Providing, of course, that the mater turned out to be one of the better class of maters and took to him from the beginning. He tried to picture Lady Wickham, and had evolved a mental portrait of a gentle, sweet-faced woman of latish middle-age when the train pulled up at a station, and a lucky glimpse of a name on one of the lamps told Dudley that this was where he alighted.

Some twenty minutes later he was being relieved of his suitcase and shown into a room that looked like a study of sorts.

'The gentleman, m'lady,' boomed the butler, and withdrew.

It was rather a rummy way of announcing the handsome guest, felt Dudley, but he was not able to give much thought to the matter, for from a chair in front of the desk at which she had been writing there now rose a most formidable person, at the sight of whom his heart missed a beat. So vivid had been that image of sweet-faced womanhood which he had fashioned that his hostess in the flesh had the effect of being a changeling.

Beauty, as it has been well said, is largely in the eye of the beholder, and it may be stated at once that Lady Wickham's particular type did not appeal to Dudley. He preferred the female eye to be a good deal less like a combination of gimlet and X-ray, and his taste in chins was something a little softer and not quite so reminiscent of a battleship going into action. Bobbie's mater might, as Bobbie had predicted, be awfully glad to see him, but she did not look it. And suddenly there came over him like a wave the realization that the check suit which he had selected so carefully was much too bright. At the tailor's, and subsequently at the Drones Club, it had had a pleasing and cheery effect, but here in this grim study he felt that it made him look like an absconding bookmaker.

'You are very late,' said Lady Wickham.

'Late?' quavered Dudley. The train had seemed to him to be making more or less good going.

'I supposed you would be here early in the afternoon. But perhaps you have brought a flashlight apparatus?'

'Flashlight apparatus?'

'Have you not brought a flashlight apparatus?'

Dudley shook his head. He prided himself on being something of an authority on what the young visitor should take with him on country-house visits, but this was a new one.

'No,' he said, 'no flashlight apparatus.'

'Then how,' demanded Lady Wickham, with some heat, 'do you imagine that you can take photographs at this time of night?'

'Ah!' said Dudley, vaguely. 'See what you mean, of course. Take a bit of doing, what?'

Lady Wickham seemed to become moderately resigned.

'Oh, well, I suppose they can send someone down to-morrow.'

'That's right,' said Dudley, brightening.

'In the meantime – this is where I work.'

'No, really?'

'Yes. All my books have been written at this desk.'

'Fancy that!' said Dudley. He remembered having heard Bobbie mention that Lady Wickham wrote novels.

'I get my inspirations, however, in the garden for the most part. Generally the rose-garden. I like to sit there in the mornings and think.'

'And what,' agreed Dudley, cordially, 'could be sweeter?'

His hostess regarded him curiously. A sense of something wrong seemed to come upon her.

'You *are* from *Milady's Boudoir*?' she asked, suddenly.

'From what was that, once again?' asked Dudley.

'Are you that man the editor of *Milady's Boudoir* was sending down to interview me?'

Dudley could answer this one.

'No,' he said.

'No?' echoed Lady Wickham.

'Most absolutely not-o,' said Dudley, firmly.

'Then who,' demanded Lady Wickham, 'are you?'

'My name's Dudley Finch.'

'And to what,' asked his hostess in a manner so extraordinarily like that of his late grandmother that Dudley's toes curled in their shoes, 'am I to attribute the honour of this visit?'

Dudley blinked.

'Why, I thought you knew all about it.'

'I know nothing whatever about it.'

'Didn't Bobbie send you a wire?'

'He did not. Nor do I know who Bobbie may be.'

'Miss Wickham, I mean. Your daughter Roberta. She told me to buzz down here for the night, and said she would send you a wire paving the way, so to speak. Oh, I say, this is a bit thick. Fancy her forgetting!'

For the second time that day a disagreeable feeling that his idol was after all not entirely perfect stole upon Dudley. A girl, he meant, oughtn't to lure a bloke down to her mater's house and then forget to send a wire tipping the old girl off. No, he meant to say! Pretty dashed casual, he meant.

'Oh,' said Lady Wickham, 'you are a friend of my daughter?'

'Absolutely.'

'I see. And where is Roberta?'

'She's tooling down in the car.'

Lady Wickham clicked her tongue.

'Roberta is becoming too erratic for endurance,' she said.

'I say, you know,' said Dudley, awkwardly, 'if I'm in the way, you know, just speak the word and I'll race off to the local pub. I mean to say, don't want to butt in, I mean.'

'Not at all, Mr—'

'Finch.'

'Not at all, Mr Finch. I am only too delighted,' said Lady Wickham, looking at him as if he were a particularly loathsome slug which had interrupted some beautiful reverie of hers in the rose-garden, 'that you were able to come.' She touched the bell. 'Oh, Simmons,' she said, as the butler appeared, 'in which room did you put Mr Finch's luggage?'

'In the Blue Room, m'lady.'

'Then perhaps you will show him the way there. He will wish to dress. Dinner,' she added to Dudley, 'will be at eight o'clock.'

'Righto!' said Dudley. He was feeling a little happier now. Formidable old bird as this old bird undoubtedly was, he was pretty confident that she would melt a bit when once he had got the good old dress-clothes draped about his person. He was prepared to stand or fall by his dress-clothes. There are a number of tailors in London who can hack up a bit of broadcloth and sew it together in some sort of shape, but there is only one who can construct a dress-suit so that it blends with the figure and seems as beautiful as a summer's dawn. It was this tailor who enjoyed the benefit of Dudley's patronage. Yes, Dudley felt as he entered the Blue Room, in about twenty minutes old Madame Lafarge was due to get her eye knocked out.

In the brief instant before he turned on the light he could dimly see that perfect suit laid out on the bed, and it was with something of the feeling of a wanderer returning home that he pressed the switch.

Light flooded the room, and Dudley stood there blinking.

But, no matter how much he blinked, the awful sight which had met his eyes refused to change itself in the slightest detail. What was laid out on the bed was not his dress-clothes, but the most ghastly collection of raiment he had ever beheld. He blinked once again as a forlorn hope, and then tottered forward.

He stood looking down at the foul things, his heart ice within him. Reading from left to right, the objects on the bed were as follows: A pair of short white woollen socks; a crimson made-up bow-tie of enormous size; a sort of middy-blouse arrangement; a pair of blue velvet knickerbockers; and finally – and it was this that seemed to Dudley to make it all so sad and hopeless – a very small sailor-hat with a broad blue ribbon, across which in large white letters ran the legend *H.M.S. See-Sik*.

On the floor were a pair of brown shoes with strap-and-buckle attachment. They seemed to be roomy number twelves.

Dudley sprang to the bell. A footman presented himself.

'Sir?' said the footman.

'What,' demanded Dudley, wildly, 'what is all this?'

'I found them in your suit-case, sir.'

'But where are my dress-clothes?'

'No dress-clothes in the suit-case, sir.'

A bright light shone upon Dudley. That argument with those two birds at the Drones had, he now recalled, been on the subject of fancy-dress. Both birds were dashing off to a fancy-dress ball that night, and one bird had appealed to Dudley to support him against the other bird in his contention that at these affairs the prudent man played for safety and went as a Pierrot. The second bird had said that he would sooner be dead in a ditch than don any such unimaginative costume. He was going as a small boy, he said, and with a pang Dudley remembered having laughed mockingly and prophesied that he would look the most priceless ass. And then he had sprinted off and collared the man's bag in mistake for his own.

'Look here,' he said, 'I can't possibly come down to dinner in those!'

'No, sir?' said the footman, respectfully, but with a really inhuman lack of interest and sympathy.

'You'd better leg it to the old girl's room— I mean,' said Dudley, recollecting himself, 'you had better go to Lady Wickham and inform her that Mr Finch presents his compliments and I'm awfully sorry but he has mislaid his dress-clothes, so he will have to come down to dinner in what I've got on at present.'

'Very good, sir.'

'I say!' A horrid thought struck Dudley. 'I say, we shall be alone, what? I mean to say, nobody else is coming to dinner?'

'Yes, sir,' said the footman, brightly. 'A number of guests are expected, sir.'

It was a sagging and demoralized Dudley who crawled into the dining-room a quarter of an hour later. In spite of what moralists say, a good conscience is not enough in itself to enable a man to bear himself jauntily in every crisis of life. Dudley had had a good upbringing, and the fact that he was dining at a strange house in a bright check suit gave him a consciousness of sin which he strove vainly to overcome.

The irony of it was that in a normal frame of mind he would have sneered loftily at the inferior garments which clothed the other male members of the party. On the left sleeve of the man opposite him was a disgraceful wrinkle. The fellow next to the girl in pink might have a good heart, but the waistcoat which covered it did not fit by a mile. And as for the tie of that other bloke down by Lady Wickham, it was not a tie at all in the deeper meaning of the word; it was just a deplorable occurrence. Yet, situated as he was, his heart ached with envy of all these tramps.

He ate but little. As a rule his appetite was of the heartiest, and many a novel had he condemned as untrue to life on the ground that its hero was stated to have pushed his food away untasted. Until to-night he had never supposed that such a feat was possible. But as course succeeded course he found himself taking almost no practical interest in the meal. All he asked was to get it over, so that he could edge away and be alone with his grief. There would doubtless be some sort of binge in the drawing-room after dinner, but it would not have the support of Dudley Finch. For Dudley Finch the quiet seclusion of the Blue Room.

It was as he was sitting there some two hours later that there drifted into his mind something Roberta had said about Roland Attwater leaving on the milk-train. At the time he had paid little attention to the remark, but now it began to be borne in upon him more and more strongly that this milk-train was going to be of great strategic importance in his life. This ghastly house was just the sort of house that fellows did naturally go away from on milk-trains, and it behoved him to be prepared.

He rang the bell once more.

'Sir?' said the footman.

'I say,' said Dudley, 'what time does the milk-train leave?'

'Milk-train, sir?'

'Yes. Train that takes the milk, you know.'

'Do you wish for milk, sir?'

'No!' Dudley fought down a desire to stun this man with one of the number twelve shoes. 'I just want to know what time the milk-train goes in the morning – in case – in – er – case I am called away unexpectedly I mean to say.'

'I will inquire, sir.'

The footman made his way to the servants' hall, the bearer of great news.

'Guess what,' said the footman.

'Well, Thomas?' asked Simmons the butler, indulgently.

'That bloke – the Great What-is-it,' said Thomas – for it was by this affectionate sobriquet that Dudley was now known below stairs – 'is planning to go off on the milk-train!'

'What?' Simmons heaved his stout form out of his chair. His face did not reflect the gay mirth of his subordinate. 'I must inform her ladyship. I must inform her ladyship at once.'

The last guest had taken his departure, and Lady Wickham was preparing to go to a well-earned bed when there entered to her Simmons, grave and concerned.

'Might I speak to your ladyship?'

'Well, Simmons?'

'Might I first take the liberty of inquiring, m'lady, if the – er – the young gentleman in the tweed suit is a personal friend of your ladyship's?'

Lady Wickham was surprised. It was not like Simmons to stroll in and start chatting about her guests, and for a moment she was inclined to say as much; then something told her that by doing so she would miss information of interest.

'He says he is a friend of Miss Roberta, Simmons,' she said graciously.

'Says!' said the butler, and there was no eluding the sinister meaning in his voice.

'What do you mean, Simmons?'

'Begging your pardon, m'lady, I am convinced that this person is here with some criminal intention. Thomas reports that his suit-case contained a complete disguise.'

'Disguise! What sort of disguise?'

'Thomas did not convey that very clearly, your ladyship, but I understand that it was of a juvenile nature. And just now, m'lady, the man has been making inquiries as to the time of departure of the milk-train.'

'Milk-train!'

'Thomas also states, m'lady, that the man was visibly took aback when he learned that there were guests expected here to-night. If you ask me, your ladyship, it was the man's intention to make what I might term a quick clean-up immediately after dinner and escape on the nine-fifty-seven. Foiled in that by the presence of the guests, he is going to endeavour to collect the swag in the small hours and get away on the milk-train.'

'Simmons!'

'That is my opinion, your ladyship.'

'Good gracious! He told me that Miss Roberta had said to him that she was coming down here to-night. She has not come!'

'A ruse, m'lady. To inspire confidence.'

'Simmons,' said Lady Wickham, rising to the crisis like the strong woman she was, 'you must sit up to-night!'

'With a gun, m'lady,' cried the butler, with a sportsman's enthusiasm.

'Yes, with a gun. And if you hear him prowling about you must come and wake me instantly.'

'Very good, your ladyship.'

'You must be very quiet, of course.'

'Like a mouse, your ladyship,' said Simmons.

Dudley, meanwhile, in his refuge in the Blue Room, had for some time past been regretting – every moment more keenly – that preoccupation with his troubles had led him to deal so sparingly with his food down there in the dining-room. The peace of the Blue Room had soothed his nervous system, and with calm had come the realization that he was most confoundedly hungry. There was something uncanny in the way Fate had worked to do him out of his proper supply of proteins and carbohydrates to-day. Hungry as he had been when waiting at Claridge's for Bobbie, the moment she appeared love had taken his mind off the menu, and he had made a singularly light lunch. Since then he had had nothing but the few scattered mouthfuls which he had forced himself to swallow at the dinner-table.

He consulted his watch. It was later than he had supposed. Much too late to ring the bell and ask for sandwiches – even supposing that his standing in this poisonous house had been such as to justify the demand.

He flung himself back on the bed and tried to doze off. That footman had said that the milk-train left at three-fifteen, and he was firmly resolved to catch it. The sooner he was out of this place the better. Meanwhile, he craved food. Any sort of food. His entire interior organism was up on its feet, shouting wildly for sustenance.

A few minutes later, Lady Wickham, waiting tensely in her

room, was informed by a knock on the door that the hour had arrived.

'Yes?' she whispered, turning the handle noiselessly and putting her head out.

'The man, m'lady,' breathed the voice of Simmons in the darkness.

'Prowling?'

'Yes, m'lady.'

Dudley Finch's unwilling hostess was a woman of character and decision. From girlhood up she had been accustomed to hunting and the other hardy sports of the aristocracy of the countryside. And though the pursuit of burglars had formed up to the present no part of her experience, she approached it without a qualm. Motioning the butler to follow, she wrapped her dressing-gown more closely about her and strode down the corridor.

There was plenty of noise to guide her to her goal. Dudley's progress from his bed-room to the dining-room, the fruit and biscuits on the sideboard of which formed his objective, had been far from quiet. Once he had tripped over a chair, and now, as his hostess and her attendant began to descend the stairs, he collided with and upset a large screen. He was endeavouring to remove the foot which he had inadvertently put through this when a quiet voice spoke from above.

'Can you see him, Simmons?'

'Yes, m'lady. Dimly but adequately.'

'Then shoot if he moves a step.'

'Very good, m'lady.'

Dudley wrenched his foot free and peered upwards, appalled.

'I say!' he quavered. 'It's only me, you know!'

Light flooded the hall.

'Only me!' repeated Dudley, feverishly. The sight of the

enormous gun in the butler's hands had raised his temperature to a painful degree.

'What,' demanded Lady Wickham, coldly, 'are you doing here, Mr Finch?'

An increased sense of the delicacy of his position flooded over Dudley. He was a young man with the nicest respect for the conventions, and he perceived that the situation required careful handling. It is not tactful, he realized, for a guest for whose benefit a hostess has only a few hours earlier provided a lavish banquet to announce to the said hostess that he has been compelled by hunger to rove the house in search of food. For a moment he stood there, licking his lips; then something like an inspiration came to him.

'The fact is,' he said, 'I couldn't sleep, you know.'

'Possibly,' said Lady Wickham, 'you would have a better chance of doing so if you were to go to bed. Is it your intention to walk about the house all night?'

'No, no, absolutely not. I couldn't sleep, so I – er – I thought I would pop down and see if I could find something to read, don't you know.'

'Oh, you want a book?'

'That's right. That's absolutely it. A book. You've put it in a nutshell.'

'I will show you to the library.'

In spite of her stern disapproval of this scoundrel who wormed his way into people's houses in quest of loot, a slight diminution of austerity came to Lady Wickham as the result of this introduction of the literary note. She was an indefatigable novelist, and it pleased her to place her works in the hands of even the vilest. Ushering Dudley into the library, she switched on the light and made her way without hesitation to the third shelf from the top nearest the fireplace. Selecting one from a row of brightly covered volumes, she offered it to him.

'Perhaps this will interest you,' she said.

Dudley eyed it dubiously.

'Oh, I say,' he protested, 'I don't know, you know. This is one of that chap, George Masterman's.'

'Well?' said Lady Wickham, frostily.

'He writes the most frightful bilge, I mean. Don't you think so?'

'I cannot say that I do. I am possibly biased, however, by the fact that George Masterman is the name I write under.'

Dudley blinked.

'Oh, do you?' he babbled. 'Do you? You do, eh? Well, I mean—' An imperative desire to be elsewhere swept over him. 'This'll do me,' he said, grabbing wildly at the nearest shelf. 'This will do me fine. Thanks awfully. Good night. I mean, thanks, thanks. I mean good night. Good night.'

Two pairs of eyes followed him as he shot up the stairs. Lady Wickham's were cold and hard; the expression in those of Simmons was wistful. It was seldom that the butler's professional duties allowed him the opportunity of indulging the passion for sport which had been his since boyhood. A very occasional pop at a rabbit was about all the shooting he got nowadays, and the receding Dudley made his mouth water. He fought the craving down with a sigh.

'A nasty fellow, m'lady,' he said.

'Quick-witted,' Lady Wickham was forced to concede.

'Full of low cunning, m'lady,' emended the butler. 'All that about wanting a book. A ruse.'

'You had better continue watching, Simmons.'

'Most decidedly, your ladyship.'

* * *

Dudley sat on his bed, panting. Nothing like this had ever happened to him before, and for a while the desire for food left him, overcome by a more spiritual misery. If there was one thing in the world that gave him the pip, it was looking like a silly idiot; and every nerve in his body told him that during the recent interview he must have looked the most perfect silly idiot. Staring bleakly before him, he re-lived every moment of the blighted scene, and the more he examined his own share in it the worse it looked. He quivered in an agony of shame. He seemed to be bathed from head to foot in a sort of prickly heat.

And then, faintly at first, but growing stronger every moment, hunger began to clamour once again.

Dudley clenched his teeth. Something must be done to combat this. Mind must somehow be enabled to triumph over matter. He glanced at the book which he had snatched from the shelf, and for the first time that night began to feel that Fate was with him. Out of a library which was probably congested with the most awful tosh, he had stumbled first pop upon Mark Twain's *Tramp Abroad*, a book which he had not read since he was a kid but had always been meaning to read again; just the sort of book, in fact, which would enable a fellow to forget the anguish of starvation until that milk-train went.

He opened it at random, and found with shock that Fate had but been playing with him.

'It has now been many months, at the present writing' (read Dudley), 'since I have had a nourishing meal, but I shall soon have one – a modest, private affair, all to myself. I have selected a few dishes, and made out a little bill of fare, which will go home in the steamer that precedes me and be hot when I arrive – as follows:–'

Dudley quailed. Memories of his boyhood came to him, of the time when he had first read what came after those last two words. The passage had stamped itself on his mind, for he had happened upon it at school, at a time when he was permanently obsessed by a wolfish hunger and too impecunious to purchase anything at the school shop to keep him going till the next meal. It had tortured him then, and it would, he knew, torture him even more keenly now.

Nothing, he resolved, should induce him to go on reading. So he immediately went on.

'Radishes. Baked apples, with cream.
'Fried oysters; stewed oysters. Frogs.
'American coffee, with real cream.
'American butter.
'Fried chicken, Southern style.
'Porterhouse steak.
'Saratoga potatoes.
'Broiled chicken, American style.'

A feeble moan escaped Dudley. He endeavoured to close the book, but it would not close. He tried to remove his eyes from the page, but they wandered back like homing pigeons.

'Brook trout, from Sierra Nevada.
'Lake trout, from Tahoe.
'Sheephead and croakers, from New Orleans.
'Black bass, from the Mississippi.
'American roast beef.
'Roast turkey, Thanksgiving style.

> 'Cranberry sauce. Celery.
> 'Roast wild turkey. Woodcock.
> 'Canvas-back duck, from Baltimore.
> 'Prairie hens, from Illinois.
> 'Missouri partridges, broiled.
> 'Possum. Coon.
> 'Boston bacon and beans.
> 'Bacon and greens, Southern style.'

Dudley rose from the bed. He could endure no more. His previous experience as a prospector after food had not been such as to encourage further efforts in that direction, but there comes a time when a man recks not of possible discomfort. He removed his shoes and tip-toed out of the room. A familiar form advanced to meet him along the now brightly lit corridor.

'Well?' said Simmons, the butler, shifting his gun to the ready and massaging the trigger with a loving forefinger.

Dudley gazed upon him with a sinking heart.

'Oh, hullo!' he said.

'What do *you* want?'

'Oh – er – oh, nothing.'

'You get back into that room.'

'I say, listen, laddie,' said Dudley, in desperation flinging reticence to the winds. 'I'm starving. Absolutely starving. I wish, like a good old bird, you would just scud down to your pantry or somewhere and get me a sandwich or two.'

'You get back into that room, you hound!' growled Simmons, with such intensity that sheer astonishment sent Dudley tottering back through the door. He had never heard a butler talk like that. He had not supposed that butlers could talk like that.

He put on his shoes again; and, lacing them up, brooded tensely on this matter. What, he asked himself, was the idea? What was the big thought that lay behind all this? That his hostess, alarmed by noises in the night, should have summoned the butler to bring firearms to her assistance was intelligible. But what was the blighter doing, camping outside his door? After all, they knew he was a friend of the daughter of the house.

He was still wrestling with this problem when a curious, sharp, tapping noise attracted his attention. It came at irregular intervals and seemed to proceed from the direction of the window. He sat up, listening. It came again. He crept to the window and looked out. As he did so, something with hard edges smote him painfully in the face.

'Oh, sorry!' said a voice.

Dudley started violently. Looking in the direction from which the voice had proceeded, he perceived that there ran out from the wall immediately to the left of his window a small balcony. On this balcony, bathed in silver moonlight, Roberta Wickham was standing. She was hauling in the slack of a length of string, to the end of which was attached a button-hook.

'Awfully sorry,' she said. 'I was trying to attract your attention.'

'You did,' said Dudley.

'I thought you might be asleep.'

'Asleep!' Dudley's face contorted itself in a dreadful sneer. 'Does anyone ever get any sleep in this house?' He leaned forward and lowered his voice. 'I say, your bally butler has gone off his onion.'

'What?'

'He's doing sentinel duty outside my door with a whacking great cannon. And when I put my head out just now he simply barked at me.'

'I'm afraid,' said Bobbie, gathering in the button-hook, 'he thinks you're a burglar.'

'A burglar? But I told your mother distinctly that I was a friend of yours.'

Something akin to embarrassment seemed to come upon the not easily embarrassed Miss Wickham.

'Yes, I want to talk to you about that,' she said. 'It was like this.'

'I say, when did you arrive, by the way?' asked Dudley, the question suddenly presenting itself to his disordered mind.

'About half an hour ago.'

'What!'

'Yes. I sneaked in through the scullery window. And the first thing I met was mother in her dressing-gown.' Miss Wickham shivered a little as at some unpleasing memory. 'You've never seen mother in her dressing-gown,' she said, in a small voice.

'Yes, I have,' retorted Dudley. 'And while it may be an experience which every chappie ought to have, let me tell you that once is sufficient.'

'I had an accident coming down here,' proceeded Miss Wickham, absorbed in her own story and paying small attention to his. 'An idiot of a man driving a dray let me run into him. My car was all smashed up. I couldn't get away for hours, and then I had to come down on a train that stopped at every station.'

It is proof, if such were needed, of the strain to which Dudley Finch had been subjected that night that the information that this girl had been in a motor-smash did not cause him that anguished concern which he would undoubtedly have felt twenty-four hours earlier. It left him almost cold.

'Well, when you saw your mother,' he said, 'didn't you tell her that I was a friend of yours?'

Miss Wickham hesitated.

'That's the part I want to explain,' she said. 'You see, it was like this. First I had to break it as gently as I could to her that the car wasn't insured. She wasn't frightfully pleased. And then she told me about you and— Dudley, old thing, whatever have you been doing since you got here? The mater seemed to think you had been behaving in the weirdest way.'

'I'll admit that I brought the wrong bag and couldn't dress for dinner, but apart from that I'm dashed if I can see what I did that was weird.'

'Well, she seems to have beccome frightfully suspicious of you almost from the start.'

'If you had sent that wire, telling her I was coming—'

Miss Wickham clicked her tongue regretfully.

'I knew there was something I had forgotten. Oh, Dudley, I'm awfully sorry.'

'Don't mention it,' said Dudley, bitterly. 'It's probably going to lead to my having my head blown off by a looney butler, but don't give it another thought. You were saying—'

'Oh, yes, when I met mother. You do see, Dudley dear, how terribly difficult it was for me, don't you? I mean, I had just broken it to her that the car was all smashed up and not insured, and then she suddenly asked me if it was true that I had invited you down here. I was just going to say I had, when she began to talk about you in such a bitter spirit that somehow the time didn't seem ripe. So when she asked me if you were a friend of mine, I—'

'You said I was?'

'Well, not in so many words.'

'How do you mean?'

'I had to be awfully tactful, you see.'

'Well?'

'So I told her I had never seen you in my life.'

Dudley uttered a sound like the breeze sighing in the tree-tops.

'But it's all right,' went on Miss Wickham, reassuringly.

'Yes, isn't it?' said Dudley. 'I noticed that.'

'I'm going to go and have a talk with Simmons and tell him he must let you escape. Then everything will be splendid. There's an excellent milk-train—'

'I know all about the milk-train, thanks.'

'I'll go and see him now. So don't you worry, old thing.'

'Worry?' said Dudley. 'Me? What have I got to worry about?'

Bobbie disappeared. Dudley turned away from the window. Faint whispering made itself heard from the passage. Somebody tapped softly on the door. Dudley opened it and found the ambassadress standing on the mat. Farther down the corridor, tactfully withdrawn into the background, Simmons the butler stood grounding arms.

'Dudley,' whispered Miss Wickham, 'have you got any money on you?'

'Yes, a certain amount.'

'Five pounds? It's for Simmons.'

Dudley felt the militant spirit of the Finches surging within him. His blood boiled.

'You don't mean to say that after what has happened the blighter has the crust to expect me to tip him?'

He glared past her at the man behind the gun, who simpered respectfully. Evidently Bobbie's explanations had convinced him that he had wronged Dudley, for the hostility which had been so marked a short while back had now gone out of his manner.

'Well, it's like this, you see,' said Bobbie. 'Poor Simmons is worried.'

'I'm glad,' said Dudley, vindictively. 'I wish he would worry himself into a decline.'

'He's afraid that mother may be angry with him when she finds that you have gone. He doesn't want to lose his place.'

'A man who doesn't want to get out of a place like this must be an ass.'

'And so, in case mother does cut up rough and dismiss him for not keeping a better watch over you, he wants to feel that he has something in hand. He started by asking for a tenner, but I got him down to five. So hand it over, Dudley, dear, and then we can get action.'

Dudley produced a five-pound note and gazed at it with a long, lingering look of affection and regret.

'Here you are,' he said. 'I hope the man spends it on drink, gets tight, trips over his feet, and breaks his neck!'

'Thanks,' said Bobbie. 'There's just one other trifling condition he made, but you needn't worry about that.'

'What was it?'

'Oh, just something very trifling. Nothing that you have to do. No need for you to worry at all. You had better start now tying knots in the sheets.'

Dudley stared.

'Knots?' he said. 'In the sheets?'

'To climb down by.'

It was Dudley's guiding rule in life never, when once he had got it brushed and brilliantined and properly arranged in the fashionable back-sweep, to touch his hair; but on this fearful night all the rules of civilized life were going by the board. He clutched upwards, collected a handful and churned it about. No lesser gesture could have expressed his consternation.

'You aren't seriously suggesting that I climb out of the window and shin down a knotted sheet?' he gasped.

'You must, I'm afraid. Simmons insists on it.'

'Why?'

'Well—'

Dudley groaned.

'I know why,' he said, bitterly. 'He's been going to the movies. It's always the way. You give a butler an evening off and he sneaks out to a picture-house and comes back with a diseased mind, thinking he's playing a star part in *The Clutching Hand* or something. Knotted sheets, indeed!' Such was his emotion that Dudley very nearly said 'Forsooth!' 'The man is simply a drivelling imbecile. Will you kindly inform me why, in the name of everything infernal, the poor, silly, dashed fish can't just let me out of the front door like an ordinary human being?'

'Why, don't you see?' reasoned Miss Wickham. 'How could he explain to mother? She must be made to think that you escaped in spite of his vigilance.'

Disordered though his faculties were, Dudley could dimly see that there was something in this. He made no further objections. Bobbie beckoned to the waiting Simmons. Money changed hands. The butler passed amiably into the room to lend assistance to the preparations.

'A little tighter, perhaps, sir,' he suggested, obsequiously, casting a critical eye upon Dudley's knots. 'It would never do for you to fall and kill yourself, sir, ha, ha!'

'Did you say "ha, ha"?' said Dudley, in a pale voice.

'I did venture—'

'Don't do it again.'

'Very good, sir.' The butler ambled to the window and looked out. 'I fear the sheets will not reach quite to the ground, sir. You will have a drop of a few feet.'

'But,' added Bobbie, hastily, 'you've got the most lovely, soft, squashy flower-bed to fall into.'

It was not till some minutes later, when he had come to the end of the sheet and had at last nerved himself to let go and complete the journey after the fashion of a parachutist whose parachute has refused to open, that Dudley discovered that there was an error in Miss Wickham's description of the terrain. The lovely soft flower-bed of which she had spoken with such pretty girlish enthusiasm was certainly there, but what she had omitted to mention was that along it at regular intervals were planted large bushes of a hard and spiky nature. It was in one of these that Dudley, descending like a shooting star, found himself entangled: and he had never supposed that anything that was not actually a cactus plant could possibly have so many and such sharp thorns.

He scrambled out and stood in the moonlight soliloquizing softly. A head protruded from the window above.

'Are you all right, sir?' inquired the voice of Simmons.

Dudley did not reply. With as much dignity as a man punctured in several hundred places could muster, he strode off.

He had reached the drive and was limping up it towards the gate which led to the road which led to the station which led to the milk-train which led to London, when the quiet of the night was suddenly shattered by the roar of a gun. Something infinitely more painful than all the thorns which had recently pierced him smote the fleshy part of his left leg. It seemed to be red-hot, and its effect on Dudley was almost miraculous. A moment before he had been slouching slowly along, a beaten and jaded man. He now appeared to become electrified. With one sharp yell he lowered the amateur record for the standing broad jump, and then, starting smartly off the mark, proceeded to try to beat the best professional time for the hundred-yard dash.

The telephone at the side of Dudley's bed had been ringing for some time before its noise woke him. Returning to his rooms in Jermyn Street shortly before seven a.m., he had quelled his great hunger with breakfast and then slipped with a groan between the sheets. It was now, he saw from a glance at his watch, nearly five in the afternoon.

'Hello?' he croaked.

'Dudley?'

It was a voice which twenty-four hours ago would have sent sharp thrills down the young man's spine. Twenty-four hours ago, if he had heard this voice on his telephone, he would have squealed with rapture. Hearing it now, he merely frowned. The heart beneath that rose-pink pyjama jacket was dead.

'Yes?' he said, coldly.

'Oh, Dudley,' purred Miss Wickham, 'are you all right?'

'As far,' replied Mr Finch, frigidly, 'as a bloke can be said to be all right whose hair has turned white to the roots and who has been starved and chucked out of windows into bushes with six-inch thorns, and chivvied and snootered and shot in the fleshy part of the leg—'

An exclamation of concern broke in upon his eloquence.

'Oh, Dudley, he didn't hit you?'

'He did hit me.'

'But he promised that he wouldn't aim at you.'

'Well, next time he goes shooting visitors, tell him to aim as carefully as he can. Then they may have a sporting chance.'

'Is there anything I can do?'

'Outside of bringing me the blighter's head on a charger, nothing, thanks.'

'He insisted on letting off the gun. That was the condition I said he had made. You remember?'

'I remember. The trifling condition I wasn't to worry about.'

'It was to make the thing seem all right to mother.'

'I hope your mother was pleased,' said Dudley, politely.

'Dudley, I do wish there was something I could do for you. I'd like to come up and nurse you. But I'm in disgrace about the car, and I'm not allowed to come to London just yet. I'm 'phoning from the Wickham Arms. I believe I shall be able to get up, though, by Saturday week. Shall I come then?'

'Do,' said Dudley, cordially.

'That's splendid! It's the seventeenth. All right, I'll try to get to London latish in the morning. Where shall we meet?'

'We shan't meet,' said Dudley. 'At lunch-time on the seventeenth I shall be tooling off to Australia. Good-bye!'

He hung up the receiver and crawled back into bed, thinking imperially.

'Right ho,' said Algy Crufts. 'Then I shall go alone.'
'Right ho,' said Ambrose Wiffin. 'Go alone.'
'Right ho,' said Algy Crufts. 'I will.'
'Right ho,' said Ambrose Wiffin. 'Do.'
'Right ho, then,' said Algy Crufts.
'Right ho,' said Ambrose Wiffin.
'Right ho,' said Algy Crufts.

Few things (said Mr Mulliner) are more painful than an altercation between two boyhood friends. Nevertheless, when these occur, the conscientious narrator must record them.

It is also, no doubt, the duty of such a narrator to be impartial. In the present instance, however, it would be impossible to avoid bias. To realize that Algy Crufts was perfectly justified in taking an even stronger tone, one has only to learn the facts. It was the season of the year when there comes upon all right-thinking young men the urge to go off to Monte Carlo: and the plan had been that he and Ambrose should catch the ten o'clock boat-train on the morning of the sixteenth of February. All the arrangements had been made – the tickets bought; the trunks packed; the 'One Hundred Systems of Winning at Roulette' studied from end to end: and here was Ambrose, on the afternoon of February the fourteenth, calmly saying that he proposed to remain in London for another fortnight.

Algy Crufts eyed him narrowly. Ambrose Wiffin was always a nattily-dressed young man, but to-day there had crept into his outer crust a sort of sinister effulgence which could have but one meaning. It shouted from his white carnation: it shrieked from his trouser-crease: and Algy read it in a flash.

'You're messing about after some beastly female,' he said.

Ambrose Wiffin reddened and brushed his top hat the wrong way.

'And I know who it is. It's that Wickham girl.'

Ambrose reddened again, and brushed his top hat once more – this time the right way, restoring the *status quo*.

'Well,' he said, 'you introduced me to her.'

'I know I did. And, if you recollect, I drew you aside immediately afterwards and warned you to watch your step.'

'If you have anything to say against Miss Wickham...'

'I haven't anything to say against her. She's one of my best pals. I've known young Bobbie Wickham since she was a kid in arms, and I'm what you might call immune where she's concerned. But you can take it from me that every other fellow who comes in contact with Bobbie finds himself sooner or later up to the Adam's apple in some ghastly mess. She lets them down with a dull, sickening thud. Look at Roland Attwater. He went to stay at her place, and he had a snake with him...'

'Why?'

'I don't know. He just happened to have a snake with him, and Bobbie put it in a fellow's bed and let everyone think it was Attwater who had done it. He had to leave by the milk-train at three in the morning.'

'Attwater had no business lugging snakes about with him to country houses,' said Ambrose primly. 'One can readily understand how a high-spirited girl would feel tempted...'

'And then there was Dudley Finch. She asked him down for the night and forgot to tell her mother he was coming, with the result that he was taken for a Society burglar and got shot in the leg by the butler as he was leaving to catch the milk-train.'

A look such as Sir Galahad might have worn on hearing gossip about Queen Guinevere lent a noble dignity to Ambrose Wiffin's pink young face.

'I don't care,' he said stoutly. 'She's the sweetest girl on earth, and I'm taking her to the Dog Show on Saturday.'

'Eh? What about our Monte Carlo binge?'

'That'll have to be postponed. Not for long. She's up in London, staying with an aunt of sorts, for another couple of weeks. I could come after that.'

'Do you mean to say you have the immortal crust to expect me to hang about for two weeks, waiting for you?'

'I don't see why not.'

'Oh, don't you? Well, I'm jolly well not going to.'

'Right ho. Just as you like.'

'Right ho. Then I shall go alone.'

'Right ho. Go alone.'

'Right ho. I will.'

'Right ho. Do.'

'Right ho, then.'

'Right ho,' said Ambrose Wiffin.

'Right ho,' said Algy Crufts.

At almost exactly the moment when this very distressing scene was taking place at the Drones Club in Dover Street,

Roberta Wickham, in the drawing-room of her aunt Marcia's house in Eaton Square, was endeavouring to reason with her mother, and finding the going a bit heavy. Lady Wickham was notoriously a difficult person to reason with. She was a woman who knew her mind.

'But, mother!'

Lady Wickham advanced her forceful chin another inch.

'It's no use arguing, Roberta...'

'But, mother! I keep telling you! Jane Falconer has just rung up and wants me to go round and help her choose the cushions for her new flat.'

'And I keep telling you that a promise is a promise. You voluntarily offered after breakfast this morning to take your cousin Wilfred and his little friend, Esmond Bates, to the moving-pictures to-day, and you cannot disappoint them now.'

'But if Jane's left to herself she'll choose the most awful things.'

'I cannot help that.'

'She's relying on me. She said so. And I swore I'd go.'

'I cannot help that.'

'I'd forgotten all about Wilfred.'

'I cannot help that. You should not have forgotten. You must ring your friend up and tell her that you are unable to see her this afternoon. I think you ought to be glad of the chance of giving pleasure to these two boys. One ought not always to be thinking of oneself. One ought to try to bring a little sunshine into the lives of others. I will go and tell Wilfred you are waiting for him.'

Left alone, Roberta wandered morosely to the window and stood looking down into the Square. From this vantage-point she was able to observe a small boy in an Eton suit sedulously hopping from the pavement to the bottom step of the house and back again. This was Esmond Bates, next door's son and heir, and the effect the sight of him had on Bobbie was to drive her from the window and send her slumping onto the sofa, where for a space she sat, gazing before her and disliking life. It may not seem to everybody the summit of human pleasure to go about London choosing cushions, but Bobbie had set her heart on it: and the iron was entering deeply into her soul when the door opened and the butler appeared.

'Mr Wiffin,' announced the butler. And Ambrose walked in, glowing with that holy reverential emotion which always surged over him at the sight of Bobbie.

Usually, there was blended with this a certain diffidence, unavoidable in one visiting the shrine of a goddess: but to-day the girl seemed so unaffectedly glad to see him that diffidence vanished. He was amazed to note how glad she was to see him. She had bounded from the sofa on his entry, and now was looking at him with shining eyes like a shipwrecked mariner who sights a sail.

'Oh, Ambrose!' said Bobbie. 'I'm so glad you came.'

Ambrose thrilled from his quiet but effective sock-clocks to his Stacombed hair. How wise, he felt, he had been to spend that long hour perfecting the minutest details of his toilet. As a glance in the mirror on the landing had just assured him, his hat was right, his coat was right, his trousers were right, his shoes were right, his buttonhole was right, and his tie was right. He was one hundred per cent, and girls appreciate such things.

'Just thought I'd look in,' he said, speaking in the guttural tones which agitated vocal cords always forced upon him when addressing the queen of her species, 'and see if you were doing anything this afternoon. If,' he added, 'you see what I mean.'

'I'm taking my cousin Wilfred and a little friend of his to the movies. Would you like to come?'

'I say! Thanks awfully! May I?'

'Yes do.'

'I say! Thanks awfully!' He gazed at her with worshipping admiration. 'But I say, how frightfully kind of you to mess up an afternoon taking a couple of kids to the movies. Awfully kind. I mean kind. I mean I call it dashed kind of you.'

'Oh, well!' said Bobbie modestly. 'I feel I ought to be glad of the chance of giving pleasure to these two boys. One ought not always to be thinking of oneself. One ought to try to bring a little sunshine into the lives of others.'

'You're an angel!'

'No, no.'

'An absolute angel,' insisted Ambrose, quivering fervently. 'Doing a thing like this is . . . well, absolutely angelic. If you follow me. I wish Algy Crufts had been here to see it.'

'Why Algy?'

'Because he was saying some very unpleasant things about you this afternoon. Most unpleasant things.'

'What did he say?'

'He said . . .' Ambrose winced. The vile words were choking him. 'He said you let people down.'

'Did he! Did he, forsooth! I'll have to have a word with young Algernon P. Crufts. He's getting above himself. He seems to forget,' said Bobbie, a dreamy look coming into her beautiful eyes, 'that we live next to each other in the country and that I know which his room is. What young Algy wants is a frog in his bed.'

'Two frogs,' amended Ambrose.

'Two frogs,' agreed Bobbie.

The door opened and there appeared on the mat a small boy. He wore an Eton suit, spectacles, and, low down over his prominent ears, a bowler hat: and Ambrose thought he had seldom seen anything fouler. He would have looked askance at Royalty itself, had Royalty interrupted a *tête-à-tête* with Miss Wickham.

'I'm ready,' said the boy.

'This is aunt Marcia's son Wilfred,' said Bobbie.

'Oh?' said Ambrose coldly.

Like so many young men, Ambrose Wiffin was accustomed to regard small boys with a slightly jaundiced eye. It was his simple creed that they wanted their heads smacked. When not having their heads smacked, they should be out of the picture altogether. He stared disparagingly at this specimen. A half-formed resolve to love him for Bobbie's sake perished at birth. Only the thought that Bobbie would be of the company enabled him to endure the prospect of being seen in public with this outstanding piece of cheese.

'Let's go,' said the boy.

'All right,' said Bobbie. 'I'm ready.'

'We'll find Old Stinker on the steps,' the boy assured her, as one promising a deserving person some delightful treat.

Old Stinker, discovered as predicted, seemed to Ambrose just the sort of boy who would be a friend of Bobbie's cousin Wilfred. He was goggle-eyed and freckled and also, as it was speedily to appear, an officious little devil who needed six of the best with a fives-bat.

'The cab's waiting,' said Old Stinker.

'How clever of you to have found a cab, Esmond,' said Bobbie indulgently.

'I didn't find it. It's his cab. I told it to wait.'

A stifled exclamation escaped Ambrose, and he shot a fevered glance at the taxi's clock. The sight of the figures on it caused him a sharp pang. Not six with a fives-bat, he felt. Ten. And of the juiciest.

'Splendid,' said Bobbie. 'Hop in. Tell him to drive to the Tivoli.'

Ambrose suppressed the words he had been about to utter; and, climbing into the cab, settled himself down and devoted his attention to trying to avoid the feet of Bobbie's cousin Wilfred, who sat opposite him. The boy seemed as liberally equipped with these as a centipede, and there was scarcely a moment when his boots were not rubbing the polish off Ambrose's glittering shoes. It was with something of the emotions of the Ten Thousand Greeks on beholding the sea that at long last he sighted the familiar architecture of the Strand. Soon he would be sitting next to Bobbie in a dimly lighted auditorium, and a man with that in prospect could afford to rough it a bit on the journey. He alighted from the cab and plunged into the queue before the box-office.

Wedged in among the crowd of pleasure-seekers, Ambrose, though physically uncomfortable, felt somehow a sort of spiritual refreshment. There is nothing a young man in love finds more delightful than the doing of some knightly service for the loved one: and, though to describe as a knightly service the act of standing in a queue and buying tickets for a motion-picture entertainment may seem straining the facts a little, to one in Ambrose's condition a service is a service. He would have preferred to be called upon to save Bobbie's life: but, this not being at the moment feasible, it was something to be jostling in a queue for her sake.

Nor was the action so free from peril as might appear at first sight. Sheer, black disaster was lying in wait for Ambrose

Wiffin. He had just forced his way to the pay-box and was turning to leave after buying the tickets when the thing happened. From somewhere behind him an arm shot out, there was an instant's sickening suspense, and then the top hat which he loved nearly as much as life itself was rolling across the lobby with a stout man in the uniform of a Czeko-Slovakian Rear-Admiral in pursuit.

In the sharp agony of this happening, it had seemed to Ambrose that he had experienced the worse moment of his career. Then he discovered that it was in reality merely the worst but one. The sorrow's crown of sorrow was achieved an instant later when the Admiral returned, bearing in his hand a battered something which for a space he was unable to recognize.

The Admiral was sympathetic. There was a bluff, sailorly sympathy in his voice as he spoke.

'Here you are, sir,' he said. 'Here's your rat. A little the worse for wear, this sat is, I'm afraid, sir. A gentleman happened to step on it. You can't step on a nat,' he said sententiously, 'not without hurting it. That tat is not the yat it was.'

Although he spoke in the easy manner of one making genial conversation, his voice had in it a certain purposeful note. He seemed like a Rear-Admiral who was waiting for something: and Ambrose, as if urged by some hypnotic spell, produced half-a-crown and pressed it into his hand. Then, placing the remains on his head, he tottered across the lobby to join the girl he loved.

That she could ever, after seeing him in a hat like that, come to love him in return seemed to him at first unbelievable. Then Hope began to steal shyly back. After all, it was in her cause that he had suffered this great blow. She would take that into account. Furthermore, girls of Roberta Wickham's fine fibre do not love a man entirely for his hat. The trousers count, so do the spats. It was in a spirit almost optimistic that he forced his way through the crowd to the spot where he had left the girl. And as he reached it the squeaky voice of Old Stinker smote his ear.

'Golly!' said Old Stinker. 'What have you done to your hat?'

Another squeaky voice spoke. Aunt Marcia's son Wilfred was regarding him with the offensive interest of a biologist examining some lower organism under the microscope.

'I say,' said Wilfred, 'I don't know if you know it, but somebody's been sitting on your hat or something. Did you ever see a hat like that, Stinker?'

'Never in my puff,' replied his friend.

Ambrose gritted his teeth.

'Never mind my hat! Where's Miss Wickham?'

'Oh, she had to go,' said Old Stinker.

It was not for a moment that the hideous meaning of the words really penetrated Ambrose's consciousness. Then his jaw fell and he stared aghast.

'Go? Go where?'

'I don't know where. She went.'

'She said she had just remembered an appointment,' explained Wilfred. 'She said . . .'

'. . . that you were to take us in and she would join us later if she could.'

'She rather thought she wouldn't be able to, but she said leave her ticket at the box-office in case.'

'She said she knew we would be all right with you,' concluded Old Stinker. 'Come on, let's beef in or we'll be missing the educational two-reel comic.'

Ambrose eyed them wanly. All his instincts urged him to smack these two heads as heads should be smacked, to curse a good deal, to wash his hands of the whole business and stride away. But Love conquers all. Reason told him that here were two small boys, a good deal ghastlier than any small boy he had yet encountered. In short, mere smack-fodder. But Love, stronger than reason, whispered that they were a sacred trust. Roberta Wickham expected him to take them to the movies and he must do it.

And such was his love that not yet had he begun to feel any resentment at this desertion of hers. No doubt, he told himself, she had had some good reason. In anyone a shade less divine, the act of sneaking off and landing him with these two disease-germs might have seemed culpable: but what he felt at the moment was that the Queen could do no wrong.

'Oh, all right,' he said dully. 'Push in.'

Old Stinker had not yet exhausted the theme of the hat.

'I say,' he observed, 'that hat looks pretty rummy, you know.'

'Absolutely weird,' assented Wilfred.

Ambrose regarded them intently for a moment, and his gloved hand twitched a little. But the iron self-control of the Wiffins stood him in good stead.

'Push in,' he said in a strained voice. 'Push in.'

In the last analysis, however many highly-salaried stars its cast may contain and however superb and luxurious the settings of its orgy-scenes, the success of a super-film's appeal to an audience must always depend on what company each unit of that audience is in when he sees it. Start wrong in the vestibule, and entertainment in the true sense is out of the question.

For the picture which the management of the Tivoli was now presenting to its patrons Hollywood had done all that Art and Money could effect. Based on Wordsworth's well-known poem 'We are Seven', it was entitled 'Where Passion Lurks', and offered such notable favourites of the silver screen as Laurette Byng, G. Cecil Terwilliger, Baby Bella, Oscar the Wonder-Poodle, and Professor Pond's Educated Sea-Lions. And yet it left Ambrose cold.

If only Bobbie had been at his side, how different it all would have been. As it was, the beauty of the story had no power to soothe him, nor could he get the slightest thrill out of the Babylonian Banquet scene which had cost five hundred thousand dollars. From start to finish he sat in a dull apathy: then, at last, the ordeal over, he stumbled out into daylight and the open air. Like G. Cecil Terwilliger at a poignant crisis in the fourth reel, he was as one on whom Life has forced its bitter cup, and who has drained it to the lees.

And it was this moment, when a strong man stood face to face with his soul, that Old Stinker with the rashness of Youth selected for beginning again about the hat.

'I say,' said Old Stinker, as they came out into the bustling Strand, 'you've no idea what a blister you look in that lid.'

'Priceless,' agreed Wilfred cordially.

'All you want is a banjo and you could make a fortune singing comic songs outside the pubs.'

On his first introduction to these little fellows it had seemed to Ambrose that they had touched the lowest possible level to which Humanity can descend. It now became apparent that there were hitherto unimagined depths which it was in their power to plumb. There is a point beyond which even a Wiffin's self-control fails to function. The next moment, above the roar of London's traffic there sounded the crisp note of a well-smacked head.

It was Wilfred who, being nearest, had received the treatment: and it was at Wilfred that an elderly lady, pausing, pointed with indignant horror in every waggle of her finger-tip.

'Why did you strike that little boy?' demanded the elderly lady.

Ambrose made no answer. He was in no mood for conundrums. Besides, to reply fully to the question, he would have been obliged to trace the whole history of his love, to dilate on the agony it had caused him to discover that his goddess had feet of clay, to explain how little by little through the recent entertainment there had grown a fever in his blood, caused by this boy sucking peppermints, shuffling his feet, giggling and reading out the sub-titles. Lastly, he would have had to discuss at length the matter of the hat.

Unequal to these things, he merely glowered: and such was the calibre of his scowl that the other supposed that here was the authentic Abysmal Brute.

'I've a good mind to call a policeman,' she said.

It is a peculiar phenomenon of life in London that the magic word 'policeman' has only to be whispered in any of its thoroughfares to attract a crowd of substantial dimensions: and Ambrose, gazing about him, now discovered that their little group had been augmented by some thirty citizens, each of whom was regarding him in much the same way that he would have regarded the accused in a big murder-trial at the Old Bailey.

A passionate desire to be elsewhere came upon the young man. Of all things in this life he disliked most a scene: and this was plainly working up into a scene of the worst kind. Seizing his sacred trusts by the elbow he ran them across the street. The crowd continued to stand and stare at the spot where the incident had occurred.

For some little time, safe on the opposite pavement, Ambrose was too busily occupied in reassembling his disintegrated nervous system to give any attention to the world about him. He was recalled to mundane matters by a piercing squeal of ecstasy from his young companions.

'Oo! Oysters!'

'Golly! Oysters!'

And he became aware that they were standing outside a restaurant whose window was deeply paved with these shellfish. On these the two lads were gloating with bulging eyes.

'I could do with an oyster!' said Old Stinker.

'So could I jolly well do with an oyster,' said Wilfred.

'I bet I could eat more oysters than you.'

'I bet you couldn't.'

'I bet I could.'

'I bet you couldn't.'

'I bet you a million pounds I could.'

'I bet you a million trillion pounds you couldn't.'

Ambrose had had no intention of presiding over the hideous sporting contest which they appeared to be planning. Apart from the nauseous idea of devouring oysters at half-past four in the afternoon, he resented the notion of spending any more of his money on these gargoyles. But at this juncture he observed, threading her way nimbly through the traffic, the elderly lady who had made the Scene. A Number 33 omnibus could quite easily have got her, but through sheer carelessness and over-confidence failed to do so: and now she was on the pavement and heading in their direction. There was not an instant to be lost.

'Push in,' he said hoarsely. 'Push in.'

A moment later, they were seated at a table and a waiter, who looked like one of the executive staff of the Black Hand, was hovering beside them with pencil and pad.

Ambrose made one last appeal to his guests' better feelings.

'You can't really want oysters at this time of day,' he said almost pleadingly.

'I bet you we can,' said Old Stinker.

'I bet you a billion pounds we can,' said Wilfred.

'Oh, all right,' said Ambrose. 'Oysters.'

He sank back in his chair and endeavoured to avert his eyes from the grim proceedings. Æons passed, and he was aware that the golluping noises at his side had ceased. All things end in time. Even the weariest river winds somewhere to the sea. Wilfred and Old Stinker had stopped eating oysters.

'Finished?' he asked in a cold voice.

There was a moment's pause. The boys seemed hesitant.

'Yes, if there aren't any more.'

'There aren't,' said Ambrose. He beckoned to the waiter, who was leaning against the wall dreaming of old, happy murders of his distant youth. 'Ladishion,' he said curtly.

'Sare?'

'The bill.'

'The pill? Oh yes, sare.'

Shrill and jovial laughter greeted the word.

'He said "pill"!' gurgled Old Stinker.

'"Pill"!' echoed Wilfred.

They punched each other delightedly to signify their appreciation of this excellent comedy. The waiter flushed darkly, muttered something in his native tongue and seemed about to reach for his stiletto. Ambrose reddened to the eyebrows. Laughing at waiters was simply one of the things that aren't done, and he felt his position acutely. It was a relief when the Black Hander returned with his change.

There was only a solitary sixpence on the plate, and Ambrose hastened to dip in his pocket for further coins to supplement this. A handsome tip would, he reasoned, show the waiter that, though circumstances had forced these two giggling outcasts upon him, spiritually he had no affiliation with them. It would be a gesture which would put him at once on an altogether different plane. The man would understand that, dubious though the company might be in which he had met him, Ambrose Wiffin himself was all right and had a heart of gold. 'Simpatico', he believed these Italians called it.

And then he sat up, tingling as from an electric shock. From pocket to pocket his fingers flew, and in each found only emptiness. The awful truth was clear. An afternoon spent in paying huge taxi-fares, buying seats for motion-picture performances, pressing half-crowns into the palms of Czeko-Slovakian Rear-Admirals and filling small boys with oysters had left him a financial ruin. That sixpence was all he had to get these two blighted boys back to Eaton Square.

Ambrose Wiffin paused at the cross-roads. In all his life he had never left a waiter untipped. He had not supposed it could be done. He had looked upon the tipping of waiters as a natural process, impossible to evade, like breathing or leaving the bottom button of your waistcoat unfastened. Ghosts of by-gone Wiffins – Wiffins who had scattered largesse to the multitude in the Middle Ages, Wiffins who in Regency days had flung landlords purses of gold – seemed to crowd at his elbow, imploring the last of their line not to disgrace the family name. On the other hand, sixpence would just pay for bus-fares and remove from him the necessity of walking two miles through the streets of London in a squashed top hat and in the society of Wilfred and Old Stinker . . .

If it had been Wilfred alone . . . Or even Old Stinker alone . . . Or if that hat did not look so extraordinarily like something off the stage of a low-class music-hall . . .

Ambrose Wiffin hesitated no longer. Pocketing the sixpence with one swift motion of the hand and breathing heavily through his nose, he sprang to his feet.

'Come on!' he growled.

He could have betted on his little friends. They acted just as he had expected they would. No tact. No reticence. Not an effort towards handling the situation. Just two bright young children of Nature, who said the first thing that came into their heads, and who, he hoped, would wake up to-morrow morning with ptomaine-poisoning.

'I say!' It was Wilfred who gave tongue first of the pair, and his clear voice rang through the restaurant like a bugle. 'You haven't tipped him!'

'I say!' Old Stinker chiming in, extraordinarily bell-like. 'Dash it all, aren't you going to tip him?'

'You haven't tipped the waiter,' said Wilfred, making his meaning clearer.

'The waiter,' explained Old Stinker, clarifying the situation of its last trace of ambiguity. 'You haven't tipped him!'

'Come on!' moaned Ambrose. 'Push out! Push out!'

A hundred dead Wiffins shrieked a ghostly shriek and covered their faces with their winding sheets. A stunned waiter clutched his napkin to his breast. And Ambrose, with bowed head, shot out of the door like a conscience-stricken rabbit. In that supreme moment he even forgot that he was wearing a top hat like a concertina. So true is it that the greater emotion swallows up the less.

A heaven-sent omnibus stopped before him in a traffic-block. He pushed his little charges in, and, as they charged in their gay, boyish way to the further end of the vehicle, seated himself next to the door, as far away from them as possible. Then, removing the hat, he sat back and closed his eyes.

Hitherto, when sitting back with closed eyes, it had always been the custom of Ambrose Wiffin to give himself up to holy thoughts about Bobbie. But now they refused to come. Plenty of thoughts, but not holy ones. It was as though the supply had petered out.

Too dashed bad of the girl, he meant, letting him in for a thing like this. Absolutely too dashed bad of her. And, mark you, she had intended from the very beginning, mind you, to let him in for it. Oh yes, she had. All that about suddenly remembering an appointment, he meant to say. Perfect rot. Wouldn't hold water for a second. She had never had the least intention of coming into that bally moving-picture place. Right from the start she had planned to lure him into the thing and then ooze off and land him with these septic kids, and what he meant was that it was too dashed bad of her.

Yes, he declined to mince his words. Too dashed bad. Not playing the game. A bit thick. In short – well, to put it in a nut-shell, too dashed bad.

The omnibus rolled on. Ambrose opened his eyes in order to note progress. He was delighted to observe that they were already nearing Hyde Park Corner. At last he permitted himself to breathe freely. His martyrdom was practically over. Only a little longer now, only a few short minutes, and he would be able to deliver the two pestilences F.O.B. at their dens in Eaton Square, wash them out of his life for ever, return to the comfort and safety of his cosy rooms, and there begin life anew.

The thought was heartening: and Ambrose, greatly restored, turned to sketching out in his mind the details of the drink which his man, under his own personal supervision, should mix for him immediately upon his return. As to this he was quite clear. Many fellows in his position – practically, you might say, saved at last from worse than death – would make it a stiff whisky-and-soda. But Ambrose, though he had no prejudice against whisky-and-soda, felt otherwise. It must be a cocktail. The cocktail of a lifetime. A cocktail that would ring down the ages, in which gin blended smoothly with Italian vermouth and the spot of old brandy nestled like a trusting child against the dash of absinthe . . .

He sat up sharply. He stared. No, his eyes had not deceived him. At the far end of the omnibus Trouble was rearing its ugly head.

On occasions of great disaster it is seldom that the spectator perceives instantly every detail of what is toward. The thing creeps upon him gradually, impinging itself upon his consciousness in progressive stages. All that the inhabitants of Pompeii, for example, observed in the early stages of that city's doom was probably a mere puff of smoke. 'Ah,' they said, 'a puff of smoke!' and let it go at that. So with Ambrose Wiffin in the case of which we are treating.

The first thing that attracted Ambrose's attention was the face of a man who had come in at the last stop and seated

himself immediately opposite Old Stinker. It was an extraordinarily solemn face, spotty in parts and bathed in a rather
remarkable crimson flush. The eyes, which were prominent,
wore a fixed far-away look. Ambrose had noted them as they
passed him. They were round, glassy eyes. They were, briefly,
the eyes of a man who has lunched.

In the casual way in which one examines one's fellow-
passengers on an omnibus, Ambrose had allowed his gaze to
flit from time to time to this person's face. For some minutes
its expression had remained unaltered. The man might have
been sitting for his photograph. But now into the eyes there
was creeping a look almost of animation. The flush had begun
to deepen. For some reason or other, it was plain, the machinery
of the brain was starting to move once more.

Ambrose watched him idly. No premonition of doom came
to him. He was simply mildly interested. And then, little by
little, there crept upon him a faint sensation of discomfort.

The man's behaviour had now begun to be definitely peculiar.
There was only one adjective to describe his manner, and that
was the adjective odd. Slowly he had heaved himself up into a
more rigid posture, and with his hands on his knees was bending
slightly forward. His eyes had taken on a still glassier expression,
and now with the glassiness was blended horror. Unmistakable
horror. He was staring fixedly at some object directly in front
of him.

It was a white mouse. Or, rather, at present merely the head
of a white mouse. This head, protruding from the breast-pocket
of Old Stinker's jacket, was moving slowly from side to side.
Then, tiring of confinement, the entire mouse left the pocket,
climbed down its proprietor's person until it reached his knee,
and, having done a little washing and brushing-up, twitched

its whiskers and looked across with benevolent pink eyes at the man opposite. The latter drew a sharp breath, swallowed, and moved his lips for a moment. It seemed to Ambrose that he was praying.

The glassy-eyed passenger was a man of resource. Possibly this sort of thing had happened to him before and he knew the procedure. He now closed his eyes, kept them closed for perhaps half a minute, then opened them again.

The mouse was still there.

It is at moments such as this that the best comes out in a man. You may impair it with a series of injudicious lunches, but you can never wholly destroy the spirit that has made Englishmen what they are. When the hour strikes, the old bull-dog strain will show itself. Shakespeare noticed the same thing. His back against the wall, an Englishman, no matter how well he has lunched, will always sell his life dearly.

The glassy-eyed man, as he would have been the first to admit, had had just that couple over the eight which make all the difference, but he was a Briton. Whipping off his hat and uttering a hoarse cry – possibly, though the words could not be distinguished, that old, heart-stirring appeal to St George which rang out over the fields of Agincourt and Crécy – he leaned forward and smacked at the mouse.

The mouse, who had seen it coming, did the only possible thing. It side-stepped and, slipping to the floor, went into retreat there. And instantaneously from every side there arose the stricken cries of women in peril.

History, dealing with the affair, will raise its eyebrows at the conductor of the omnibus. He was patently inadequate. He pulled a cord, stopped the vehicle, and, advancing into the interior, said ''Ere!' Napoleon might just as well have said ''Ere!'

at the battle of Waterloo. Forces far beyond the control of mere words had been unchained. Old Stinker was kicking the glassy-eyed passenger's shin. The glassy-eyed man was protesting that he was a gentleman. Three women were endeavouring to get through an exit planned by the omnibus's architect to accommodate but one traveller alone.

And then a massive, uniformed figure was in their midst.

'Wot's this?'

Ambrose waited no longer. He had had sufficient. Edging round the newcomer, he dropped from the omnibus and with swift strides vanished into the darkness.

The morning of February the fifteenth came murkily to London in a mantle of fog. It found Ambrose Wiffin breakfasting in bed. On the tray before him was a letter. The handwriting was the handwriting that once he had loved, but now it left him cold. His heart was dead, he regarded the opposite sex as a wash-out, and letters from Bobbie Wickham could stir no chord.

He had already perused this letter, but now he took it up once more and, his lips curved in a bitter smile, ran his eyes over it again, noting some of its high spots.

'... *very disappointed in you ... cannot understand how you could have behaved in such an extraordinary way* ...'

Ha!

'... *did think I could have trusted you to look after ... And then you go and leave the poor little fellows alone in the middle of London* ...'

Oh, ha, ha!

'*...Wilfred arrived home in charge of a policeman, and mother is furious. I don't think I have ever seen her so pre-War...*'

Ambrose Wiffin threw the letter down and picked up the telephone.

'Hullo.'

'Hullo.'

'Algy?'

'Yes. Who's that?'

'Ambrose Wiffin.'

'Oh? What ho!'

'What ho!'

'What ho!'

'What ho!'

'I say,' said Algy Crufts. 'What became of you yesterday afternoon? I kept trying to get you on the 'phone and you were out.'

'Sorry,' said Ambrose Wiffin. 'I was taking a couple of kids to the movies.'

'What on earth for?'

'Oh, well, one likes to get the chance of giving a little pleasure to people, don't you know. One ought not always to be thinking of oneself. One ought to try to bring a little sunshine into the lives of others.'

'I suppose,' said Algy sceptically, 'that as a matter of fact, young Bobbie Wickham was with you, too, and you held her bally hand all the time.'

'Nothing of the kind,' replied Ambrose Wiffin with dignity. 'Miss Wickham was not among those present. What were you trying to get me on the 'phone about yesterday?'

'To ask you not to be a chump and stay hanging around London in this beastly weather. Ambrose, old bird, you simply must come to-morrow.'

'Algy, old cork, I was just going to ring you up to say I would.'

'You were?'

'Absolutely.'

'Great work! Sound egg! Right ho, then, I'll meet you under the clock at Charing Cross at half-past nine.'

'Right ho. I'll be there.'

'Right ho. Under the clock.'

'Right ho. The good old clock.'

'Right ho,' said Algy Crufts.

'Right ho,' said Ambrose Wiffin.

P. G. Wodehouse

IN ARROW BOOKS

If you have enjoyed Mr Mulliner, you'll love Uncle Fred

FROM

Cocktail Time

The train of events leading up to the publication of the novel *Cocktail Time*, a volume which, priced at twelve shillings and sixpence, was destined to create considerably more than twelve and a half bobsworth of alarm and despondency in one quarter and another, was set in motion in the smoking-room of the Drones Club in the early afternoon of a Friday in July. An Egg and a Bean were digesting their lunch there over a pot of coffee, when they were joined by Pongo Twistleton and a tall, slim, Guards-officer-looking man some thirty years his senior, who walked with a jaunty step and bore his cigar as if it had been a banner with the strange device Excelsior.

'Yo ho,' said the Egg.

'Yo ho,' said the Bean.

'Yo ho,' said Pongo. 'You know my uncle, Lord Ickenham, don't you?'

'Oh, rather,' said the Egg. 'Yo ho, Lord Ickenham.'

'Yo ho,' said the Bean.

'Yo ho,' said Lord Ickenham. 'In fact, I will go further. Yo frightfully ho,' and it was plain to both Bean and Egg that they were in the presence of one who was sitting on top of the world and who, had he been wearing a hat, would have worn it on the side of his head. He looked, they thought, about as bumps-a-daisy as billy-o.

And, indeed, Lord Ickenham was feeling as bumps-a-daisy as he looked. It was a lovely day, all blue skies and ridges of high pressure extending over the greater part of the United Kingdom south of the Shetland Isles: he had just learned that his godson, Johnny Pearce, had at last succeeded in letting that house of his, Hammer Lodge, which had been lying empty for years, and on the strength of this had become engaged to a perfectly charming girl, always pleasant news for an affectionate godfather: and his wife had allowed him to come up to London for the Eton and Harrow match. For the greater part of the year Lady Ickenham kept him firmly down in the country with a watchful eye on him, a policy wholeheartedly applauded by all who knew him, particularly Pongo.

He seated himself, dodged a lump of sugar which a friendly hand had thrown from a neighbouring table, and beamed on his young friends like a Cheshire cat. It was his considered view that joy reigned supreme. If at this moment the poet Browning had come along and suggested to him that the lark was on the wing, the snail on the thorn, God in His heaven and all right with the world, he would have assented with a cheery 'You put it in a nutshell, my dear fellow! How right you are!'

'God bless my soul,' he said, 'it really is extraordinary how fit I'm feeling today. Bright eyes, rosy cheeks, and the sap rising strongly in my veins, as I believe the expression is. It's the London air. It always has that effect on me.'

Pongo started violently, not because another lump of sugar had struck him on the side of the head, for in the smoking-room of the Drones one takes these in one's stride, but because he found the words sinister and ominous. From earliest boyhood the loopiness of this uncle had been an open book to him and, grown to man's estate, he had become more than ever convinced that in failing to add him to their membership list such institutions as Colney Hatch and Hanwell were passing up a good thing, and he quailed when he heard him speak of the London air causing the sap to rise strongly in his veins. It seemed to suggest that his relative was planning to express and fulfil himself again, and when Frederick Altamont Cornwallis Twistleton, fifth Earl of Ickenham, began to express and fulfil himself, strong men – Pongo was one of them – quivered like tuning forks.

'The trouble with Pongo's Uncle Fred,' a thoughtful Crumpet had once observed in this same smoking-room, 'and what, when he is around, makes Pongo blench to the core and call for a couple of quick ones, is that, though well stricken in years, he becomes, on arriving in London, as young as he feels and proceeds to step high, wide and plentiful. It is as though, cooped up in the country all the year round with no way of working it off, he generates, if that's the word I want, a store of loopiness which expends itself with terrific violence on his rare visits to the centre of things. I don't know if you happen to know what the word "excesses" means, but those are what, the moment he sniffs the bracing air of the metropolis, Pongo's Uncle Fred invariably commits. Get Pongo to tell you some time about the day they had together at the dog races.'

Little wonder, then, that as he spoke, the young Twistleton was conscious of a nameless fear. He had been so hoping that it would have been possible to get through today's lunch without the old son of a bachelor perpetrating some major outrage on the public weal. Was this hope to prove an idle one?

It being the opening day of the Eton and Harrow match, the conversation naturally turned to that topic, and the Bean and the Egg, who had received what education they possessed at the Thames-side seminary, were scornful of the opposition's chances. Harrow, they predicted, were in for a sticky week-end and would slink home on the morrow with their ears pinned back.

'Talking of Harrow, by the way,' said the Bean, 'that kid of Barmy Phipps's is with us once more. I saw him in there with Barmy, stoking up on ginger pop and what appeared to be cold steak-and-kidney pie with two veg.'

'You mean Barmy's cousin Egbert from Harrow?'

'That's right. The one who shoots Brazil nuts.'

Lord Ickenham was intrigued. He always welcomed these opportunities to broaden his mind and bring himself abreast of modern thought. The great advantage of lunching at the Drones, he often said, was that you met such interesting people.

'Shoots Brazil nuts, does he? You stir me strangely. In my time I have shot many things – grouse, pheasants, partridges, tigers, gnus and once, when a boy, an aunt by marriage in the seat of her sensible tweed dress with an airgun – but I have never shot a Brazil nut. The fact that, if I understand you aright, this stripling makes a practice of this form of marksmanship shows once again that it takes all sorts to do the world's work. Not sitting Brazil nuts, I trust?'

It was apparent to the Egg that the old gentleman had missed the gist.

'He shoots things *with* Brazil nuts,' he explained.

'Puts them in his catapult and whangs off at people's hats,' said the Bean, clarifying the thing still further. 'Very seldom misses, either. Practically every nut a hat. We think a lot of him here.'

'Why?'

'Well, it's a great gift.'

'Nonsense,' said Lord Ickenham. 'Kindergarten stuff. The sort of thing one learns at one's mother's knee. It is many years since I owned a catapult and was generally referred to in the sporting world as England's answer to Annie Oakley, but if I had one now I would guarantee to go through the hats of London like a dose of salts. Would this child of whom you speak have the murder weapon on his person, do you suppose?'

'Bound to have,' said the Egg.

'Never travels without it,' said the Bean.

'Then present my compliments to him and ask if I might borrow it for a moment. And bring me a Brazil nut.'

A quick shudder shook Pongo from his upper slopes to the extremities of his clocked socks. The fears he had entertained about the shape of things to come had been realized. Even now, if his words meant what they seemed to mean, his uncle was preparing to be off again on one of those effervescent jaunts of his which had done so much to rock civilization and bleach the hair of his nearest and dearest.

He shuddered, accordingly, and in addition to shuddering uttered a sharp quack of anguish such as might have proceeded from some duck which, sauntering in a reverie beside the duck pond, has inadvertently stubbed its toe on a broken soda-water bottle.

'You spoke, Junior?' said Lord Ickenham courteously.

'No, really, Uncle Fred! I mean, dash it, Uncle Fred! I mean really, Uncle Fred, dash it all!'

'I am not sure that I quite follow you, my boy.'

'Are you going to take a pop at someone's hat?'

'It would, I think, be rash not to. One doesn't often get hold of a catapult. And a point we must not overlook is that, toppers being obligatory at the Eton and Harrow match, the spinneys

5